"I hate how you stare at me."

"A lot of men stare at you, Quinn," Wyatt said.

"Not like you do."

Wyatt didn't just look at her. He studied her. He made her think of all the things he wanted to do to her, to do with her, to do inside her.

"I am attracted to you," he said softly as he stared into her eyes. "But I'll never act on it."

"Why not?"

His gaze dropped to her mouth and Quinn had to clear her suddenly dry throat.

"My biological clock is ticking."

Quinn had been expecting many things—like he was gay, or celibate, or asexual—but that his biological clock was ticking?

He smiled. A small, awkward one, but it was there. Dimples on both cheeks flashed. Quinn gripped the armrests as all-out lust spread through her body and caused her thighs to clench. Where had he been hiding that smile?

"I want a family. I want kids. I'm ready for that," he explained.

"But you're a man."

"I'm glad you finally notic

Books by Tamara Sneed

Kimani Romance

At First Sight
At First Touch

Kimani Arabesque

Love Undercover
A Royal Vow
When I Fall in Love

TAMARA SNEED

was born and raised in the Los Angeles area. She currently is an attorney, practicing civil litigation in Southern California. Her first novel, *Love Undercover,* was published by BET Books in September 2000 and became an instant reader and reviewer smash. Tamara's third book, *When I Fall in Love,* won the EMMA for Favorite Romantic Comedy at the 2003 Romance Slam Jam. Tamara's work has appeared in *Cosmopolitan,* and she was a contributor to the anthology *An All Night Man,* which Borders awarded as the Best Selling African American Romance in 2005.

Tamara has been a lifelong romance reader and writer and enjoys stories where brave heroes and heroines laugh their way through life and love. To learn more about her visit www.tamarasneed.com. Tamara also enjoys hearing from readers at tamara@tamarasneed.com.

At First
TOUCH

Tamara Sneed

KIMANI PRESS™

ISBN-13: 978-0-373-86046-3
ISBN-10:   0-373-86046-3

AT FIRST TOUCH

Copyright © 2007 by Sekret T. Sneed

www.kimanipress.com

Printed in U.S.A.

Dear Reader,

Welcome back to Sibleyville, California! I enjoyed writing about Sibleyville so much in *At First Sight* that I had to return again. At this time of year, Sibleyville is perfect. The shops on Main Street are decorated with twinkling holiday lights and smell of cinnamon and sugar. The towering Christmas tree sits in the town square waiting to be lit in the annual tree-lighting ceremony. And all of the residents are just a little friendlier and smile a little bit brighter as they pass each other on the streets.

Yes, I know that Sibleyville is not real, but I hope you all become so engrossed in my story that it feels just as real to you as it does to me. Besides, you never know, there could be a real Sibleyville out there. At this time of year, anything is possible…even a down-on-her-luck actress falling in love with a small-town mortician. So, settle back, grab a couple of Christmas cookies and some eggnog and become reacquainted with old friends!

Happy Holidays!

Tamara Sneed

To the Creators, Actors and Supporters of "Soap Operas"

Chapter 1

Judging from the heavy pounding on the front door of the Granger Funeral Home, Wyatt Granger figured either the defensive line of the Oakland Raiders had come to pay a visit or someone had died. Since Wyatt did own and operate a funeral home—and the average member of the Oakland Raiders, along with most other people in California, had no idea that Sibleyville existed—that left the latter proposition. Wyatt's luck had run out, and someone was dead.

Wyatt cursed and slowly set down the newspaper on the nearby coffee table. It appeared that his late evening ritual of reading the paper was not going to happen tonight. He suspected that most funeral directors did not curse when they were faced with the prospect of potential customers. But, then again, Wyatt was not like most funeral directors.

Unfortunately for Wyatt though, he was the last Granger left in Sibleyville and by default that left him to answer the door and pretend to be like most funeral directors. After all, the Granger Funeral Home motto was not Burying Your Dead Since 1919 for nothing.

Wyatt forced himself to stand from his father's favorite easy chair and walked through the foyer to the front door. He took a deep breath and stood frozen at the front door. He cursed at himself again. He needed to stop acting like a wuss and open the door.

Wyatt pasted his best funeral director smile on his face and opened the door. He was immediately blinded by a bright white light and the sound of applause. He shielded his eyes with a hand and squinted into the light. At least ten people stood crowded on the covered front porch. There were two cameras, one man holding the blinding light overhead and another guy holding a large microphone. And in front of the entire circus stood Quinn Sibley.

Wyatt felt the sudden urge to vomit. It was the same reaction every time he saw her. Like a sledgehammer in his gut. She was too beautiful, too perfect. And entirely too much out of his league.

His gaze drifted from her perfectly formed, heart-shaped lips to the deep V of the skintight dark green halter dress that skimmed every famous and well-photographed curve of her body. Her brown hair held hints of dark blond and honey and hung like a curtain of silk down her back. Her honey-brown skin was flawless, and her hazel eyes flashed more green one moment, then more brown another. He would have sworn they were contacts if he hadn't spent so much time studying her to know they were 100% real. And then there were her breasts.

Men could spend hours writing poems to her breasts. Wyatt had spent enough time staring at them over the last year to know every curve by heart. They were a little too perky and round and perfect to be God-given, but they were absolutely perfect. Any man who turned up his nose at them was either blind or a complete fool.

And with all things that came in a package that promised to be too good to be true, Wyatt had stayed far away from her. No, sir. Not him. Besides, he had other plans for himself this holiday season, like getting to know Dorrie Diamond better. Dorrie was petite, cute and most importantly, one of the only single women in town under the age of sixty and over the age of eighteen. Not to mention that she was black, this was even rarer in Sibleyville. She was 28 years old and Wyatt had decided that she was perfect for his plan. He wanted to start a family and judging from the longing he saw in her eyes when she saw babies, so did she. Quinn Sibley was nowhere in that plan. Not one beautiful inch of her.

"Wyatt!" Quinn exclaimed, as if he were a long lost friend.

When Wyatt only gaped in response, Quinn threw her arms around him and squeezed her ample breasts against his chest and, God help him, Wyatt moved closer to her, allowing himself for a moment to accept that this was not a fantasy.

Ever since he had first met Quinn Sibley in Sibleyville last year, she had been the name in lights in his daydreams and fantasies. She and her two sisters had come to Sibleyville to live in their grandfather's

boyhood home for a few weeks in hopes of inherit-
ing Max Sibley's considerable fortune. There had
been no fortune, but the women had left a mark on Sibleyville. Quinn's sister, Charlie, had married Wyatt's
best friend, Graham, and the two had spent the last
year essentially disgusting everyone with their
lovesick, puppy-dog looks and cuddly exchanges.
Thankfully, Charlie and Graham spent most of their
time in Los Angeles.

The few times Wyatt had seen Quinn since she and
her sisters had left town had been just enough to let him
know that it hadn't been a joke: this woman had a hold
on him. She knew it, which probably explained why she
treated him like snail dung on the bottom of her shoe.
And glutton for punishment that he was, Wyatt still
could not stop thinking about her. Or her body and those
lips, to put it more accurately. It was pure lust, and lust
could be controlled. Or so Wyatt had heard.

"You're looking good, Wyatt," Quinn gushed, as she
not so subtly positioned him so that they both faced the
camera. "What has it been? Five, six months? Too long,
right? We're practically family. We shouldn't wait this
long to see each other."

It took him a while because he did have the most
perfect pair of breasts pressed against him a few seconds
ago, but Wyatt finally realized that it was not an accident
that Quinn and a camera crew were hogging his porch.

"Quinn," he finally said.

He glanced at the cameras and the men in flannel shirts
and khaki shirts standing around the porch, watching the
scene with bored expressions. One man blew a bubble,
then popped it and continued to chew like a cow.

Wyatt stepped closer to her and turned his back to the cameras. He asked, flatly, "What is going on?"

"I've got a chance of a lifetime for you, Wyatt," Quinn continued excitedly, ignoring his question. She flashed a smile at the camera, then turned back to Wyatt, "I'm documenting one of the most exciting moments of my life—my homecoming to Sibleyville—"

"Homecoming?" he repeated, blankly. "You're not from—"

She squeezed his arm—*hard*—and continued to smile at the camera. "I have been picked to star in a Helmut Ledenhault movie. Yes, that's right, Wyatt, *the* Helmut Ledenhault. And, even more, exciting, Helmut has chosen to film the movie here in Sibleyville. Our little town. And here is the really best part, Wyatt. Are you ready for this?"

"No."

Like a runaway train, she ignored his distinct lack of enthusiasm and plodded on. "We want to film the movie here in the Granger Funeral Home!" Wyatt shook his head in disbelief, and this time she pinched him on the back of his arm. He flinched in surprise. Her camera-worthy smile never faltered. "Two weeks, at the most, Wyatt. What do you stay? Are you ready to be a star?"

Wyatt stared at her uncomprehendingly for a moment. For the first time, her bright smile faltered for a second as she nervously glanced at the camera and then back to him.

Wyatt cleared his throat, then said to the crew, "Can you guys give us a minute?"

"Cut, cut, cut!" roared an irritated male voice.

Wyatt squinted against the lights as a man walked up

the porch steps from the darkness of the front lawn. The man stood no taller than Quinn's shoulder, and while Quinn wasn't a short woman at close to five-foot-eight, that meant the man wasn't exactly tall. He had a bad hairpiece that sat askew atop his head, and thick black-rimmed eyeglasses covered beady blue eyes that were perched above a beady nose and a beady mouth, if a mouth could be beady. He was dressed in an all-khaki outfit for a day on safari—or at least how movie stars in the 1940s dressed for a day on safari—with the white scarf tied around his neck.

"Quinn, what the hell is going on here?" the man shouted in a thick German accent, jabbing his hands on his hips. "You said that this wouldn't be a problem. That this was all just a formality. That you had this cowboy wrapped around your little finger. It doesn't look like he's wrapped around your little finger. In fact, it looks to me like he's on the verge of saying no, and he cannot be saying no when we need to start filming this movie in one week."

Wyatt stepped in between Quinn and the fuming man. Wyatt kept his voice even as he pinned the man with a hard glare and said, "I don't know where exactly you're from, little man, and I don't care, but around here we don't talk to ladies like that. *Comprende?*"

Some of the anger drained from the man's expression as he shot an uncertain glance over his shoulder at the camera crew.

"Were you filming that? I said to cut. Don't you idiots know the meaning of the word? I'll put it more simple for the un-evolved around us. Turn! Off! The! Cameras!" Helmut screamed at the crew, since he realized that screaming at Quinn was no longer an option.

The other men did a poor show of hiding their smiles and nods of appreciation at Wyatt. The lights and cameras went out.

"Wyatt, please," Quinn snapped, irritated, stepping around Wyatt. She sent the man an apologetic smile. "He's from Sibleyville, Helmut. He doesn't know any better. He's really sorry for threatening you."

"I did not sign up for amateur hour," Helmut spat at her. He waved to the enraptured camera crew. "Let's leave this town before we start to smell like it."

"Helmut, wait," Quinn pleaded, running around the man to block the porch steps. "Wyatt will let us use the house, right, Wyatt?" She stared at him imploringly.

Wyatt ignored Quinn and pinned Helmut with another hard glare.

Helmut flinched, then turned to Quinn. "You need me much more than I need you, Quinn. Remember that. You have one week, and then I find a new location and a new lead actress. One week."

"One week?" she sputtered in disbelief. "But, it's Christmas—"

"Merry Christmas, Quinn."

With pat of his proverbial hair, he descended the steps towards a waiting van. The camera crew mumbled amongst themselves and slowly followed. There was no sound in the neighborhood as the two minivans filled up and drove down the oak tree-lined street toward the highway.

Wyatt glanced down the dark street at the other houses. There were several other houses on the wide street, but gossip traveled around their neighborhood as if they all lived on top of each other He didn't see any curious faces peeking out the windows, so at least none of his neighbors had seen the cameras. Wyatt did not want his mother hear about the *60 Minutes* surprise show on their front yard, until he could explain. Beatrice did not handle surprises well.

Wyatt glanced at Quinn and found her staring at him. She frowned and snapped, "Thank you very much, Wyatt." She groaned and raked hands through her hair, disturbing the carefully coifed curls. Wyatt tried not to notice that now she looked as if she had just gotten out of bed. She muttered to herself, "What am I going to do?"

"Quinn—"

She whirled around to face him. He coughed to cover the desire that slammed into his body. Quinn had never been angry with him. She had never been *anything* with him. As far as she was concerned, he was white paint on the wall.

Fire flashed in her hazel eyes, her cheeks flushed and her breasts heaving. If he still cared about Quinn Sibley, he would be raging hard right now because she looked like an Amazon warrior princess come to life. Well, maybe he could stop caring tomorrow because right now he was raging hard.

"You stalk me around Sibleyville and whenever you find an excuse to come to L.A. Now I give you a chance to stare at me for hours on end, without anyone stopping you, and you ruin it."

Wyatt was jerked from whatever X-rated fantasies had been developing in his head. "I don't stalk you, Quinn. I haven't seen you since…I can't remember when."

He remembered when. Five months ago, he saw her

for five minutes when he had been visiting Graham and Charlie at their home in Los Angeles. He hadn't known that Quinn lived in their pool house until Quinn had breezed into the house, glared at Wyatt, then grabbed Charlie and walked into the kitchen. It had taken everything in Wyatt's power not to follow her into the kitchen like a starstruck teenager.

Quinn crossed her arms over her chest and studied him, as if she knew exactly what he was thinking. And she probably did. A woman that beautiful did not spend more than a week alive without knowing how to tell when a man was bullshitting her.

"Are you going to let me use your house or not?"

"I don't know," he said with a shrug.

"You don't know? You don't know?" she repeated, growing more outraged with each word.

"I don't know," he confirmed.

"What is there to know?" she sputtered.

"There are things to consider—"

"What things? It's not like you have to worry about having a funeral in a funeral home. From what Graham says, there hasn't been a death in this town in eight months."

Wyatt inwardly cursed his best friend. *Thank you, Graham.* Ever since Graham had married Charlie, Graham had been the regular *New York Times*. Graham couldn't let a conversation pass without telling Wyatt about Quinn. And apparently Quinn was getting the Wyatt updates on the other end. Except Wyatt remembered that there wasn't really much to update when his life consisted of going home and going to work.

"My mother lives in this house on the second floor,"

he said calmly. "This is not just a mortuary. It's also a family living space. I have to talk to her."

"You better not ruin this for me," she threatened, with glowering eyes. When he didn't respond, she snorted in disgust, then dug a sleek, black cell phone from an oversized purse on the stairs of the porch. "Great. My reception is out again. Damn Sibleyville. But it's not like I could call a taxi around here anyway. I need a ride back to the house."

Without another word, she stomped toward his SUV. Because it was Sibleyville, the SUV was unlocked and she climbed inside the passenger side and slammed the door.

Wyatt stuffed his hands in his jeans pocket and watched her, fuming, as she sat in the SUV with her arms crossed. Wyatt was tempted to walk back inside his house, close the door and turn off the front porch light. He was in the middle of a tempting crossword puzzle in the newspaper. And he did have big plans for Dorrie Diamond and white picket fences and minivans. He stared at Quinn again.

Despite his better judgment, he made his way toward theSUV before Quinn changed her mind and walked the several miles back to her home. In her stilettos, no less. He wouldn't put anything past this woman.

Chapter 2

Quinn knew when a man wanted her. It was the way he looked at her, followed her with his eyes, stared at her breasts and her mouth when he thought she wasn't looking. Quinn knew how to handle men like that. Either she ignored them completely until they got the hint, or she flirted mercilessly until they gave her exactly what she wanted. But only with Wyatt Granger did she turn into a surly teenager who snarled and rolled her eyes just because he looked at her.

She had tried to be nice to him. She really had. But, for some reason, she just could not be nice to Wyatt. And she had had more than enough chances. She had seen Wyatt several times over the last year, ever since her sister had married Wyatt's best friend, and each time, she forgot her vow to be nice to him and instead snarled and snapped. It was surprising since she could fake liking even the most vile creatures. She had gone on a date with L.A. actors, after all.

Quinn didn't bother to hide her scrutiny of Wyatt as he directed his SUV down the dark, deserted highway that led from town, where the funeral home was located, to the Sibley house on the outskirts of the town limits.

It was not as if he were ugly. In fact, if she thought about it for too long, she would admit that he was handsome…in that Sibleyville cowboy way. Long, lean and confident. He had honey-brown skin, dark curly black hair that he kept a tad too long and intense dark brown eyes that she always found looking at her, whenever she was within ten feet of him.

She had only ever seen him in jeans and a button-down shirt, or a T-shirt. And she found herself thinking about that sight when she least expected it. Like sitting in the beauty salon, or in the middle of shopping, or when she had spent the entire four-hour drive from Los Angeles to Sibleyville preparing to see Wyatt, instead of preparing to meet with the director who could change her life.

Quinn shook her head to erase thoughts of Wyatt in snug jeans and instead glared at him. Now she remembered why he annoyed her. He never spoke. He just stared and watched.

She gritted her teeth and quickly rolled down the passenger window. It was much colder in Sibleyville than it had been in Los Angeles. She frowned as she thought of Los Angeles, or more accurately, her movie career. Leave it to Sibleyville. She had been in the dump of a town less than three hours, just enough time to ruin her career *again*.

Quinn shifted in the seat and glanced at Wyatt. Aside

from being a mute, he was so damn nice. He opened doors, said "please" and "thank you," and probably helped little old ladies cross the street in his spare time. Only her sister and her sister's too-perfect husband would know someone like Wyatt. No one in Hollywood would believe that someone like him existed. Quinn barely believed it herself.

"Do you ever talk?" she abruptly demanded, angry at him for being so damn quiet and angry at herself for caring.

Silence followed. Quinn sighed again and raked a hand through her hair, then quickly moved her hair back in place to cover her too large ears. Only one other person brought out this visceral reaction in her. Her oldest sister, Kendra.

There was a long silence before he said evenly, "How are Graham and Charlie?"

"It took you a long time to come up with that one, didn't it?" she said, with a short laugh. When more silence followed, she added, "They're fine. Still in domestic wedded bliss. In other words, as sickening as always."

"So, tell me about this movie. Why is it so important to you?"

"Who said it was important to me?" she shot back.

"The fact that you would willingly talk to me tells me how important it is to you."

She rolled her eyes, but felt a small stab of guilt. She acted like a shrew around this man. And he was nothing but nice and polite to her. Sure, he watched her with those unsettling eyes, but when she thought about the type of fan mail she had received from men in prison—

and a few women—when she had been at the height of her popularity on the daytime drama *Diamond Valley*, then Wyatt really wasn't so bad.

She reluctantly answered, "I haven't worked since I left *Diamond Valley*."

"Diamond Valley?" he repeated, curious.

"The soap opera I reigned over as the character Sephora Burston for the last ten years before I was carelessly tossed aside like a bag of outdated wigs," she snapped, more annoyed than she wanted to admit that Wyatt had no idea about the name of her show. She had been on the cover of *Us Weekly* magazine six times. She didn't count the *Us Weekly* cover that came out when she had been kicked off the show.

"Oh, yes, I remember now. Graham mentioned that you had been fired."

"I wasn't *fired*. My contract was not renewed," she corrected through clenched teeth. "Anyway, it's been one year and….this movie is my only shot."

"Shot for what?"

Quinn hesitated. She hadn't even told her sisters about her fears of never working again, of being ordinary. But she had the sudden urge to tell Wyatt. It was something about how quiet both he and of the SUV were. She almost felt as if she could tell him anything, and he would just nod. No judgment.

"I haven't worked in a year. That's a lifetime in the entertainment business. I'm 28 years old, in another couple of years, it'll be too late for me to even make it. On top of the age and the forced semiretirement, I'm trying to switch from television, daytime television, to movies. Do you know how difficult that is?"

"Why do you want to switch from television to movies?"

"I can't stay a soap actress all of my life, Wyatt," she said, attempting to sound patient. "The next logical step is movies. Movie stars are the cream of the A-List crop. All of the tabloid covers, the covers of magazines, the features. When you're a movie star, you can pick your own projects. And possibly start a perfume line or a clothing line."

He didn't respond but continued to stare down the dark road as he carefully drove the SUV within the speed limit.

"Helmut was the first director to even consider me for a part that did not involve my breasts as the second and third characters on screen. But I had to sweeten the pot."

He actually took his eyes off the road to shoot her a look. He asked, carefully, "What does that mean?"

"I don't sleep with men for roles," she snapped, annoyed, and then added with a shrug, "Not anymore."

"So how exactly are you planning to sweeten the pot?"

"Helmut is a brilliant director, but, as you probably noticed, he's not a…a people person. He's difficult. And so insistent on having total creative control of his projects that he can rarely get in the door at the big studios. So he has to make this film, *On Livermore Road*, on the lower end of the average Hollywood film budget."

"How much on the lower end?"

"Enough where Helmut is considering filming in this town."

Wyatt stared at her for a moment and then asked with a sigh, "So this guy is a jerk, no one in Hollywood likes him and he has no money to make his movie. Why do you want to be in this movie again?"

"Helmut is also a star-maker. If you survive a movie with him, any director or agent in town will take your calls because everyone knows that Helmut does not work with talentless hacks. And this film has a great role for me. Do you know how hard it is to find a dramatic role as a black actress in this town? But, this role has my name written all over it. Every black actress in Hollywood wanted it, but I got it. Or, I will have it. I needed to get Helmut's attention. And great locations that cost next to nothing are all you need to grab any independent director's attention. Your house, this town. It's perfect."

"Use your house," Wyatt suggested.

Quinn rolled her eyes in annoyance. "Helmut said my house looked like…what were his exact words… Oh, yes, a 'gingerbread house on crack.' Your house is bigger, more creepy…er, I mean, it has more character."

"Have you talked to Boyd?"

Quinn inwardly shivered at the mention of the mayor's name. The man was ex-military, mean and old. He also didn't crack a smile for anyone but his wife, Alma. In other words, she had no idea how to deal with him.

At her answering silence, Wyatt said, "You can't have a film crew traipsing through town without getting approval from the mayor or the city council."

Quinn narrowed her eyes at him. "My grandfather was the only man I ever allowed to lecture me, and he's dead."

"It wasn't a lecture, Quinn," he said evenly. "Just an observation."

She thought she saw the flash of a smile, but if there was a smile, it faded as quickly as it appeared. "I don't need your observations, either."

Through the darkness of the highway, Quinn spotted

the porch lights she had left on at the Sibley house and sighed in relief. The house had not been much when she and her two sisters had first moved in, but with the work and love that Charlie and Graham had put into the house over the last few months, it now felt like a home. Or as much as a place without a fitness center, valet service and a sauna could feel like home. In fact, Quinn was somewhat surprised by her sense of attachment to the little house because regardless of what it looked like, it was hers. She owned it. Or, at least, she owned one third of it.

Wyatt parked the SUV in front of the house and turned off the engine. The sudden quiet surprised her. The house, set back from the road, was surrounded by dirt and grass-covered hills rolling like waves behind it. Their closest neighbor was miles away. If she closed her eyes, it would almost seem as if she were alone in the world, which was either good or bad, depending on how many agents had rejected her that day.

Wyatt turned to her and asked in a deep, too-calm voice, "Why do you dislike me so much?"

"I don't know what you mean," she lied. His gaze was unwavering, and Quinn had a sinking sensation that she could not lie to this man. She averted her gaze and muttered, "I don't know. I guess…I don't like how you stare at me."

"A lot of men stare at you, Quinn," he reminded her in an almost gentle tone.

"Not like you."

He didn't just look at her. He studied her. Watched her. Made her think of all the things he wanted to do to her, with her, inside her. And sometimes when she wasn't careful, she found herself wanting the same things, which was very wrong. Wyatt Granger was not her type. He was only three years older than her, he didn't have a private plan and, most important, he was a mortician. Definitely not her type.

"I am attracted to you," he said softly, staring at her. Drinking her in. "I'd be blind not to be. But I'll never act on it."

"Why?" she blurted out, before she could remind herself to feel relieved.

"Does it matter?" he said with a small shrug.

"Not really, but I want to know. I mean, if it's because I'm an actress and you're a nobody…I totally understand that. It's an insurmountable hurdle that few men can get past. But for the sake of argument, I should note that a lot of nobodies marry women like me. Look at Julia Roberts and her husband, what's-his-name. And then there's…"

He stared at her again, and Quinn's voice trailed off as his gaze dropped to her mouth. She had to clear her suddenly dry throat as one corner of his mouth lifted in a mysterious smile that she hadn't thought a boring man like Wyatt capable of.

Wow. She had finally seen his smile, and she had to admit that she wanted to see it again.

"That's not it, Quinn," he finally said, leaning back in the leather seat and looking entirely too comfortable for a spurned suitor.

His scent began to wrap around her. Fresh soap that smelled like the ocean or the grass-covered hills behind the house after a hard rain. Quinn once more cleared her throat. "Then what is it?"

Wyatt studied the house for a moment and then admitted, "My biological clock is ticking."

Quinn had been expecting many things—maybe he was gay, or celibate, or asexual—but that his biological clock was ticking?

"I don't understand."

He smiled. A small, awkward one, but it was there. Dimples on both cheeks flashed. Quinn gripped the armrests as something akin to all-out lust spread in her body and caused her thighs to clench. Where had he been hiding that smile?

"I want a family. I want kids. I'm ready for that," he explained.

"But, you're a man."

"I'm glad you finally noticed." Before she could retort, he quickly said, "I don't know how it started or why it started, but over the last three years, all I think about is having children. I see other men with their children and I feel resentful. When my friends complain about their wives, in ways that you know it's not really a complaint, but a small prayer that they have a wife to complain about, I get jealous. I want a daughter to spoil and a son to play football with. I want the whole package—diapers, a dog, temper tantrums. The warmth of waking up at night and knowing that no matter what else is going on in the world, for that one moment, it's okay because my family is safe and warm. I know it's strange, but…. At some point, most men feel this way, they just don't tell beautiful women."

"And what does any of that have to do with your attraction to me?"

Wyatt smiled again then shook his head. "You're a

walking contradiction, Quinn. You can't decide if you want me to want you or not."

"Trust me, Wyatt, I don't want you to want me," she said quickly. "But, I find it odd that you don't, especially since a man like you is in my core audience. Thirties, heterosexual. So I want to know why."

"My wife will never have to worry about me running around her. I don't even want her to think about worrying about it. It'll be just her and me for the rest of our lives. In Sibleyville. With our children. Running the family mortuary because that's what Grangers have done for the last three generations. I need a woman who will fit into that life, be a mortician's wife without cringing or running away in disgust. Someone who will fit into Sibleyville."

"And you don't think I could be that woman," Quinn said, understanding dawning.

"I know you can't be that woman," Wyatt responded simply. "And since you have no desire to be that woman, I guess it works out for everyone."

She tried to conceal the bitterness in her voice as she asked dryly, "And where exactly do you plan to meet this paragon of virtue who will be Mrs. Wyatt Granger, town heroine, bearer of the fruit of your loins and Ms. Congeniality?"

He laughed and then said, "I know she won't be perfect, but I'm not looking for perfect. I'm just looking for someone who will be happy to see me at the end of the day and who will be happy with what I can offer her. Maybe bake an apple pie once in a while, even if it's awful. Sing to our children after their nightmares. Someone who can make a home anywhere, even in a drafty funeral home."

"You're a romantic," she accused, smiling.

"I don't know about that," he said, shaking his head, amused. "But, I know what I want. And I may have found her."

"Who?"

He sent her another smile and shook his head. Quinn forced a smile and playfully jabbed his arm. "Come on, Wyatt. We're being honest here."

"Her name is Dorrie Diamond."

Quinn couldn't stop the note of sarcasm that entered her voice as she said, "She sounds like a comic book superhero."

"She's an accountant. She moved here last year from Danville and opened an office on Main Street."

"Does Miss Diamond know that she's the future womb for your children?"

"Not yet," he said, grinning, taking no offense at her anger. "We've gone on a couple of dates. Well, not dates, actually, but we've met for coffee. Dorrie is very shy, but my mother likes her. She's a sweet person and I'm happy with my decision."

"Well, that's that," Quinn drawled, imitating a Sibleyville slow accent. "So, tell me more about the amazing Dorrie."

"There's not much to tell."

"Where did you meet?"

Wyatt studied her suspiciously. "Why?"

"Curiosity," she said, with a shrug. "What are her hobbies? What are her likes, dislikes?"

He hesitated, then said, "She likes church."

Quinn paused. "Church? All you know about the love of your life is that she likes church?"

"That's important. My faith is important to me and I want it to be important to the mother of my children."

"Hmm…Katherine also is very pious. It's probably her biggest downfall."

"Katherine?"

Quinn pursed her lips in irritation. "My character in *On Livermore Road*."

He glanced at her uncertainly, then asked, "What type of character are you playing exactly?"

"You say that as if you expect me to be playing a hooker or something."

"There's nothing wrong with hookers."

She laughed at his suddenly careful expression. "Wyatt Granger, what exactly do you know about hookers? You're pleading the Fifth on that one," she noted with a grin. When he still stared straight ahead, she answered, "If you must know, I am playing a housewife."

"A housewife?" he repeated, in disbelief.

"I know that you think I could never be anything as wholesome as a housewife, but that's why it's called acting," she muttered. She squared her shoulders and continued in a calmer tone, "The night of her honeymoon, where Katherine is set to lose her virginity—don't laugh—with her husband, a man bursts into their hotel room, beats Katherine's husband unconscious and rapes her. She becomes pregnant. They live in a small town and no one suspects that the child is not the husband's, but Katherine and Clint know and it is slowly driving a wedge in their marriage. Five years later, Clint is driving the child home from school and there is a car accident. Their son dies. The movie follows Clint's spiral into relief, guilt, an affair with a kindly, older waitress and ultimately salvation in his love for Katherine."

"So it's a comedy?"

Quinn smiled at his attempt at humor, then said, "Comedies don't win Oscars."

"That's what you want? An Oscar?"

"Of course. It's what every actor wants. It's why you become an actor."

"I thought you became an actor to…I don't know, act."

"I'm a serious actor, Wyatt," she snapped.

"I never said you weren't."

"Just because I want an Oscar doesn't mean that I'm not serious about my craft. It's just when you've been… when you've been through what I've been through…it's not enough to work again. I have to prove to everyone that they were wrong about me." Embarrassed by her admission, she glared at him and said, "It's a great script and it's going to be a great movie."

"I don't doubt it," he said, not sounding the least bit sarcastic. When she had no response, he reached for the key in the ignition, which was her not-so-subtle clue to get out of the car. "At any rate, I'll stop staring at you. In fact, you won't have to worry about me at all. I don't have any more trips planned to L.A. for another year, and I'm assuming you'll be leaving Sibleyville as soon as you get an answer about the house, which I'll let you know by tomorrow when I talk to my mother. And, if things go according to plan with Dorrie, the next time you see me, I'll be too busy changing diapers to stare at you."

Quinn racked her brain for something to say, besides a protest that Wyatt didn't need to marry an accountant who's name sounded like a comic book character.

She settled on an awkward, "Good luck."

She quickly moved from the car and slammed the door, uncertain why she had to force herself to walk to the house. Wyatt didn't drive away until she had closed the door to the house. She leaned against the door and closed her eyes. She couldn't wait to leave Sibleyville. This town always made her forget the important things in life. Like being on the cover of *People* again.

Chapter 3

Quinn was having a pleasant dream about eating a tub of rocky road ice cream without worrying about gaining weight, when an annoying shrill ring intruded. She groaned as she recognized the sound of her cell phone in her dream. She opened her eyes and squinted at the bright sunlight streaming through the windows of her designated bedroom in the Sibley house.

Graham and Charlie had barely touched her room in their home improvement stage. Everything was exactly where Quinn remembered it from her last visit during their wedding. There was a queen-sized lumpy mattress on an old-fashioned wood bedframe that squeaked and creaked when she breathed, that had been in the room on the first day she and her sisters had walked into the house, along with the matching antique dresser and chest of drawers that squeaked in dramatic protest every time Quinn tried to grab a pair of clothes. At least the windows had been replaced and the hardwood floor had been buffed and polished until it sparkled. No one had gotten around to putting curtains or blinds over the new windows, which meant Quinn was now squinting against the sunlight and her lack of sleep.

Quinn blindly reached for the cell phone on the mattress next to her and groaned again when she saw Charlie's name flashing on the small screen. Charlie was the only person Quinn knew who would call her at seven o'clock in the morning. Actually, Charlie was the only person Quinn knew who was awake at seven o'clock in the morning.

"What?" Quinn groaned into the telephone.

"Good morning, beautiful," Charlie sang.

Quinn rolled her eyes at Charlie's cheerful greeting. But then again, Quinn would be that cheerful too if she went to sleep every night next to a millionaire who adored her and gave her carte blanche to his seven-figure bank account. Of course, Charlie being Charlie, the bank account meant nothing to her.

Not that Quinn begrudged Charlie's happiness, or her obvious love with Graham. In fact, Quinn thought of all three Sibley sisters, Charlie deserved happiness the most. While Quinn and Kendra had moved away as soon as possible from under their grandfather's authoritarian rule, Charlie had remained by Max Sibley's side until his death two years ago. And Charlie had been the one to bring the three sisters together and to keep them together. But all the same, if Quinn didn't love Charlie so much, she would have hated her.

"I haven't had caffeine in twenty-four hours. Be very careful," she muttered in greeting.

"How did it go with Wyatt? Did he say yes?"

Quinn came wide awake at the mention of Wyatt. When she hadn't been dreaming about guilt-free, calorie-free ice cream, she had been dreaming about Wyatt and that smile. The snug-fitting jean-encased body. Even now, her stomach did a little flip. Although it could have been hunger, since Sibleyville's local cuisine—beef, beef and more beef—was not exactly in her diet.

"You never told me he was a momma's boy on top of being a creepy mortician. He has to talk to Mommy Dearest before he'll let me know the final answer."

"How did Helmut like Sibleyville?"

Quinn thought about Helmut placing a handkerchief over his mouth the moment he got out the minivan in Sibleyville. "He loved it," she lied brightly.

"And how do you feel about Sibleyville?"

"Is that a trick question?"

"You know, Quinn, I think you'd actually like Sibleyville. I've spent a lot of time there with Graham over the last year, and there's something about the place. It grows on you-"

"Like a bad rash."

Charlie ignored Quinn's dry remark. "If I didn't have the museum and Graham didn't have his business here, we'd move to Sibleyville permanently."

"Of course you would," she muttered sarcastically. "Because then you'd have your perfect husband with your perfect relationship in the perfect town."

She realized that she sounded more bitter than she intended and silently cursed. Sometimes she forgot that

Charlie was not Kendra. Kendra did not take insults personally because Kendra was made of Teflon or some equally indestructible material that had been found in space. Charlie took everything personally.

"Graham is not perfect and our relationship is not perfect. We have our ups and downs, just like every couple," Charlie said, sounding hurt.

"I know, Charlie," Quinn said immediately. "I'm sorry. I warned you that I hadn't had my coffee yet."

"Quinn—"

Quinn groaned loudly, hearing the concern in Charlie's voice. "It's too early in the morning for a heart-to-heart talk, Charlie."

"I'm not trying to have a heart-to-heart talk. I just want to talk to you. Some families actually do that every once in a while."

"Can we talk later?"

"Quinn—"

"I have to figure out where to hunt and kill breakfast in this hick town and then I have to intimidate Wyatt and his mother into doing what I want them to do so I can get out of here and back to civilization. I expect to be eating dinner tonight at my favorite sushi restaurant on Sunset. Whenever I step foot in this town, I immediately start craving fish."

"I wish you would stay an extra day. Graham and I will be there tomorrow. We're going to spend Christmas in Sibleyville."

"I know. You've told me that a million times."

"There's no reason for you to drive all the way back to Los Angeles just to turn around in a few days to come back."

"There is one reason that you're forgetting. I won't be in Sibleyville."

Charlie laughed, then said, "Call me when you're on the road and drive safely."

Quinn pressed the Disconnect button, then stared at the ceiling. She didn't want to get out of the bed and face this horrid town, where everyone stared at her as if she were a freak. She was used to being stared at, but not as if she were the town harlot who needed to be run out of town. And these people didn't know *half* of the things she had done.

But no matter how miserable she was this morning, at least she could make Wyatt more miserable. That prospect actually made her smile and get out of bed. She even whistled a little on her way to the shower.

"Good morning, Mom," Wyatt greeted as he walked into her kitchen.

Beatrice Granger looked up from the stove and angled her face for a kiss. Wyatt smiled and pressed a kiss against her smooth peanut butter-colored cheek. His mother patted his cheek and went back to scrambling eggs.

The bottom floor of the Granger Funeral Home was comprised of several viewing rooms of various sizes, a reception area and a small office. The back of the house and the second level were the family's living quarters. Most people had thought it was strange for Wyatt to grow up in the mortuary, but to him, it had just been the way it was. He would come home from soccer practice to find the county coroner dropping off body bags, his dad in a smock covered with blood and his mother holding a tray of oatmeal cookies. Just another day in the Granger Funeral Home.

During Wyatt's last year in college, his father had died. The usually unflappable Beatrice had been inconsolable, and had fallen into a depression that had scared Wyatt into moving back home into the small apartment over the garage in the back of the house.

The move was supposed to be temporary, but someone had to keep the family tradition alive and his mother needed him. So here he was, years later, still living over the garage.

"I'm going to string up the Christmas lights this morning," he said as he sat at kitchen counter where his mother had set a table setting for him.

Even though Wyatt was thirty-two years old and didn't technically live in the house with his mother, Beatrice still made him breakfast every morning. Wyatt could just imagine Quinn's reaction to that little tidbit about the exciting life of Wyatt Granger.

He grimaced and drained the glass of fresh-squeezed orange juice on the counter. But it was too late. He was thinking about Quinn now. Damn it. He had been dreading asking his mother about the film all morning. Beatrice did not like change, and she definitely did not like change that would involve Quinn Sibley. Beatrice had seen Quinn dancing with a groomsman at Charlie and Graham's wedding in a tangle of arms and legs that had not been fit for public viewing, and she had gone on for two weeks about the spectacle Quinn had made. Wyatt had been more pissed about the display than his mother, especially since Quinn had kept giving him smug smiles while she twisted in the other man's arms, but Wyatt had kept that to himself.

"Do you want bacon?" Beatrice asked.

"Don't I always want bacon?"

Beatrice smiled in response and placed a plate of steaming food in front of him. Wyatt grinned and dug in.

"I spoke to Dorrie this morning," Beatrice said in a casual tone that was anything but casual. "She was telling me that her kitchen sink is clogged. I told her that you'd come take a look at it this afternoon."

Wyatt tried to keep his tone level, "You just happened to speak to Dorrie this morning?"

At least Beatrice had the decency to look ashamed. "She called me, Wyatt."

"Returning your call, no doubt."

"She's a polite girl. I called her about the quilting circle. We're looking for another member, and I suggested her."

Wyatt rolled his eyes and groaned. "How in the world did you talk your friends into letting Dorrie into the quilting circle? You all haven't allowed any new members since the Lyndon administration."

"Well, I haven't exactly gotten the group's approval," Beatrice admitted reluctantly, then added with a smile, "But, I don't anticipate any problems. We need some new blood and Dorrie is a wonderful person. Sweet, kind, respectful—"

"I get it, Mom. You like her," he said tiredly. His mother wasn't exactly a subtle person, and she had not been subtle in the least over the last few months about how much she liked Dorrie. "I like her, too. But as much as you and I both like her, I don't need you setting up dates for me. I am a grown man."

"I know you're a grown man, sweetie. Do you need me to butter your toast?"

Wyatt shook his head in surrender as his mother began to busily spread butter on a slice of toast for him.

"So, what time should I tell Dorrie you're coming over?"

"Mom—"

"Well, are you not going to go just because I arranged it? She's in need. I raised you better."

"Mom…"

Beatrice sighed heavily and set the plate of toast in front of him. "I know you like Dorrie. Dorrie knows that you like that Dorrie. The whole town knows that you like Dorrie. What's taking you so long? Just ask her out for a real date. We don't get young single women in this town. This may be your last chance. And if you don't claim her, I hear that Miles Logan has been sniffing around her office, claiming to need help on his finances when we all know the man has an MBA from Harvard. Susan Logan certainly bragged about it enough."

"Mom…"

Beatrice signed heavily then said, "Fine, have it your way. I'll just tell her that you're not coming over—"

"Tell her I'll be there at eleven," Wyatt groaned.

His mother's smug silence almost made him change his mind, but she was right. He had to make his move sooner rather than later, especially if Miles Logan was "sniffing around." Dorrie was the type who might actually care about a Harvard MBA even though watching paint dry was more fun than talking to Miles.

Both Wyatt and Beatrice startled at a sudden knock on the front door. Beatrice looked wide-eyed at Wyatt. Some morticians' wives learned to live with the job; Beatrice was not one of those women.

Wyatt tried to keep his expression calm for his mother. Twice in two days. This couldn't be a false alarm.

"Do you think…" Beatrice's voice trailed off as she looked toward the hallway that led to the front door.

"I'll get it," Wyatt said, mentally congratulating himself on how calm he sounded.

Wyatt ignored his mother's worried gaze and walked through the highly polished and spotless family living area and into the mortuary's reception area to the front door. He sighed, relieved when he saw Quinn's silhouette through the stained glass in the front door. Then he frowned. The chances of Quinn knocking on his door twice in two days were about as likely as the Oakland Raiders making their appearance.

Quinn pounded on the door again and Wyatt quickly opened it before she knocked the door off its hinges. For a small woman, she sure could knock.

A blast of cold air rushed into the warm house as Quinn stood on the porch, looking more beautiful than she had last night and even more pissed. He silently cursed. He had lied last night. He would never be able to ignore her when she was near. The world became Technicolor, Dolby Surround sound. How could he ignore that?

"Quinn," he greeted calmly.

She pushed designer sunglasses to the top of her head, then quickly took them off to brush her hair into perfect waves again. "So?"

"So…what?"

"So, can we use your house or not?" she demanded, crossing her arms over her chest, which drew his gaze to the cleavage. He suddenly felt a little sweat bead on his forehead. Quinn's honey-brown cleavage could do that to a man. "I have places to be, things to do. I need a decision."

Wyatt stared at her for a moment, then leaned against the door frame. She returned his stare with a lift of her chin. And a small part of him wanted to take her up on it. To just lose his nice-guy, patient image and to just grab her around the waist and…Wyatt shook his head at his thoughts. He wouldn't be touching Quinn Sibley. No matter what. He should just turn and walk away. Ignore her. Leave her alone.

"I told you that I'd let you know as soon as I knew."

"Have you even asked your mother yet?"

"I can't just spring something like this on my mother. She is very set in her ways, and she's very traditional. It'll take some gentle persuasion, but she'll come around. Hopefully. I'll let you know as soon as she does."

"That's not good enough, Wyatt. I have a whole production waiting on this. I told you what's at stake. I need to know now."

"I'm doing the best I can," he said, with a shrug. When she only glared at him, he moved to close the door.

She placed a hand on the door, stopping him. If possible, laser beams shot from her eyes and bored into his brain. "We're not done here, Wyatt," she said huskily.

Wyatt told himself to remain calm. He knew Quinn liked to pout and shout and act like a brat. Hell, half of him liked for her to pout and shout and act like a brat. But the other half of him wanted her to respect him and treat him like a man.

He closed the distance between them until he could feel the heat from her body stroke his. She craned her neck to look at him. She no longer looked defiant and angry. Now there was a question in her eyes. Maybe even nerves. Something male and powerful snaked around Wyatt's heart.

He kept his voice low and even as he said, "We're done when I say we're done, Quinn. And, trust me, we're done."

He actually heard her gulp. The tip of her pink tongue nervously wet her bottom lip, and her bright eyes darted from his eyes to his mouth. Her gaze finally lingered on his mouth. Wyatt's body tightened in response as if it knew something that he didn't. As if it felt that maybe— just maybe—Quinn was beginning to feel that *something* Wyatt always felt around her.

Of course, Beatrice picked that moment to stand beside Wyatt. Quinn instantly averted her gaze, and Wyatt coughed to cover the desire clogging his throat.

Beatrice's gaze hardened as she pointedly stared from Quinn's tight sweater and blinged-out gold bomber jacket to the skintight expensive jeans and stiletto heels. Beatrice's mouth narrowed, and Wyatt silently cursed. That expression from his mother was not a good thing.

Quinn turned her sweet smile on Beatrice, which prompted Beatrice's eyes to narrow even more. Wyatt thought about warning Quinn because he could tell she was going to bring up the movie, but what good would that do? All the warnings in the world would not help Quinn now.

"May I help you?" Beatrice asked, as if she had no idea who Quinn was.

"I'm Quinn Sibley," Quinn said brightly. "I don't believe we've met—"

"We met at your sister's wedding," Beatrice replied in a stiff tone that told them both that Beatrice had not considered it a pleasant experience. Her eyes once more traveled over Quinn's outfit.

Quinn soldiered on. "We did? I'm sure I would have remembered a woman as beautiful as you. Are you Wyatt's sister?"

Beatrice did not crack a smile at the lame attempt at sucking up. Wyatt told himself to remain silent, but then he saw the brief flash of discomfort across Quinn's face before she could hide it. And since he was a genuine sucker for Quinn, he couldn't just stand by while his mother pulverized her.

"Quinn, this is my mother, Beatrice Granger," Wyatt quickly covered the awkward silence. "Quinn was actually just leaving—"

"Since I'm here, Mrs. Granger, we may as well talk," Quinn interrupted Wyatt, her gaze flickering to him in annoyance before she turned that smile back on Beatrice. "You may have heard that I'm planning to film a movie right here in our very own Sibleyville. We had the pick of places in town, but we've chosen your beautiful home as our prime location for filming. This house is such a testament to this town and there's obviously so much love and time put into each and every room in this house. We would pay for your inconvenience, of course, and even paint and—"

"No," Beatrice said, flatly. "We're a funeral home, not a movie studio. Your father would roll over in his grave if he saw movie cameras traipsing around his home."

Wyatt was surprised by his mother's flat refusal and her open hostility to Quinn. Beatrice was not the friendliest person, but she also didn't usually express her dislike so openly. Well, maybe she did, but Wyatt couldn't really recall ever seeing it.

Beatrice effectively dismissed Quinn and said to Wyatt, "Close the door. You're letting all the heat out. And remember Dorrie is waiting for you. You should try to get over there soon. She wants to take you to lunch to repay you, but I think she wants to just spend some time with you."

Quinn watched in disbelief as Beatrice walked back into the house, without another glance in Quinn's direction. Wyatt sighed in relief. That could have gone much worse.

Chapter 4

Quinn was an actress. A black actress, no less. She was used to rejection. The last few months, she had taken two steps into audition rooms and been told, "Thanks, but no thanks," before she even had opened her mouth. But, Beatrice Granger could give Hollywood casting agents a run for their money. In just a few short words, she had made Quinn feel really small.

Quinn turned to Wyatt. The sympathy in his eyes actually made her want to crawl into his arms and just be near his warmth.

"I'm sorry," he said.

Quinn's world collapsed to Wyatt's mouth as cold sweat broke out between her shoulder blades. "So that's it?" she asked, hoarsely.

"I told you to let me handle it. I told you that she needed some time to get used to the idea," he said quietly.

She clutched his arm and tried to keep the desperation out of her voice, as she said, "I need this, Wyatt."

He looked uncomfortable. "I don't know what to tell you. Mom says no."

"Who's house is this? Hers or yours?"

His discomfort magnified. "Both of ours."

Quinn didn't realize that she was squeezing his arm until she saw a wince cross his face. "Then tell her that you want me to use it. You have to tell her."

He gently disengaged himself from her grasp and still did not meet her eyes. "I'm sorry, Quinn. I really am."

Quinn's mouth flapped open in disbelief. And then the anger started. "You're doing this on purpose," she accused in an angry whisper. "You knew She-Dragon would say no, and you're doing this to punish me."

His eyes widened in surprise as he finally looked at her. "Punish you?"

"For not wanting you as much as you've wanted me all this time."

He actually looked amused as he said, "That's not what's happening. Trust me."

She squared her shoulders and said in her best Sephora voice of promise of retribution, "This is not over, Wyatt."

"What do you want me to do?"

"I want you to tell your mother that you want the movie to be filmed here."

He released an impatient sigh. "Quinn, I told you to wait. You didn't listen to me. It would have taken a while but I could have talked her into it. Now her position is set. She's not going to budge."

She narrowed her eyes and said threateningly, "I will make your life hell until this is resolved, Wyatt."

He stared at her for a moment and then smiled. She resented him even more for making her stomach strangely clench. It was that damn smile. He was much too sexy when he flashed that smile. And because he did it so rarely, the smile and her reaction to it always took her by surprise.

"What are you going to do, Quinn? Toilet paper the house?"

"I hadn't thought of that, but thanks for the idea."

He rolled his eyes in frustration. "Mother doesn't change her mind."

"Neither do I. This is not over, Wyatt. You may as well surrender now because a Sibley always gets what she wants." She flipped hair over her shoulder and stalked to her car.

She turned back to yell at him again and was rendered breathless when she realized that he had been staring at her ass as if he could find the answers to life. He didn't even seem embarrassed when she caught him.

Normally, such blatant male hunger would have annoyed her, at the least pissed her off. But for some reason she became nervous. There was something about the frank male appreciation in his eyes that made her uncertain. As if no man had ever stared at her ass before.

As he stared at her expectantly, Quinn realized that she couldn't speak. Her throat was clogged with nerves. She sat in her Mercedes convertible and jerked the door shut angrily. Her tires squealed as she stomped down on the gas pedal. She really needed to get the hell out of this town if Wyatt Granger was making her speechless.

Ten minutes later, Quinn stormed into her house and slammed the front door. She kicked off her heels and smiled in satisfaction as they flew across the room into a wall. She paced the length of the living room. She couldn't return to L.A. without the location. Helmut had made that clear. And Helmut had only given her a week. It would take longer than a week to convince Beatrice Granger that Quinn was not the devil; it would probably take about a century.

Not that Quinn blamed her. Quinn had never been very good with mothers. It was something about the miniskirts and halter tops. Most moms didn't like a woman like her around their precious sons.

Quinn rolled her eyes in annoyance. Beatrice Granger was not standing in the way of her career comeback. She needed a plan, and she needed a plan fast. Quinn suddenly smiled. Only one person she knew was evil enough and brave enough to take on the likes of Beatrice Granger. Kendra. Beatrice was no match for Kendra. Hell, a Roman legion would have been no match for Kendra.

Quinn plopped onto the sofa in the living room and grabbed the telephone. She dialed her sister's telephone number in New York.

"Hello," Kendra mumbled into the telephone.

Quinn glanced at the clock on the VCR. It was nearly one o'clock in the afternoon, which meant that it was nearly four o'clock in the afternoon in New York. She had never known Kendra to sleep past six o'clock in the morning or to take naps. Something had to be wrong.

"Are you asleep?"

"I was," Kendra snapped, sounding like her usual annoyed self.

Quinn instantly dismissed her worries. "I need your help, Kendra."

"What? Why?" Kendra asked, suddenly sounding wide awake and concerned. "Are you hurt? I'll be there as soon as I can."

"Thank God. I'm in Sibleyville." There was a long pause on the phone line. "Kendra? Are you still there?"

"Are any limbs broken?" Kendra demanded.

"No."

"Are you in jail?"

"Of course not."

"Are you pregnant?"

"Kendra—"

"Then I'm not coming to Sibleyville and I have to go—"

"Kendra, wait," Quinn ordered. "I need you."

"What in the world do you possibly need from me that involves me traveling from New York to that hellhole?"

"It's almost Christmas, and Charlie and I will be here for Christmas. You can't spend Christmas alone."

"I won't be alone. There are almost three million people in Manhattan, and I'm sure there are one or two of them who hate the holidays almost as much as I do. If I hear 'We Wish You a Merry Christmas' one more time, I will not be responsible for my actions."

"Kendra, I need you here by tomorrow."

Kendra sighed. "I know that you wouldn't be in Sibleyville unless your life depended on it, and since your life is solely focused on acting, I'm going to assume that all of this has something to do with that movie you've been talking about nonstop for the last few weeks."

"Not just a movie, but *the* movie. My come-back

movie. All I have to do is convince this town and Wyatt Granger to go along with it."

"Quinn, quit the dramatics and give me the short version," Kendra snapped.

"I finally got Helmut Ledenhault to let me audition for his movie. It's a great role. The character is—"

"You're giving me the short version, remember?"

"I'm trying. After reading the script for *On Livermore Road*, I knew that Sibleyville would be perfect for it. I talked Helmut into driving to Sibleyville because he needs a cheap location. Anyways, Helmut saw the town, fell in love with the price and in particular fell in love with the Granger Funeral Home. He's given me one week to get the approval and permits, and I have one huge, unsightly obstacle blocking my way to future Oscar renown. Wyatt Granger."

"I'm not sure what I'm having more trouble understanding. The fact that you're actually acting again, or the fact that someone believes that Sibleyville is good for something."

"Kendra, this is serious," Quinn snapped.

"I'm still not sure how I fit into all of this."

"Wyatt wants to give me the house, but his mother doesn't. I need some way to force Wyatt to make his mother agree."

"Just bat your fake eyelashes and wiggle your fake breasts at him. Doesn't that usually do the trick?"

"Wyatt is different from most men," Quinn said, frustrated. "He doesn't want me. He's convinced that he wants to marry some Pollyanna here in town, and he plans to be married to her and popping out little Sibleyvillians—if that's a word—by next year. I have no practice in convincing a man who doesn't like me to do something I want, so I need your help. I'm sure you've found yourself in this situation numerous times."

"If you're trying to sweet-talk me, it's not working," Kendra replied dryly.

Quinn ignored her sister's sarcastic tone. "What should I do, Kendra? The director won't make this movie without Wyatt's house, and Wyatt refuses to talk his mother into doing it."

"As you remind me every five minutes, you're Quinn Sibley. Daytime Emmy winner and one of *People's* 50 Most Beautiful People three years in a row. You can convince a man to do anything, Pollyanna or not."

"Usually, that's right, but Wyatt...he's not exactly normal. He's a funeral director."

"You have a point," Kendra agreed, which instantly annoyed Quinn. There was nothing *per se* wrong with being a funeral director. Quinn would put Wyatt up against any of those suit-wearing losers that Kendra used and abused and dumped climbing up her corporate ladder.

"Regardless of Wyatt's supposed Pollyanna fixation, he's obsessed with you. He'll do whatever you want," Kendra said firmly.

"You think so?" she asked uncertainly.

"Put on a tight dress, shake your ass and your breasts that you've certainly paid enough for, and get that house."

"It's not that simple, Kendra."

"Of course, it is. Or, maybe, you need to go about it another way," Kendra said with a short burst of laughter.

"What do you mean?"

"Are Wyatt and his Pollyanna actually dating?"

"Not yet."

"I can't believe you didn't think about this. What did Sephora do when her sister—the nun, not the ex-secret agent—met that rebel in the Colombian jungle?"

"She came on to the priest whenever Elizabeth was around because she knew it would make Elizabeth jealous and hate the rebel, and then Elizabeth would return back to the convent and Sephora could take over the family business—"

"Precisely. Sephora drove a wedge straight between the couple, even though she and the rebel never even touched. But the sister wouldn't believe him, and he got angry that she wouldn't believe him and went back to the Colombian jungle where he was eaten by a crocodile."

"It was an anaconda, and his death led Elizabeth to leave the convent and to move back to town, where she locked Sephora in the dungeon built behind the wine cellar of the family mansion for a month. That was such a horrible time. I had to wear the same hideous fuchsia dress for four months—"

"Quinn, focus."

Quinn was silent as she squeezed the telephone receiver. She suddenly grinned. "Kendra, you're a genius. Or, more accurately, the writers of *Diamond Valley* are geniuses."

"You become Wyatt's worst nightmare. You're on him like white on rice. Flirting, laughing, whispering in his ear, wanting him like Sephora wanted that Bulgarian prince. Pollyanna will never believe Wyatt when he claims there's nothing going on. Of course, you'll stop the campaign of terror just before Pollyanna vows to never speak to him again if he lets you film the movie in his house. And the perfect part is that Wyatt will have no control over the situation. No one will believe that he's not into it."

"You're evil, Kendra."

"Thank you."

Quinn laughed. "Only you would take that as a compliment."

"Glad to help, and don't lay it on too thick. You wouldn't want the poor thing to self-combust. Remember this is Sibleyville."

"So, I'll see you tomorrow."

"Tomorrow?" Kendra squeaked. "You don't need me there. I've give you the perfect plan. All you have to do is execute it."

"I'll see you tomorrow, or I'll sic Charlie on you."

There was a long silence on the telephone and then Kendra said flatly, "Apparently, I'm not the only evil Sibley sister. I'll see you tomorrow."

"Perfect." Quinn pressed the Disconnect button then ran up the stairs to her room with a grin. She had to find the perfect outfit for lunch. Wyatt hadn't said where he was taking Dorrie for lunch, but considering the options around town, Quinn had a feeling she would find them sooner or later.

Chapter 5

Wyatt smiled across the table at Dorrie. Dorrie sent him a shy smile in return, then went back to pushing her food around her plate. Wyatt went back to his own plate. He had taken his mother's advice. He had driven to Dorrie's small apartment above her office on Main Street and he had fixed her drain, then he had asked her to lunch. The two had walked the few short blocks from her place to Annie's Diner, the most popular of the town's few diners.

It had been perfect. The men they had passed on the way to the café had smiled knowingly at Wyatt, and the women had smiled excitedly at Dorrie. Obviously, Sibleyville was ready for another wedding. Although given that Quinn was still suffering repercussions from the last one, Wyatt thought maybe it was best that weddings didn't happen that often around town.

Wyatt forcibly pushed those thoughts out of his head. Quinn was probably long gone by now, on her way back to Los Angeles, looking for another movie director to harass. And Wyatt was here with Dorrie, the woman he could build a life with. A life of complete and utter silence, because Dorrie hadn't said more than six words since they had sat at the table.

Wyatt didn't necessarily need to talk for the sake of talking—he was a mortician, after all—but he didn't think that an occasional exchange of words was asking too much. He could barely get Quinn to shut up.

Wyatt glanced around the diner and noticed more than a few of the older couples at the various tables throughout the diner staring at him. Vera Spears winked at him and gave him an encouraging nod. Wyatt inwardly groaned. Sometimes, he really hated living in a small town.

Wyatt turned back to Dorrie, who was staring at him and quickly looked back down at her plate. She really was cute. She had sun-kissed golden skin, bright brown eyes and dark hair that she wore parted down the middle. She barely reached his shoulders in her sensible pumps. The word *stiletto* probably wasn't even a part of her vocabulary. She was petite, sweet and soft in all the right places. Just like a wife should be.

Wyatt cleared his throat and asked, "So—you like the pot pie?"

"Yes."

"My mom makes a great pot pie."

Dorrie murmured in response and continued pushing around her food. Wyatt thought about banging his head on the table. Maybe that would get a reaction beyond mild politeness. Quinn probably would have gone on a ten-minute monologue about her movie character's dining proclivities.

Wyatt felt guilty once more. He shouldn't be thinking about Quinn, let alone comparing Dorrie to Quinn.

Dorrie suddenly looked up at him and asked hesitantly, "Your mother said that you're interested in plants and flowers?"

"I am," he said, trying to hide his surprise that she had asked him a personal question. "I mean, it's just a hobby but it's something I really enjoy. You know, dealing with flowers kind of offsets the mortuary business. We haven't seen a lot of deaths in the last two years, but it's always the prospect—"

"Beatrice said that you even have a little nursery behind the house," she interjected quickly, obviously uncomfortable with the subject of death.

Wyatt tried not to take offense at the description *little*. Last year, he had made more money from his "little" nursery, planning and tending the town's landscape and growing flowers for people in the area, than his father had ever made from the mortuary in a year.

"It's a side project," he finally said.

"What's your favorite flower?"

"Favorite flower? I don't know."

"I like roses."

Wyatt refrained from his numerous complaints about the most oversold flower in the States. "Roses are nice. I have a greenhouse behind the house. I even have a small section of orchids. They're a very delicate plant to grow, but I portioned off a section of the greenhouse and tried to make conditions perfect. I think it's working. I also have gardenias and hydrangeas and…"

His voice trailed off as Dorrie put her hand on his. Her smile was gentle, which made him realize that he had been blabbing. She removed her hand and said, "Maybe you can show me some time."

"I'd like that," he said, grinning probably wide enough for his mother to see it back at the house. Dorrie returned his smile.

Wyatt noticed a sudden shift in the air. He also noticed that no one in the diner was staring at them anymore. Instead, they were staring at the door. Wyatt followed their stares and couldn't suppress the cough of disbelief as Quinn stood in the door frame. She didn't just stand. She posed, as if allowing everyone to get a full look at her. And every man in the place was incredibly grateful.

She wore a teensy-weensy, barely-there black skirt, black fishnets, black pointy-toed, calf-length boots and a sweater that dipped too low to really be considered a sweater. Wyatt supposed it was Quinn's version of a winter outfit, but he couldn't understand how she could prance around in so few clothes when it was close to fifty degrees outside.

Quinn flipped her now straight hair over her shoulder and sauntered across the restaurant toward Wyatt. She kept her gaze on him the entire time, ignoring everyone else. She stopped in front of his table and leaned down, giving him a view of the front and everyone else in the restaurant a view of the back. His body hardened and tightened, as if it knew what was near and didn't appreciate Wyatt not doing what his body obviously wanted to do.

"Hi, Wyatt," she breathed, her lips so close to his ear that he could feel her breath heat the shell of his ear.

If Wyatt didn't know better, he would think that "Hi, Wyatt," meant "Take me back to my house and pound into me until I can't walk anymore." He wanted to bury his face in her hair and smell it and touch it and pull it as he entered her—

Wyatt swallowed the lump in his throat and met her gaze. Everything about her screamed sex, but the look in her eyes twinkled with something else. Mischief.

"Quinn," Wyatt greeted carefully.

"Mind if I join you?" she purred.

Without waiting for a response, she slid into the booth next to Wyatt, her thigh pressing into his. Wyatt grimaced and moved farther over until he was pressed against the window, but she only followed him until every inch of her thigh pressed against every inch of his. Quinn had never willingly sat next to him, let alone touched him, since he had known her. Something was definitely up, and it had nothing to do with what was in his pants.

Quinn smiled at Dorrie, who looked transfixed with awe, and offered her hand. "I don't think we've met. I'm Quinn Sibley. I hope I'm not intruding."

Dorrie stared at Quinn for a moment, then appeared to snap out of whatever daze she was in and shook Quinn's hand. "I know who you are. I watch *Diamond Valley*, or…I used to, until they killed you off."

Quinn's pleasure was evident as she said, "Really?" Quinn playfully jabbed Wyatt in the arm and asked, "Why didn't you tell me you were having lunch with a woman with such good taste?" Wyatt narrowed his eyes at her, and Quinn turned to Dorrie. "Sometimes Wyatt has the worst manners. What is your name?"

"Dorrie Diamond."

"What a beautiful name," Quinn gushed, obviously not remembering her comic book comment from yesterday. "You stopped watching *Diamond Valley* because of me?"

"Of course," Dorrie said, nodding eagerly. "Sephora was the best part of that show. The only reason to watch it."

"I thought so, too," Quinn agreed.

Wyatt decided that whatever game Quinn was playing had gone on long enough, especially since she had placed her elbow on the table, touching his.

He cleared his throat and said, "Quinn—"

Dorrie interrupted him, her gaze still on Quinn. "Ms. Sibley—"

"Please call me Quinn," Quinn said, patting Dorrie's arm.

Dorrie gave Quinn a wide smile that she had never given him. "Quinn, I always wondered, what is Gregory like in real life?"

Quinn laughed and tossed her hair over her shoulder in a cascading waterfall of brown silk. "I'm not surprised. Every woman in America wants the lowdown about Gregory Rotelle. He seems so debonair and sophisticated on television, but believe me, honey, the man deserves an Emmy for even being able to portray a human. In real life, he's an ass. He spent more time in hair and makeup than most of the women. And, for the record, the hair is not real."

Dorrie giggled, her pale skin coloring slightly. "No!" she gasped, moving her hand to cover her mouth.

Wyatt grew more annoyed. He still hadn't gotten a laugh out of Dorrie.

"Oh, yes. His real hairline starts somewhere around

the top of his ears," Quinn said with a conspiratorial wink, causing Dorrie to collapse into laughter.

"Quinn," Wyatt said in a low, quiet voice that neither woman could ignore. Dorrie glanced at him and stared back down at her plate, her smile disappearing, while Quinn looked at him with an innocent expression that would have fooled only a blind man. He clenched his teeth and demanded, "What do you want?"

"Wyatt!" Dorrie admonished in a whisper, as if Quinn wouldn't be able to hear her.

"It's all right, Dorrie," Quinn said sweetly, patting the woman's arm again. "I'm used to Wyatt's moods."

"Moods?" Dorrie repeated hesitantly.

"Quinn," Wyatt said, a little louder this time. Quinn sent him another innocent smile. "What are you doing here?"

"Wyatt, I'm not sure I like your tone," Dorrie said, sounding offended on Quinn's behalf.

Quinn bit her bottom lip to hide her smile from Dorrie, but she didn't hide the twinkle of amusement in her eyes as she turned to Wyatt.

Dorrie sent Wyatt a death stare, then smiled at Quinn. "I apologize for Wyatt's behavior. You're obviously here for lunch and just stopped by to say hello. That's very nice—"

"I'm not here for lunch, unless they've changed the menu to include items that don't automatically turn you into a cow," Quinn said, then turned to Wyatt with a lovestruck look in her eyes. She placed a hand on his arm. "I came here because I heard that Wyatt would be here. He and I had a small argument this morning and I wanted to apologize."

Wyatt could almost hear some cheesy soap opera music

playing in the background. He glanced at Dorrie. She looked as if she had swallowed something distasteful. And Wyatt instantly knew what Quinn's little show was about.

Wyatt narrowed his eyes at Quinn, who blinked at him. He moved his arm from her touch. "Apology accepted, Quinn. You can go now."

"Will I see you later tonight?" Quinn waited a dramatic beat, then added, "When Graham and Charlie get here."

"Quinn, we'll talk later," he replied tightly. "You can go. Now.

Quinn jumped from the booth, pulling down the skirt that had ridden up her thighs. Then he got distracted by the fishnets. He gulped. Hard.

Quinn avoided his eyes and smiled at Dorrie, who was looking at Quinn as if she wasn't her favorite soap actress anymore.

"Dorrie, it was wonderful to meet you. Maybe we can get together and I'll give you more dirt about the show."

Dorrie murmured noncommittally, then sent Quinn a wan smile. Quinn glanced at Wyatt, then quickly turned and nearly ran out the diner. Wyatt would have felt some satisfaction, but Dorrie was looking at him with a strange expression. Two steps forward and twelve steps back.

"Can we go?" Dorrie asked, glancing around the diner for the owner, Annie. "I have a client coming at one-thirty."

"Of course." Wyatt pulled out his wallet, dug out enough cash to cover the bill and stood.

He offered his hand to Dorrie, but she ignored it and stood on her own. She grabbed her coat from the booth, then walked out the diner without another glance in Wyatt's direction.

"Nice going, Wyatt," someone yelled out dryly.

Wyatt ignored the catcalls that followed and shrugged into his own coat before he hurried out the diner after her. Dorrie was already halfway down the street to her office. He ran to catch up with her.

Quinn had said that it wasn't over, and obviously it wasn't. She was now determined to ruin his life.

"Dorrie, wait," he said, grabbing her arm.

They stopped in the middle of the sidewalk. The withering look Dorrie gave his hand on her arm made him quickly release her. She relaxed a fraction, then glanced around Main Street. Thankfully, the street was almost deserted. Most people had gone back to their ranches, farms or stores. The lunch hour—as much as there was one in Sibleyville—was over.

"I told you that I have an appointment," Dorrie said stiffly.

"I'm sorry about that," he said, motioning back toward the diner. "Quinn and I had a little argument this morning when she stopped by the house—uninvited, I might add—and that's all. There was nothing more to it."

"Quinn's reaction to you didn't seem like nothing," Dorrie said quietly, avoiding his eyes.

"Quinn is an actress."

"I'm not an idiot, Wyatt," she said icily, her cheeks flushing with anger. Wyatt didn't know whether to feel excited that he had finally gotten a reaction out of Dorrie or worried. "I saw the way you looked at her, and I saw the way she looked at you. The whole diner did."

"Quinn and I are friends," he said, attempting to carefully walk through the minefield without losing any limbs.

She snorted in disbelief, then appeared surprised that

she had done anything so unladylike. She shook her head as the anger slowly drained from her face. "I don't know why I'm getting so upset. You don't owe me anything."

"Not yet."

Her expression grew guarded as she studied him. "What do you mean?"

"I think you know how I feel about you, Dorrie. I really like you. I think you and I have a lot in common and want the same things for the future. I want to get to know you better."

A smile bloomed across her face and she instantly stared at the ground, as if she hadn't meant to smile like that. Wyatt smiled, relieved.

"I want to get to know you better, too," she said softly.

"Lunch? Same time tomorrow?"

"I'd like that," she said, finally meeting his eyes again.

She waved, then walked into her office. Wyatt waited until the door closed, then cursed. Quinn wanted to know if he ever spoke. Well, he now had plenty to say to her. A lot, in fact.

Chapter 6

Quinn didn't like to reward herself with food, but sometimes only the ability to eat anything she wanted could sufficiently reward a woman who normally ate no more than fifteen hundred calories a day. Quinn bit into the oversized cheeseburger she had picked up from another diner outside town, then stuffed several French fries in her mouth. She moaned in pleasure and leaned back against the pillows of the porch swing on the back porch of the house.

She would never admit it, but this was her favorite spot in Sibleyville. Two large trees shadowed the back porch from the overhead sun. There were gentle rolling green hills as far as the eye could see punctuated by little bursts of wildflowers that bloomed in the summer.

This afternoon there was a chill in the air, but the sun shone and the all-encompassing quiet was only interrupted by the occasional shrill of a bird call.

She had changed out of her come-hither clothes into a pair of comfortable, worn jeans and one of Graham's sweatshirts. As a result, she was warm for the first time since she had driven into Sibleyville last night. And she was actually eating. Real food. She almost felt content; maybe Sibleyville was not exactly the pit of hell she had always pictured. But then again, she was drowning her insides with fat and grease, and a girl was liable to feel anything under that influence.

She chuckled to herself as she remembered Wyatt's expression in the diner. An hour later and she still got a good laugh out of it. He had been furious. Annoyed. Pushed to the limit. Completely outmatched. By the time Charlie and Graham arrived in town in another few hours, Wyatt would have admitted defeat and Quinn would be packed and ready to return to Los Angeles. Of course, Kendra would not be happy to arrive here and not find Quinn, but Quinn would thank Kendra in her Oscar acceptance speech.

Quinn smiled again, then lifted her wineglass to her imagined enraptured audience. No, she would first thank Wyatt in her Oscar speech. He could fume while he changed all those babies' diapers he was so looking forward to changing.

"Celebrating something?" came a dry voice.

Quinn screeched in fear at the sight of Wyatt standing in the yard. She screamed again when she realized that she had spilled wine all over her jeans. She jumped to her feet and swiped at her jeans with the towel she had been using as a napkin.

"Damn it, Wyatt. You scared me," she snapped, annoyed.

She glared at him and was surprised by the sudden shiver that raced through her body. He was gorgeous. All brown skin and denim-clad legs and eyelashes. It was ridiculous to think of a man as simply legs and eyelashes, but she did. And he even wore a tan cowboy hat. And he didn't look ridiculous in the least.

"Where are the fishnets?" he demanded, walking up the porch stairs to tower over her.

Quinn ignored him and quickly walked into the house to the kitchen. He followed her.

"These jeans cost one hundred and fifty dollars," she growled as she wet the towel and began to blot the stains. "Not to mention I spilled wine all over my lunch."

"One pair of jeans and a burger and fries for my future with Dorrie. It's a good start," he said flatly.

"What are you talking about?"

"You know exactly what I'm talking about. Your little act in the diner," he said angrily. "I have to admit, it was a brilliant performance, Quinn."

She threw the towel in the sink disgustedly, giving up on her jeans and then glared at him. He was much closer than she had realized. And there was that scent again. The Wyatt scent. Her nerves tingled.

"I have no idea what you're talking about," she managed.

He laughed in disbelief and sat at the table to lean back and study her. She refused to believe that she was nervous in the least. But she sure felt something akin to nervous. Very nervous.

"I know you think that all Sibleyville natives are hicks, and maybe you're right. We are. But this hick knew exactly what you were doing when you sauntered into the diner in those fishnets." He paused in his speech to sputter, outraged, "Fishnets, Quinn? It's nearly fifty degrees outside. You're going to catch pneumonia."

For some reason, she found it amusing and a tad touching that he was so focused on her health. She hid her smile and said, while pretending to stifle a yawn, "You're really going to have to stop speaking in codes because I have no idea what you're talking about and I'm getting bored."

Wyatt's eyes narrowed and Quinn wondered if she had finally pushed him too far. He stood and moved across the kitchen toward her. Actually, he stalked across the kitchen to her. She took a defensive step back and bumped into a counter. She placed her hands behind her and tried to hold Wyatt's dark gaze.

"You upset Dorrie today, and you pissed me off with that little show," he said in a low voice that threatened either ecstasy or hell. "If you think that I'm going to roll over for you because you attempt to throw a little wrench in my budding relationship with Dorrie, then you don't know me very well. If anything, you've made me more resolved than ever to date Dorrie and you also have made me more resolved than ever to make certain that you and your film crew never set foot in my house."

"That's not fair," she squeaked.

"Not fair," he repeated, in disbelief. "After your performance in the diner, Dorrie and half the town think you and I are sleeping together. By the end of the day, the entire town will think we're on the verge of getting married. *That's* not fair, Quinn. You know that I'm trying to build a life with Dorrie. She walked out on me in the diner and almost walked out on me entirely."

"Almost?" Quinn repeated, disappointed.

"Yes, almost. I managed to salvage our growing friendship, no thanks to you. But even though she pretended to believe me, there was doubt in her eyes that was not there before."

"I see I'm not the only one bitten by the drama bug around here. All I did was act a little friendly, Wyatt."

"Do you really think that I'll talk my mother into letting you use the house just because you're threatening to sabotage my relationship with Dorrie?"

"That's exactly what I think," she said flatly. He appeared surprised, as if he didn't expect her to admit it. She smiled. "You know I can do it, Wyatt. One smile. A well-placed hand or, a kiss even, and Dorrie will never talk to you again."

"Are you threatening me?" he asked in disbelief.

"Whatever you think of me, I am an actress. An extraordinary actress, actually. I can make anybody believe whatever I want, which means I can make this town— including Dorrie—believe that you and I are having a torrid, no-holds-barred affair and that we're madly in love," she said simply. "Without any participation from you. And no one will believe your denials because everyone knows how you've followed me around like a puppy ever since Graham and Charlie met."

"You wouldn't."

"Oh, I would. I intend to, actually, unless…well, you know what I want," she said then lifted her left eyebrow in challenge. When he only stared at her, his face a blank mask, she sighed in frustration. "Come on, Wyatt. Why put me through this? Just give me what I want— the house for the film—and I'll be out of your hair, and you and Dorrie and continue your inevitable march toward white picket fences and dirty diapers."

He stepped closer until the heat from his body mingled with hers. She suddenly found herself breathing hard. Her gaze dropped to his mouth, and she found herself licking her lips.

"You have gone too far, Quinn. This is war."

"War?" she croaked. She shook her head confused. "I don't want—"

"War, Quinn. You want a battle. You have a battle."

She choked out a nervous laugh. "Be reasonable, Wyatt."

"I'm done being reasonable with you. You don't understand reasonable. Here are the rules of engagement. One week. One week for you to try whatever you can to turn Dorrie against me. If you succeed, then you'll have the mortuary for your film because you'd have done me a favor in showing me that Dorrie is not the woman I thought she was. If, on the other hand, Dorrie ignores all of your underhanded attempts, then you'll never mention that film or my house again."

"Wyatt, I'm not—"

"Is it a deal or not?" he demanded, moving even closer.

They stared at each other for a moment. Then his gaze subtly dropped. To her breasts. Even though she wore a sweatshirt at least two sizes too big, she felt vulnerable and dainty. It made her instantly more nervous.

She crossed her arms over her breasts, and Wyatt instantly lifted his gaze to hers. He didn't smile this time. He just watched her. Waiting.

"You're really confident in Mission—Find a Wife, aren't you?"

"I'm confident in Dorrie."

"I watched you two before I walked into the diner. It looked painful. When you're the big talker at the table, there definitely is trouble." Her eyes widened as Wyatt leaned even closer and placed his finger on her lips, effectively silencing her.

"Don't worry about my relationship with Dorrie," he said quietly, his eyes boring into hers. "You should be worrying about finding your next movie role. Do we have a deal or not?"

She couldn't resist the grin that spread across her face. "A Sibley always gets what she wants, Wyatt. You're in over your head."

She placed her hand in his to shake on the deal. Wyatt laughed, seeming almost as delighted as she was. And there it was. The two were smiling at each other. Enjoying each other, even, with the threat of mutual destruction.

At the same time, they both realized that they were smiling at each other, alone, in the house, holding hands. His hand was large and warm, slightly callused. And even though Quinn felt weird touching Wyatt, it also felt strangely comfortable, as if she had been holding his hand for most of her life.

Time stopped. His smile faded and a strange expression crossed his face, as if he couldn't quite believe that she was standing there, near him. His lips parted slightly. Quinn thought that Wyatt leaned toward her. She knew that she leaned toward him.

"We're home!" came an excited cry from the living room.

Wyatt jumped away from Quinn, and Quinn bumped into the counter once more. Charlie walked into the kitchen, looking cute and impossibly sweet, loaded down with brown grocery bags. She set the bags on the counter and grinned when she saw Quinn. She raced across the kitchen to wrap Quinn in a tight embrace that left Quinn gasping for air.

"You're still here," Charlie said, excitedly. "I saw your car out front, and I was so excited. We can go pick a Christmas tree."

Graham walked into the kitchen and appeared to be on the verge of speaking, then just looked from Quinn to Wyatt. Quinn widened her eyes at Graham, silently begging him not to say anything that would draw Charlie's attention the strange undercurrents in the kitchen.

"And did you hear that Kendra will be here tomorrow?" Charlie practically jumped up and down as she released Quinn. "I don't think the three of us have been together for Christmas since…I don't know when. This is going to be so exciting. I have to start baking cookies and making popcorn for the tree—"

"Calm down, baby. We have a few more days until Christmas. You can torture us with Christmas cheer after you've had a chance to relax a little," Graham said with a gentle smile in Charlie's direction before he pinned Quinn with a hard look and then turned to Wyatt. "Wyatt, nice to see you. What are you doing here? Helping Quinn prepare for our arrival?"

"Wyatt, what a nice surprise," Charlie exclaimed, walking across the room to throw her arms around him.

Quinn tried not to feel jealous at the sight of her sister touching Wyatt and Wyatt touching her back. Quinn couldn't hug Wyatt. Quinn frowned when she caught Graham staring at her with a knowing smirk. She resisted the urge to stick her tongue out at him. She had never had a brother before and as brothers went Graham was fine, but he did have the annoying part down.

"It's nice to see you, too, Charlie," Wyatt said, smiling. He nodded at Graham then glanced at his watch. "We should all catch up later. I have to…I have to get to something in town. A meeting."

He hugged Charlie once more, pounded fists with Graham, then glanced at Quinn. Quinn instantly turned to the grocery bags on the counter to unload them. She heard Wyatt's boots pound on the wooden floor as he walked out the kitchen and tried not to feel as if all the air had just left the room.

"Leaving so soon?"

Wyatt rolled his eyes in frustration when he heard Graham follow him out the house. Wyatt thought about ignoring his best friend and just getting into his car and driving away. But Graham would probably follow him. The two had known each other their entire lives. Graham was not the type of man who would allow anyone to ignore him. Especially Wyatt.

"So what exactly were you helping Quinn with?" Graham asked, with a smirk.

"It's not what you think, Graham."

"Of course it's not," Graham said in the most condescending tone he could manage, which was pretty condescending—even for Graham.

"Nothing is going on with Quinn and me," he said firmly as he leaned against his truck.

"I know you're lying. Your left eyelid is twitching. It always twitches when you lie."

Wyatt instantly touched his eyelid, which made Graham howl with laughter. Wyatt rolled his eyes annoyed. "What are you? Twelve?"

"No, I'm actually thirty-three," Graham said, attempting to keep a straight face. "Now, you and Quinn. Spill it before Charlie realizes how strange it was for you and Quinn to be alone together and she comes out here to investigate. Trust me, she won't be as nice as I'm being."

"Quinn wants to film a movie in Sibleyville, and, for some reason, she thinks the funeral home would be perfect for it."

"The mortuary?" Graham asked perplexed.

Wyatt shrugged in response. "I'm as shocked as you. Quinn, in her usual Quinn way, asked my mother, and Mom, in her usual Mom way, won't even entertain the idea. And, of course, Quinn won't take no for an answer and has decided that it's all my fault and is now relentlessly harassing me."

"Of course," Graham said with a grin. "And what exactly does any of this has to do with you being here making goo-goo eyes at her in my kitchen?"

"I'm a grown man. I don't make goo-goo eyes at anyone."

"Then I'll just say there was some serious silent movie action going on in that kitchen when I walked in. Quinn didn't even look at you when you left. Usually, she at least manages to sneer at you."

"For the last time, Graham, nothing is going on between Quinn and me. She's an attractive woman. Downright, drop-dead gorgeous. I won't deny that. But I'm interested in someone else. In fact, I plan for her to be my wife. And I won't let Quinn stand in the way of that."

"Marriage?" Graham choked out. "Who? When I was here for Easter, you were complaining that you may as well join the priesthood for the action you get around here."

"And then I went to a church picnic and had one of Dorrie Diamond's famous chocolate almond balls." Wyatt sent Graham a silent grin of male appreciation. "It could make a grown man weep. I hear that her meat loaf is even better."

"Meat loaf? Chocolate almond balls?" Graham shook his head in disbelief. "Do you want a personal chef or a wife?"

"She's a good woman, Graham."

"Dorrie Diamond, huh? That's the new accountant on Main Street who never looks anyone in the eye."

"She looks me in the eye," Wyatt said defensively, then added, "sort of."

Graham wisely chose not to comment further and, instead, asked, "Why do you think that Quinn wants to stand in the way of your relationship with Dorrie?"

"That woman has no respect for anyone or anything. She practically demanded that I turn over my house to her for her movie. As if I owe her."

Graham hesitated before muttering, "It's not like you have a full house over there. When was the last time you had a funeral?"

"That's not the point," Wyatt snapped, irritably. "I'm operating a funeral home. A respectable establishment. We've been serving Sibleyville's dead since—"

"Since 1919," Graham intoned dully. He rolled his eyes. "I know, Wyatt, I know. I was the one standing next to you when your dad would go on and on about the importance of the Granger Funeral Home. You would think he was solving world hunger."

"He was proud of the Granger legacy," Wyatt said, defensively.

"And he should be," Graham quickly agreed, then asked, "but is allowing a movie to be filmed there really damaging that legacy? No one has died in town in over eight months. It's not like you have a line of funeral goers waiting to use the space."

"You don't understand, Graham. This is not a carnival ride. This is a funeral home. People come here to bury their loved ones. We have to make certain that the absolute solemnity of that occasion is never compromised."

Graham rolled his eyes once more, and Wyatt resisted the urge to roll his eyes himself. He had heard that speech so many times from his mother and father over the years that he couldn't believe that it had somehow transfered into his own speech.

Wyatt shook his head and admitted, reluctantly, "I actually don't have a problem letting her film the movie there, but Mom nixed the idea. I haven't been home since the meltdown this morning."

"I wouldn't have gone home, either."

"I can change Mom's mind. It won't be pleasant, but I can find a way to do it."

Graham laughed and shook his head. "You better find a way because Quinn does not like being told no. She's going to hound you unmercifully until you relent."

"I know, I know. I can handle Quinn."

Graham suddenly became extremely still and said quietly, "She may annoy the hell out of me and she could possibly drive a monk to drink, but Quinn is

Charlie's sister. Charlie loves her, so I love her. You hurt Quinn, you hurt Charlie, which you definitely don't want to do if you want to be able to walk upright for the rest of your life."

Wyatt bit his bottom lip to hold back the laughter. He was being warned off by Graham Forbes, the biggest playboy that Wyatt had ever known. Or at least until Charlie entered the scene.

"You are so whipped," he finally said, unable to control his laughter anymore.

Graham raked both hands over his hair, looking slightly embarrassed. He shrugged, even as a smile played across his lips. Then he frowned as he said, "I'm serious, Wyatt. Quinn is family now. I don't want her hurt, no matter what she says or does to you. No matter how grown-up she tries to act, she's still just a kid."

Wyatt hid his snort of disbelief. Only a man as deeply in love with his wife as Graham was would consider Quinn Sibley a kid. There was nothing remotely child-like about that woman—or her body.

"I would never hurt Quinn. You know that."

Graham glowered, and Wyatt glowered back. Graham finally sighed heavily and threw up his hands in surrender. "Just don't do anything that I'll have to answer to Charlie for. She's real sensitive when it comes to her sisters, especially Quinn."

"For God's sake, Graham, you've known me your whole life," he snapped.

"Exactly, and that's why I'm worried, because I know how long you've wanted Quinn. She's treated you like shit for a long time, and sometimes when a man gets close to a woman who's been torturing him for a year, he…well…. Just don't hurt her."

Wyatt didn't bother to deny Graham's observation. For a spilt second in Quinn's kitchen, maybe he had forgotten that the word *gentleman* existed. He had wanted to kiss her. To devour her. And he probably would have if Charlie hadn't walked into the kitchen. And then his life would have been in a bigger mess than it was now.

"I'm not interested in Quinn anymore. I told you that. I'm looking for marriage and kids, and we both know that Quinn is about as ready for that as…any young Hollywood actress with the body and looks Quinn has." Wyatt cleared his throat when he realized that Graham's gaze had hardened. He forced a smile and said lightly, "Quinn will be fine. Whether I will be after Mom hears that we may have half of Hollywood running around the house is another subject."

Graham shuddered in agreement.

Chapter 7

Wyatt sagged onto his sofa, then took a drag from a chilled bottle of beer. It had been a long day, from Quinn showing up on his doorstep to almost taking Quinn in the middle of his best friend's kitchen. So basically, Wyatt had started the day hard as a rod and was ending the day as hard as a rod. Not to mention the fact that he had to come up with a way to get Dorrie to take his phone calls again and to rub Quinn's face in it.

Wyatt flipped on the television and sighed in contentment as an NBA game filled the fifty-six-inch plasma screen. One of the things he would miss once he married was being to relax with a beer in front of the plasma without any interruptions. Basketball in high-def. It was about as perfect as a bachelor could get, without his woman sitting next to him in stilettos and little else while feeding him a plate of buffalo wings.

A knock on the front door of his apartment instantly nixed his fantasy of two uninterrupted hours of basketball.

"Come in, Mom," he called.

Beatrice opened the door and walked into the living room carrying a foil-covered plate of food. Wyatt's stomach immediately grumbled as the smell of pot roast and potatoes assaulted his senses. His mother did not fight fair.

"I figured you were in here sulking about our little argument this morning, so I brought you dinner," Beatrice announced as she set the plate on the wood coffee table in front of the sofa.

"I'm not sulking, and thanks for dinner," he muttered as he reached for the food. He briefly closed his eyes in ecstasy when he saw that large piece of peach cobbler on the corner of the plate.

Beatrice propped the decorative pillows on the easy chair next to sofa and sat. She watched Wyatt inhale the food for a moment, then said evenly, "As long as I'm alive, I will not allow that woman to desecrate our business or your father's memory by making an adult movie in the house."

Wyatt choked on his food and coughed to clear his throat. He took a quick swig of beer. "Quinn does not want to make a porno in the house. In fact, it's about as far from a porno as you can get. It's some depressing and serious independent movie. Come on, Mom. Do you really think I'd allow that? Do you really think Boyd would allow that in this town?"

"Now, that you mention it, I spoke to Mayor Robbins this morning, and he has not heard of any movie being made in town. Not only was he surprised to hear the news, but he was mortified. This is a peaceful town. The last thing we need is a bunch of Hollywood types running around here causing problems."

"You spoke to Boyd about this?" he asked, annoyed.

Beatrice bristled. "I didn't think this movie was a secret. She does need Boyd's permission. I thought he already knew."

"You should have called me first."

"You wouldn't answer your cell phone. Besides, this is my town, and my home that that woman wants to corrupt. I had to talk to someone since you obviously don't see the danger."

"I told you that she's not making a porno or anything close to a porno."

"Well, I don't see what other movie anyone would put her in," Beatrice said with a sniff.

"You know Quinn. You know her family. You always go on and on about what a lucky man Graham is."

"Charlie is a decent, sweet woman. Eliza did not raise a fool, so I know Graham would not marry a woman who was not worthy. She's nothing like the other two sisters. Everyone in town knows that. All you had to do was watch the other two at Graham's wedding. Kendra was stumbling around drunk, while Quinn was grinding against every man she could find, married or not."

Wyatt resisted the urge to correct his mother. Quinn had grinded against every man at the wedding except him.

Beatrice continued, "And look at the way she dresses. I'm surprised the poor thing hasn't died of pneumonia with the clothes she flounces around in this weather."

"Her clothes are her business, and she's not making

a porno. What valid objections do you have to the movie being shot in the mortuary?" he demanded.

"I know trouble, Wyatt, and that girl is trouble. I already heard about what happened today in the diner." Wyatt groaned, then took another swig of his beer. Beatrice nodded, knowingly, "Yes, I heard how she sauntered into the diner—wearing next to nothing, I might add—and poured herself all over you while Dorrie sat on the other side of the table. How could you do that to Dorrie? Dorrie is a decent, good woman. She didn't deserve that. Not to mention that I heard she read you the riot act in the middle of Main Street."

He set down the beer bottle a little harder than he meant to, which caused Beatrice to flinch in surprise. "I'm going to say this once, Mother, so listen closely. Quinn is my friend and the sister of my best friend's wife. As such, I expect you to be cordial to her."

Beatrice's eyes narrowed and she said in a tight voice, "Wyatt, please tell me that you are not dating this girl?"

"Quinn is my friend, Mom. That should be all you need to know to treat her with some semblance of respect. Understand?" Wyatt waited for his mother's response, but she only stared at him in shock.

The two rarely argued. Beatrice bullied, and Wyatt didn't resist. He knew his mother was wondering why it was different this time. Wyatt wondered too.

Beatrice's expression softened as she said gently, "I'm sorry, sweetie. I just want you to be happy, and I think Dorrie will make you happy."

"Don't count me out yet, Mom," he said with a wink. "I haven't given up on Dorrie."

Beatrice smiled and walked across the floor to caress

his cheek. "I didn't think you'd be distracted by someone like Quinn. I raised you better than that."

Beatrice walked out the apartment, closing the door. Wyatt covered the plate again, suddenly not hungry anymore.

Quinn looked up from the script she had been trying to read for the last hour as her bedroom door flew open. She couldn't help but smile as Charlie bounded into the bedroom, wearing a silly nightgown with panda bears and fluffy slippers. Charlie looked as if she were eight years old.

"You're still awake. Good," Charlie exclaimed, climbing onto the bed next to Quinn. "Whenever we visit Sibleyville, Graham resorts back to his rancher sleep hours. Awake at the crack of dawn and in bed by eight."

"Or maybe it's because you had him running around all day, buying Christmas trees, stringing lights on the house and baking Christmas cookies."

"Wait until we start our Christmas shopping," Charlie said, giggling. "He'll probably be in bed by four-thirty every afternoon just to have enough energy to keep up."

Quinn laughed and studied the sheer happiness on Charlie's face. For a moment, she felt an intense jab of envy. She wanted what Charlie had, and she knew that she would never get it. Women like her didn't marry men who would climb on houses to hang Christmas lights. Women like her married men who paid other men to hang the Christmas lights and then left as soon as wrinkles appeared and skin started to sag.

"Do you want to run lines?" Charlie asked, while tapping the script in Quinn's hands.

"Not particularly," Quinn muttered, tossing the script aside.

"Do you want to talk about what was going on in the kitchen with you and Wyatt when Graham and I got here?"

Quinn looked at Charlie, surprised. She had thought Charlie hadn't noticed Quinn's strange behavior that afternoon in the kitchen. If Charlie hadn't walked into the kitchen at that moment, Quinn knew that she and Wyatt would have kissed. Then Wyatt would have fallen in love with Quinn even more, and Quinn would not have been able to use his house for the movie without going on a date with him.

She could imagine trying to force Wyatt to talk for two hours while he stared at her with those beautiful eyes and the occasional dimpled smile…. Quinn frowned, not at all pleased about the direction of her thoughts.

"I don't know what you're talking about," Quinn said, simply.

"The sexual tension in the air could have been cut with a knife."

Quinn laughed too loudly, then stood from the bed and walked to the dresser. She picked up a hairbrush and began to brush out the tangles in her hair as she stared at her reflection in the mirror. "My pores are looking large enough to swallow a makeup brush. How about we give each other facials?"

"Now I'm intrigued. You're avoiding the subject," Charlie noted, sitting up on the bed to cross her legs. "Are you attracted to Wyatt, Quinn?"

"Don't be ridiculous," she snapped, more heatedly than she intended.

"Wyatt is a great guy. He's gorgeous, kind—"

"A mortician who lives with his mother."

"He lives in an apartment over the garage—"

"So he has even less money that I first thought."

"In case you've forgotten, you're not exactly rolling in dough, either, dear sister."

Quinn set down the brush and turned to Charlie . "Which is exactly why I need a man who makes more in a year than what I used to tip my valets in a month. I can do poor on my own."

Charlie continued to grin as she said, "I think you're protesting a tad too much."

"Oh, please," Quinn huffed in indignation while rolling her eyes. "As if I'd be interested in him. He wouldn't know Versace from Prada. He's probably never even flown first-class."

"All definite strikes against his character," Charlie agreed, then coughed to hide her obvious laughter.

"Definitely," Quinn agreed.

"Now that you've unsuccessfully tried to change the subject, can we get back to what I really wanted to know? What happened between you and Wyatt in the kitchen? And you can also throw in an explanation about what happened at Annie's Diner."

Quinn froze, then asked hesitantly, "You heard about the diner?"

"You know how Sibleyville is," Charlie responded with a shrug, then ordered, "now, spill it."

Quinn blurted out, "Wyatt won't let us film in his house."

"Have you gotten filming permits yet from Boyd?"

"Just a technicality." Quinn cleared her throat at the alarm that crossed Charlie's face and said quickly, "I have an appointment with him tomorrow…or maybe the day after."

"Quinn—"

"I'm taking care of it."

"What does any of this have to do with the scene in the kitchen?"

"As I said, Wyatt won't let us film in his house. And the Granger Funeral Home is the only place where Helmut wants to film. Without the house, Helmut doesn't want the town…or me. I told Wyatt all of this, and he could give a damn. Since he has little regard for my future, I've chosen to have little regard for his future."

Charlie lifted one eyebrow suspiciously. "What is that supposed to mean, Quinn?"

"Don't worry about your precious Wyatt, Charlie. He'll be just fine…as long as he does exactly what I want."

"Quinn, Wyatt is not like the usual men you date…"

Now Quinn didn't have to act to pretend indignation. "And what is that supposed to mean?"

"Sibleyville is Wyatt's home and my home, too, for that matter. Don't embarrass him."

Quinn felt hurt by the suspicious note in her sister's voice. She stretched her arms over her head and murmured, "I'm bored by this conversation. I need my beauty rest. Can we finish this titillating conversation tomorrow?"

Charlie slid off the bed and crossed the room to Quinn. Concern was etched on her face as she studied Quinn. "Did I offend you? You know that I would never purposely hurt you."

"I really am tired, Charlie. Can we—"

Charlie continued, undeterred. "I'm sorry, Quinn. I just don't think you realize how much Wyatt likes you—"

Quinn couldn't disguise her snort of disbelief. "*Likes me?* He barely talks around me. All he does is stare. I'll agree that he's attracted to me and acts like a lovesick idiot around me, salivating over my breasts. All heterosexual men—and most gay man—do, but I highly doubt that Wyatt likes me."

"He does, Quinn. I think he…" Charlie's voice trailed off and she averted her gaze.

"What?" Quinn prodded, interested despite her attempts at aloofness.

Charlie shook her head, then forced a smile. "Nothing. You're both adults. It's none of my business."

Charlie pecked Quinn on the cheek, then walked out the room. Quinn sat on her bed and stared at the closed door. Now she would never be able to go to sleep tonight, wondering what her sister had been about to say about Wyatt's feelings for her. And wondering what had been in Wyatt's eyes when he had leaned toward her in the kitchen. She knew lust. And there hadn't just been lust in his eyes. It had been something more.

Chapter 8

Quinn walked into the kitchen the next morning. She sighed in relief to find it empty. She could not deal with Wyatt questions from Charlie this morning. She had too many herself to answer Charlie's questions.

She raked hands through her tangled curls and found the coffeepot still full with steaming coffee. She poured coffee into Kendra's favorite mug, which she took particular joy drinking out of, then walked to the living room. No sign of Charlie and Graham in there, either.

She pushed aside a lace curtain in one of the front windows and didn't see Graham's Porsche. But she did, unfortunately, see Boyd Robbins climbing from his truck. She quickly released the curtain, but it was too late. Boyd had seen her. It wasn't fair. She was in pajamas and a robe. Hardly proper attire for a confrontation with Sibleyville's cantankerous mayor.

Boyd pounded on the front door. "Ms. Sibley! Ms. Sibley, I know you're in there! I need to talk to you."

Quinn grimaced, then gulped down the cup of coffee, knowing that she would need all the caffeine she could handle to deal with Boyd. She set the cup on a nearby table and opened the door.

She tried her best smile and the semblance of a country drawl, "Good morning, Mayor Robbins."

Boyd didn't smile back. He was a former Marine and damn proud of it. He still kept his military buzz cut, lean, muscular figure and ramrod-straight posture, even decades after having retired from the Corps. The problem was, Boyd also still kept his Marine attitude. He ordered people around. And because the Sibleyville residents thought it would do more harm than good to let him run around complaining about not being mayor, he was in the middle of his fifteenth consecutive term as mayor.

"Let's cut the small talk, Ms. Sibley," Boyd said, his country drawl thick, even though Sibleyville sat in the middle of California. He planted his feet wide apart, rocked back on his heels and hooked his hands on his oversized silver belt buckle. "I heard that you're trying to make a movie in my town. I find that damn surprising, since no one has called my office and asked for permission, and since I would never grant permission for any Hollywood types to run around my town, messing with my citizens and causing general havoc in this town."

"Mayor Robbins, I'm sure we can reach some type of agreement—"

"That's funny because I'm pretty damn confident that we can't reach any type of agreement," he shouted. She had been waiting for the shouting to begin. Mayor Robbins was not exactly known for his poise and grace. "In fact, I'm pretty damn confident that no Hollywood types are going to set foot in my town with any damn cameras."

"We will not disrupt the town in any way," Quinn spoke quickly. "We'll be filming a few exterior shots on the outskirts of town and maybe one or two on Main Street. The majority of the shooting will take place at the Granger Funeral Home—"

"Now I know you're lying," Boyd said, with a loud guffaw of disbelief. "I heard from a very reliable source that you will not be filming at the mortuary under any circumstances."

"I'm working on that," Quinn conceded.

Boyd smiled in that way of his that meant he was nowhere near close to being amused. "If you get permission to film at the Granger Funeral Home, I will personally chauffer you and the film crew anywhere in this town that you want."

Quinn lifted one eyebrow, amused. "Everyone will love being shown around by the mayor. It'll add that down-home touch that will make the cast and crew fall in love with Sibleyville."

His smile fell, and his eyes narrowed at her. "You really are a Sibley, aren't you? Arrogance runs in the family."

"You set the terms of the deal, Mayor, and I'm just accepting them."

"You're awfully sure of yourself. You think you can bat your eyelashes at Wyatt Granger and he'll go against his mother. That is never going to happen. Wyatt is a good boy. He will not be tempted by you."

"Who said anything about tempting Wyatt?" she demanded angrily. "Some people would love to have their homes featured in a movie. Only in this town is Hollywood still considered Sodom and Gomorrah."

"We're not the only town. We're just the most vocal about it," he said, becoming calmer the more angry she became.

"Boyd, what a pleasant surprise," came Graham's sardonic voice from the still open front door.

Charlie quickly stepped into the house to stand by Quinn's side and to frown at Boyd.

"Are you all right, Quinn?" Charlie asked, grabbing her hand.

"Of course she's all right," Boyd snapped. "She and I just reached an understanding. There's nothing like having a good understanding."

"Oh, we understand each other all right, Boyd. And I can't wait to let the crew know how happy you'll be to see all of us," Quinn replied, with a sugary sweet smile.

Boyd practically growled at her, then stomped toward the front door. He cast one look last disgusted look at Quinn and Charlie, then stormed down the porch and toward his truck.

"Always good to see you, Boyd," Graham called after him, then slammed the door and turned to Quinn. "What did that asshole want?"

"Nothing," Quinn said, shaking her head. She ignored both of their questioning glances and said, "I'm going to take a shower and then I'm heading into town. I have a few errands to run."

She walked up the stairs and to her room, her nerves making her nearly break into a run. She had to convince Wyatt to give her the house, and she had to convince him now.

* * *

Wyatt parked his SUV in front of Dorrie's office for their lunch date. He had gotten up with a renewed purpose that morning. Not only would he woo Dorrie in a manner that this town would talk about for years, but he also would be teaching Quinn a lesson that she should have learned a long time ago: don't underestimate a determined man.

Wyatt grabbed the bunches of daffodils wrapped in green paper on the passenger seat and got out the car. Not many women could resist daffodils, especially bright pink ones that were hard to find in the middle of winter.

Fortunately, Wyatt had such daffodils in the greenhouse he had built from scratch and filled with all varieties of flowers. He could not bear to bring her boring roses.

Wyatt was not just the town mortician; he as also the town's unofficial gardener and florist. He didn't garden for the money, he did it because he loved to garden. He loved to have people visit the greenhouse and admire his flowers.

Wyatt grinned as he checked his reflection in the sideview mirror. He wasn't usually a vain, check-him-self-in-the-mirror type of man, but a man had to look his best when he was wooing, and Wyatt would definitely be wooing today.

"Flowers?" came a deep drawl behind him. "Nice touch."

Wyatt turned to face Graham's father, Lance, and Lance's best friend and partner in crime, Angus Affleck. The two men could have been advertisements for cowboys. Their weathered, lined faces were usually covered by hats, their attire was denim, boots and plaid shirts, and their legs were bowed from being more comfortable on a horse than in a car. They were tough, old-time cowboys with ranches and farms, and the deep lines etched in their leathery brown skin reflected that. Wyatt could not have asked for better substitute fathers after his own died.

Lance touched the rim of his Chicago Cubs baseball hat and said, "From what I heard about the row you and Dorrie had in the street yesterday, I don't think those flowers are going to be enough."

Angus laughed and added, "Not to mention the little scene in the diner with the Sibley girl."

"That's right. Quinn. You are in trouble if that one has you in her sights," Lance said, an amused twinkle in his brown eyes.

"I definitely wouldn't mind being in her sights. I can tell you that much," Angus said, causing both the men guffaw in laughter.

Wyatt hid his own smile and said dryly, "If you two are done with the Laurel and Hardy routine, I have some wooing to do."

"Now that sounds downright serious," Lance said, while nudging an obviously amused Angus.

"We definitely wouldn't want to get in the way of wooing," Angus managed to agree, without laughing too much.

"But, let's not be hasty, young buck," Angus said, while placing a firm grip on Wyatt's arm. "Talk to two old men for a moment."

"Yes, talk to us," Angus said.

Wyatt narrowed his eyes suspiciously then glanced from one man to the other. "What is this about?"

"Dorrie is a sweet girl, but if Quinn is as lovestruck for you as people say she was in the diner—"

Angus interrupted Lance to say, "I think the most popular description so far is lovestruck calf—"

"Then you need to reassess the situation," Lance concluded.

Angus added, "There's nothing like a good reassessment of the situation."

"Because Quinn is a wonderful woman," Lance said, finishing Angus's sentence. "Not saying that Dorrie isn't, but you and Quinn would be good together."

"And not so much with Dorrie…as great as she is," Angus murmured.

"Because we've watched you watching Quinn for the last year, and now that you're getting your chance, we'd hate to see you blow it," Lance concluded, followed by a confirming nod from Angus.

Wyatt gently extracted his arm from Angus's grip and said, "Have you two thought about joining the local quilting circle? I'm sure you could add valuable gossip and meddling."

"Easy there," Angus growled as Lance laughed.

Wyatt ignored Angus and said to Lance, "There's nothing to reassess. Quinn likes to play games and, because she's bored, I'm her plaything for right now."

"I would pay money to be that young girl's plaything," Angus said, sounding a tad too serious. Lance stared at him surprised, and Angus shrugged innocently. "I watched *Diamond Valley*. She's a pistol."

"The point is," Wyatt continued while shooting Angus an annoyed look, "Quinn was putting on a show in the diner because she knew that people were watching. I'm not going to let her distract me from trying to build a relationship with Dorrie."

Angus and Lance stared at each other for a moment, speechless. Then they both simultaneously began to laugh. Wyatt stared at them, confused.

"We obviously can't do any good around here," Lance said, shaking his head. "Let's grab some lunch."

"Poor idiot," Angus muttered, glancing at Wyatt.

The two men walked down the street still laughing and jabbing each other in the sides.

Wyatt shook his head at the two men, then walked into the accountant's office. There was a large desk in the center of the room, several chairs and a sofa against the wall. A door led to a private bathroom. She had numerous pictures of her nieces and nephews in Seattle and their drawings framed on the walls, not to mention the stitched pillows. Anyone who walked into the office would instantly feel at home. Comfortable. Wyatt could imagine that their home would feel like this too.

Dorrie stood at a filing cabinet at the back of the room. She turned when she heard the door open and smiled in welcome. She looked the picture of small-town beauty in dark gray slacks and a crisp white blouse. She even wore pearls. Perfect and feminine and sweet. Wyatt waited for that unsteady, rock-the-world sensation he got whenever Quinn smiled at him, but he felt nothing.

"Hi, Wyatt," she greeted. "I was just about to call you."

He walked across the room and offered her the flowers. "Pretty flowers for a pretty lady."

She looked at them, as if they were snakes. Then her eyes welled with tears and she sneezed. Loudly.

"Excuse me," she said then grabbed a tissue from the box on the top of the desk.

Wyatt offered her the flowers again. She sneezed again. Louder.

"You're allergic," he guessed with a grimace.

"Notice the plant-free, flower-free decor," came Quinn's loud voice from the door leading to the bathroom.

Wyatt's mouth dropped open as Quinn sauntered into the room. Wearing skin-tight corduroy pants, equally tight turtle-neck sweater and knee-high boots. In theory, it was a conservative outfit, but on Quinn... He hadn't heard the door open or noticed that someone else had been in the office. Quinn sent Wyatt a smug smile, then beamed a supposedly sympathetic at Dorrie, who was sniffling into a tissue.

"What are you doing here?" Wyatt demanded.

"Talking to Dorrie, silly. Why else would I be here?" she asked with a carefree laugh.

She crossed the room to loop her arms through one of his. He glared down at her and asked suspiciously, "What in the world do you have to talk to Dorrie about?"

"I just wanted to tell her that whatever she heard about you and me is a complete lie," Quinn said, then became distracted as she brushed imaginary lint off his shoulder. Once that was done, she met his gaze and said sweetly, "I told Dorrie that you and I are strictly friends and she has nothing to worry about."

"You told her that?" The disbelief was evident in his voice.

"Of course I did," Quinn said, pretending moral outrage. "You have made it more than clear that you want Dorrie, not me. I want you to be happy. And if Dorrie makes you happy, then she's who I want for you."

Dorrie sneezed again, and Wyatt and Quinn both turned to her with guilty expressions. Wyatt had momentarily forgotten that Dorrie was in the room. Judging from Quinn's smirk at him, she obviously had not.

"So how about the three of us go to lunch?" Quinn asked, grinning as she turned to Dorrie.

"No," Wyatt practically screamed. Dorrie and Quinn both looked at him with surprised expressions.

"You don't want to have lunch with Dorrie?" Quinn asked innocently.

"Of course, I want to have lunch with Dorrie. Dorrie and I have a lunch date *alone*," Wyatt snapped. When Quinn pretended to pout, Wyatt turned to Dorrie, who appeared to be trying to breathe while sniffing into a tissue.

Dorrie started to speak, but instead unleashed another torrential sneeze. Her eyes watered and she reached for another tissue.

"Wyatt, you're going to send the poor thing into a seizure," Quinn said, while pulling him toward the door. "Maybe you should try lunch tomorrow."

"Dorrie—"

"She's right," Dorrie said, nodding at Wyatt with an apologetic smile. "I need to take my allergy medicine and lie down for a few minutes. I'm so sorry."

Wyatt silently cursed while Quinn squeezed his arm. He tried subtly to shake her off, but she clung to him.

He turned to Dorrie. "Are you sure?"

"I'm sure, Wyatt. And for the record, I believe Quinn."

Wyatt smiled and moved towards her to hug her, but a resounding sneeze stopped him. He held up his hands in surrender, then walked out of the office with Quinn close on his heels.

"Well, since you're busy—" Quinn screeched when Wyatt grabbed her arm and led her to the SUV.

He yanked open the passenger door and practically threw her inside. He stormed around to the driver's side, stopping briefly to toss the flowers into a nearby garbage can. He slid behind the steering wheel and slammed the door.

"Where are you taking me?" Quinn demanded.

"You wanted to have lunch, so we're having lunch," he growled and then reversed out the parking spot, leaving tire tracks in the street. He ignored her protests and slammed down on the gas pedal. He noticed several neighbors turn on the sidewalk to stare at his SUV. For once, he didn't care.

Chapter 9

At some point during the hour-long ride where Wyatt sat in silence, glaring at the road, Quinn quit being scared and just enjoyed the scenery. The cool winter air blew into the car through the lowered windows. Wyatt had conceded to some noise and allowed her to turn on the radio, and there was nothing for miles and miles except trees and grass. It was kind of nice in a backward, country way.

She would never admit this to Wyatt, but for the first time in a long time she felt completely relaxed. She didn't have to worry about her makeup or her clothes or her hair. And she couldn't study her lines, or worry about the movie or her sisters because she was being kidnapped. No one in the world knew where she was.

Sure, Quinn had been a little frightened of what Wyatt had intended during the first two silent-filled minutes of the ride. Then she realized that no matter how angry Wyatt was with her, he would never hurt her. It wasn't in his genetic makeup. She didn't know how she knew that, but she did. And there was a certain level of comfort in that knowledge that made her lean back against the seat and just enjoy the moment.

A few minutes later, Wyatt turned off the highway and into the dirt parking lot of a brick building. It appeared to be a restaurant, but there was no name on the building. Cars and trucks were packed on the lot around the building and smoke billowed from the back of the building. The distinct smell of barbecue and cooked meat filled the air.

Wyatt stood from the truck and slammed the door. Quinn scrambled after him, smoothing her hair behind her ears and then moving it back.

"You really are taking me to lunch," she said, surprised.

He looked at her for the first time since he had thrown her into the SUV. "What did you expect?"

"You were trying to scare me," she accused.

He smiled, making that jolt of emotion quiver through her that only came up when he was around. "Nothing could scare you, Quinn. I think you Sibleys are incapable of feeling fear."

Quinn studied him for a moment, then smiled back. "You're right."

He shook his head, then walked into the restaurant. Quinn hesitantly followed him and stepped into another time. She glanced around the one-room restaurant filled with men in overalls and cowboy hats and knew that the place had never heard of trans fat and didn't give a damn about low-carb.

Wyatt waved to a man who appeared to be in charge, since his T-shirt looked a little more clean than those of some of the patrons. The man nodded in return, then motioned to a wood booth near an open window. Wyatt slid into the booth, and Quinn hesitantly sat across from him, wondering how she could sit without actually touching anything.

"So this is lunch?" she asked, glancing around at the other diners, who appeared more interested in their food than her. That was the first time that had happened. Ever. Quinn always made an entrance.

"Why did you tell Dorrie that we were just friends?"

"Classic bait-and-switch maneuver. Sephora used it many times on *Diamond Valley*," she said, distracted, as she brushed crumbs off the table and then wiped her hand on her skirt.

"Bait-and-switch."

"Tell the mark exactly what she wants to hear, then do exactly what you want, which is more often the exact opposite. When Sephora wanted the countess to sell the Irresistible perfume line to her, Sephora pretended not to want it. It worked like a charm. The countess actually begged Sephora to buy the line because she was convinced it was on the verge of folding and she would not be able to keep up the family castle. Of course, the countess didn't know that her husband was embezzling funds, but Sephora knew—"

"Dorrie is not a mark, Quinn," he interrupted, shaking his head.

"I wasn't talking about Dorrie. I was talking about you."

"Ah. You do realize that Dorrie is a human being

with feelings, and that your manipulation of those feelings could be considered cruel and callous."

"And this explains your participation in the bet how?"

"I was asking Dorrie out before you came to town. The fact that my pursuit coincides with making you eat crow is just icing on the cake."

Quinn slowly leaned across the table closer to him. She smiled when his gaze dropped to her mouth, but resisted the victory dance. She had him exactly where she wanted him. She lowered her voice to a seductive whisper. "There's one way to end this whole charade. Allow Helmut to film the movie in your home."

"Nice try," he muttered, shaking his head.

"Then the challenge continues," she said simply.

"But how did you know I'd be there?" Wyatt pressed.

"You're very predictable," she responded with a shrug. "I knew you'd do something predictable in order to apologize to Dorrie, although I might add that you have nothing to apologize for. And I figured you'd try to take her to lunch again, so I just got to her office a little early and made small talk until I saw your car drive by."

"You think I'm predictable."

"Most men are. It's not meant as an insult." Before she could stop herself, she tucked her hair behind her ears, then realized what she was doing and instantly rearranged her hair.

"Why do you do that?" he demanded, looking annoyed for some reason.

"What?"

"You always move your hair behind your ears, then quickly move it back, as if you're trying to hide something."

"I am. Big ears," she admitted. "I have freakishly large ears, so I try to never wear my hair back. You'd be surprised how much the camera magnifies a person's ears."

"I don't think your ears are freakishly large. Maybe strangely large, noticeably large, but freakishly…I wouldn't go that far. In fact, some people—y'know people with ear fetishes—would think your ears are just perfect."

Quinn's mouth dropped open in surprise. Then she realized that Wyatt was laughing.

She smiled. "Wyatt, I do believe you're demonstrating signs of a sense of humor."

He sent her one of his knee-shaking grins. "Just signs, huh?"

Quinn pretended not to be affected by his smile as she murmured, "I'll need more proof to determine if you actually have one or not."

When he only stared at her in response, with a slight smile, Quinn averted her gaze. There was something about the way he stared at her, as if he wanted to know every single detail about her and could learn it all just by looking at her.

"Is there a menu?" she asked abruptly.

He stopped staring at her to glance around the restaurant. "The menu stays the same. Ribs, potato salad and beer. Or chicken, potato salad and beer. And then there's the steak, potato salad and beer—"

"I'm sensing a high-caloric theme here."

"And the best part is that you never know what you're going to get. Cletus, the owner, brings you whatever he feels like bringing you or whatever happens to be ready."

"Sounds charming," she muttered dryly.

"My dad always brought me here. And his dad

brought him here. It's almost as much a Granger tradition as the mortuary."

"And your mother?"

"Wouldn't step foot in this place to save her life," he responded, laughing, then studied her obvious discomfort. "You two probably have more in common than either one of you realize."

Quinn shuddered to think that she had anything in common with Beatrice Granger. The woman looked brittle enough to break. She also had wrinkles. Quinn religiously checked her face every night for wrinkles because the moment one appeared she planned to hightail it to the nearest plastic surgeon.

"So…is your mother's distaste for this place the reason your father likes it so much?" she asked.

Wyatt laughed, then shrugged. "He'd never admit it."

"I don't think I've ever met your father. Did he come to Graham and Charlie's wedding?"

He hesitated, then cleared his voice and murmured, "He died when I was twenty. Cancer."

Quinn swallowed hard at the obvious pain on his face. "I'm sorry. I didn't know…" Her voice trailed off as she realized that there was no way she would know because she had never asked Wyatt a personal question in the time she had known him.

Wyatt cleared his throat again. "You'd think that eleven years later I'd be able to talk about him without choking up."

"I wouldn't think that." He sent her a grateful smile but continued to stare out the window at the parking lot. Quinn said softly, "Tell me about him."

He turned back to her, surprised, and Quinn

suddenly felt guilty that she had been so dismissive of him for so long.

"It's just I don't talk about him much. I realized a long time ago that it made my mother too sad to think about," he said, quietly. "He was just a good man. You know that saying…*he never met a stranger?* That was my dad. He could talk to anyone about anything, get along with anyone, and he would give a stranger the clothes off his back. He was a good dad. A great dad, actually."

"He was a mortician, too?"

"He actually liked it," Wyatt murmured while shaking his head. "And he was very good at it. He always knew exactly what to say, when to be gentle, when to tell someone to snap out of it. He just made people feel comfortable."

"It must be a hard job."

He studied her for a moment, as if looking for her next joke at his expense or insult, then said, "It is. Being that close to people in so much pain is… It's a constant reminder of what's important in life and how none of us are promised tomorrow."

"And makes you want a wife and kids as soon as possible," she added, gently.

He suddenly looked nervous. "That's not why I want a family, Quinn."

"I know," she murmured, only because he looked so panicked at the thought. She took a deep breath, then said, "My parents died when I was seven."

The sympathy in his eyes felt like a physical thing that reached across the table and touched her. "Graham told me."

"I barely remember them," she admitted. "Even

before they died, my sisters and I spent most of our time with Grandpa Max. Our parents traveled a lot. Not for work, but from one party to the next. I try to miss them. I really do, but I… Charlie and Kendra remember them, but I don't. Sometimes I try to imagine how different things would have been if they had lived. Grandpa Max probably wouldn't have been so hard on us because he wouldn't have been so scared that we'd end up like them. Maybe I wouldn't have been an actress and then all of this wouldn't have happened…"

Her voice trailed off and she started to laugh. He quirked one eyebrow and asked, "What?"

"I always complain about your silence, but I guess the positive side is that you're very easy to talk to."

"First you admit that I *might* have a sense of humor. And now you actually admit that I'm easy to talk to."

"It's all the grease in the air," she quickly explained. "It's warping my normal brain functions."

"Obviously," he murmured, amused.

The large man with the stained and torn T-shirt walked over and placed two heaping plates of food in front of them and two frothy jugs of beer on the table. Quinn forgot to be disgusted at the sight of heaps of meat smothered in barbecue sauce and the mound of potato salad, greens and bread, because everything just smelled so delicious. Her stomach growled, reminding her that she hadn't eaten since the greasefest last night.

The man towered over them for a moment until Quinn looked up at him. He was staring at her with a blank expression that reminded her he knew where to hide bodies after he killed them. Quinn glanced across the table at Wyatt, who shrugged in response to her silent question. Quinn glanced back at the man.

"Hey, Cletus," Wyatt greeted. "How's it going?"

Cletus ignored Wyatt and grunted to Quinn, "I stopped watching *Diamond Valley* after they kicked you off. You were the best thing on that show, and it was their loss."

Without another word, he walked away, making his way through the tables and other customers, who looked over in awe at the person who had made Cletus talk.

"That's the most I've ever heard him say at one time in years," Wyatt whispered to her, his eyes wide.

"Sephora fans are intensely loyal."

"Obviously," he said, still staring in awe after Cletus. He shook his head, then pointed towards the plate of food. "Dig in."

Quinn hesitantly complied and dug into the plate of food. At the first taste of real food—not diet, low-carb, low-fat gunk—on her tongue, she closed her eyes in sheer ecstasy.

"It is delicious," she sighed, opening her eyes.

The food became a lump in her throat as she met Wyatt's suddenly hot gaze. He wanted her. And for the first time that knowledge didn't make her uncomfortable or annoyed. She wanted him, too.

He cleared his throat and averted his gaze to his own plate. A strange silence hung between them as they both focused a little too much on their food. Quinn hadn't realized how easy things were between them until suddenly they weren't. Conversation was never truly easy between her and a man. Either he was trying to get in her pants, or she wanted something from him. There was always an edge. There was no edge with Wyatt, and she realized that the lack of edge was actually nice.

"I never watched *Diamond Valley*," he said, breaking the silence. "What's it about?"

She lifted her head to stare at him, surprised. "You really want to know?"

"It's obviously important to you. Of course I want to know."

Quinn met his gaze as pure liquid heat pooled in her center. He wanted to know about her. And she wanted to glue herself to his mouth.

"It's your typical soap opera. Two rich and powerful families and their children, the Barstows and the Childresses. My character, Sephora, is the youngest sibling in the Barstow family. She had been stolen by a nanny as a child and didn't know she was a Barstow until she turned eighteen… Well, frankly, until the writers wanted to add some spice to the show one summer… Anyway, I auditioned and suddenly I was Sephora, the long-lost Barstow. It was my first real acting job. My first real job, period. I had a great time until…until I didn't."

"What happened?" Wyatt asked hesitantly. When she only stared at him, he laughed nervously and said, "Forget I asked. It's none of my business—"

"No, it's okay. I forget that not everyone read the *Enquirer* or Internet celebrity gossip blogs." She took a swig from the beer for courage then said, "Do you want to know the official version or the unofficial version?"

Confusion crossed his face as he studied her for a moment. "I want to know the truth."

"I told my sisters that an ex-boyfriend got me kicked off the show. Y'know, the usual story. Handsome, suave, debonair man sweeps gorgeous, talented actress off her feet. He claims to be a financial guru and tells her to invest her money with him. She does, and at his gentle persuasion, talks most of the cast and crew on her highly-rated soap opera into doing the same with guarantees of fabulous returns… And then the gorgeous actress wakes up one morning to find her money gone, the man gone and all of her friends' money gone too."

"I'm sorry, Quinn—"

She held up her hand at the genuine concern shining in his eyes. "That's not the whole truth, or even the half-truth, but the truth is pretty boring. Predictable, even."

Wyatt looked confused again. Quinn realized it was because he probably never lied and the concept confused him. "You lied to your sisters?"

"It wasn't a complete lie," she said, defensively. "I did give my money to a self-proclaimed financial guru, and he did steal a lot from me, but I got it all back. The NYPD is much better than I thought."

"Why the lie?"

"Because the truth is so much more embarrassing," she muttered with a sigh. "When I first landed the role of Sephora, I was so grateful to get a job, any job, but then…then Sephora became a phenomenon, one of the most popular characters in daytime television. The network did a poll and announced that more people knew who Sephora Barstow was than knew who the vice-president of the United States was. Some people claim that after my popularity took off, I became different."

"Did you?"

For the first time since Quinn had been fired from the show, she could admit the truth. "I was a bitch. Nothing was good enough—not the wardrobe, the hair, the makeup, the script. I alienated all of my cast mates and the directors. I threw things at people, near people, around people. I was a terror to work with." At his horrified expression, she laughed and said, "Relax, Wyatt. The evil bitch got her comeuppance in the end."

"I'm sorry."

"I deserved it. After I screamed at an extra to stop looking at me and tipped over his wheelchair because he was in my way—I didn't know he was really disabled, I thought the wheelchair was a prop—the cast and crew collectively went to the show's producers and said they would all quit if I wasn't fired. The producers had tolerated me for years because I was Sephora and the fans loved me, but they couldn't risk losing the entire show. So the next week, Sephora was diagnosed with a rare flesh-eating illness and died. It was an open-casket funeral."

"Oh, Quinn. The show meant a lot to you."

She wiped at an errant tear, surprised that she still was able to cry over it. "But I'll show them," she said, firmly. "When I'm standing on the stage of the Kodak Theatre with my Oscar, I'll thank them for getting rid of me because it forced me to elevate my career to the next level." When Wyatt continued to stare at her with that sympathetic expression, she murmured softly, "But I do miss it. I miss it a lot."

"You were on that show for most of your adult life. Of course you miss it. No one would expect anything less."

She laughed through her suddenly blurred vision. "I haven't admitted that to anyone, even myself. I can't believe I told you."

Wyatt smiled and held up his beer glass. "To Sephora."

Quinn laughed and clinked her glass against his. "To Sephora."

The two drank their beers, their gazes holding, until Wyatt abruptly looked away. Quinn slowly set the glass down, feeling something monumental shift into place. She didn't know what it was, but something was different between them.

She asked softly, "Why are you so nice to me, Wyatt?"

His cheeks flushed with embarrassment, and he dropped his gaze to his plate. He finally mumbled, "I'm nice to everyone."

"But I don't deserve it."

"No, you probably don't," he agreed, then sent her one of his earth-shattering smiles.

"And I haven't been very nice to you, have I?"

His smile faded. "No, you haven't."

"I'm sorry."

"I'm not. It kept me in reality. I would have made a fool of myself over you by now with as much as I wanted you. But, because you always kept me at arm's length—hell, the length of the state of Wyoming—we can be friends now. And I can truly say that I like having you as a friend." He abruptly laughed and added, "Of course, that doesn't mean you're getting the house. You still have to work for it, but I do promise I'll talk to Mom because that's what friends are for."

"Friends," she murmured with a forced smile.

For some reason, being friends with Wyatt made her lose her appetite. She pushed the plate away and focused on her beer, while her new "friend" devoured his food and hers.

* * *

Wyatt parked his SUV in front of the Sibley house and turned to Quinn, who sat trying to look innocent. Innocent, his ass. She had tortured him throughout lunch with soft moans and flirtatious laughs, and then had spent the entire car ride twirling her hair and playing with the buttons on her cardigan. Wyatt doubted that Quinn was doing any of it on purpose, but being in such a small space with her for such a long time had made him more conscious of her. Her sweet smell. The honey-blond glints in her hair. Her long legs. Even the sound of her breathing set his blood on fire.

"Thanks for lunch," Quinn murmured.

Wyatt clenched the steering wheel to force himself not to move toward her. As the scent of apples and sugar washed over him, his gaze dropped to her lips. They were so perfect. So beautiful. So close to his…Wyatt snapped himself out of his daze. He could not think about kissing Quinn. He was in love—well, close to being in serious like—with Dorrie.

"Wyatt, look at me," Quinn whispered. Against his will, he turned to her. She leaned toward him and his gaze instantly dropped to her mouth. The sound of his gulp filled the quiet interior of the car. "I know you've wanted to kiss me for a long time, and I'm going to give you your chance. Your last chance before you become chained to Dorrie."

He laughed in disbelief and amazement at her arrogance, but then again, she had every reason to be arrogant. "Quinn—"

She didn't wait for him to finish; she pressed her lips against his. He gripped the steering wheel as a shock of emotions slammed into his body, instantly making him hard. Her lips were so soft, so sweet. So damn perfect. It was one of the most innocent kisses he had experienced since junior high school—and the most erotic.

She leaned back with that secret smile of hers, and he cursed and grabbed her arms. Her cry of surprise was cut off as his mouth slammed against hers. She tensed as he dragged her across the seat to practically sit in his lap. He used her shock to slip his tongue into her mouth and search for all the hidden cavities. He found them. Honey and peaches. Her mouth reminded him of honey and peaches on a hot summer day.

Then her tongue touched his. Tentatively. He moaned and silently encouraged her, his hands caressing her arms, itching to travel over every inch of the body that he had worshipped from afar for so long. She became more bold and her tongue became more bold, dipping into his mouth, dueling with his tongue. All of her wet sweetness poured into his mouth.

He groaned and dragged one hand into her hair, the silk strands falling over his hand, adding another layer of sweetness. One of her hands moved to the back of his neck, trying to pull him closer. She wanted him. Quinn Sibley wanted him, and it scared the hell out of him. He tried to pull away, but she clung to his bottom lip, nipped his top one. Hung on to the back of his neck, her other hand wrapped around his right biceps.

They devoured each other's mouths with sweeping, drugging kisses that lasted for days and hours. Kissing away all of the sexual tension that had been between them since they shook hands in the kitchen. Her tongue was like a spark that lit pinpricks of arousal everywhere it swept. Her hands on him were demanding, wanting.

Wyatt was getting too hot, too aroused. His hand on her arm began to travel to her breast. Then through the last vestige of common decency, he remembered where they were and pulled from her lips.

Their heavy breathing filled the cabin of the car. Wyatt dragged a hand down his face, then chanced looking at her. Bad move. Her lips were swollen, and her hair was tangled from his hands. It was her eyes that did him in, though. She wanted him. He could doubt himself with the kiss, but not with that smoldering look in her eyes.

She bit her swollen bottom lip, sending him a look that should have been bronzed in a statue, then quickly moved out the car.

Wyatt told himself to drive away. He needed to drive away and rethink, regroup. But instead he opened the door and started after her.

"Quinn—" She turned to him with an expectant look in her eyes and Wyatt's next sentence stuck in his throat.

The two stared at each other, and Wyatt wondered how long it would take to throw her in the backseat and drive to the closest place that would not include her sister or Graham being within screaming distance.

"Quinn!" Kendra shouted, storming down the porch steps.

Quinn turned from Wyatt to her sister, and Wyatt suddenly was able to breathe again. To think again. He didn't want to sleep with Quinn. Well, of course, he did. Especially after that kiss. But he wouldn't because he wanted a future with... What was her name again? Dorrie. He shook his head. Had Quinn really just kissed him? His body was still trembling, so she must have, but his mind hadn't quite caught up with the speed of events.

"Where the hell have you been?" Kendra demanded as she dragged Quinn into a tight embrace. Wearing a black pin-striped minisuit and stiletto heels, she looked like the power broker she was.

Wyatt didn't like to admit it, but Kendra scared him slightly. But then again, Kendra probably scared hardened criminals. Kendra was as frighteningly beautiful as her two sisters—the same delicate-shaped almond eyes, unblemished skin and tall frame. But there was also a hardness about Kendra, probably due to the fact that she could bench-press Wyatt with one arm. She didn't have overly defined muscles, but everything about her was muscled and athletic. Nothing was impossible as far as Kendra was concerned.

Kendra pushed Quinn away, as if the hug had lasted too long, then blew her silky, dark chin-length hair from her face and pointed toward the roof. "There is a Santa Claus on the roof, Quinn. I am actually staying in a house that has a Santa Claus on the roof."

Wyatt hid his laugh at the six-foot, helium-filled dark brown-skinned Santa Clause slightly waving in the wind on the roof of the house. The round figure held one hand up in a wave and another hand held reins to—what else—the reindeer. It was giant and tacky, and Wyatt could just imagine Graham biting his tongue as he did Charlie's bidding.

"Charlie," Quinn guessed, staring at the Santa Claus.

"Who else?" Kendra turned her back on the house to study Quinn from head to foot. "I can see you've already gotten started on the holiday eating."

"Bite me, Kendra," Quinn snapped.

Wyatt shook his head, amused. The two sisters definitely did not relate in the traditional sister way. They related more like two prizefighters who had engaged in multiple bouts and now had a wary, healthy respect for each other.

"What are you laughing at, cowboy?" Kendra snarled, glaring at Wyatt.

"Kendra," Quinn warned.

"Hello, Kendra. It's good to see you again," Wyatt said, then moved cautiously toward her for a hug. He never knew if Kendra would bite or kick. Instead, she hugged him back. Hard. Wyatt tried to hide his surprise at how thin she felt under the suit she wore. He pulled back and studied her, and noticed with surprise that she didn't meet his gaze but was instead glaring at Quinn.

"You and I need to talk," Kendra said while pointing a finger at Quinn. "You order me out here, then disappear on the morning I'm supposed to arrive. I just spent three hours stringing popcorn. Stringing popcorn, Quinn?" She turned to Wyatt and demanded, "Do I look like a woman who strings popcorn?"

"No," Wyatt instantly responded since she looked like she actually wanted an answer.

"Exactly," Kendra said, firmly. "Quinn owes me. Big."

"Is the party out here?" Charlie greeted as she walked out the house and down the stairs toward them. She placed an arm around Kendra, who looked distinctly uncomfortable at the touch. "Kendra got here just in time, didn't she, Quinn? The church choir is going caroling tomorrow night and has invited all members to join."

Kendra looked horrified as she stated, "I don't sing under any circumstances, let alone Christmas carols."

"We're singing Christmas carols," Charlie said, with a rare glint in her eye that meant business.

"Apparently, I'm singing Christmas carols," Kendra said dully.

"Welcome to hell, Kendra," Graham said, lifting a cup of eggnog in salute as he joined the group in the yard. Charlie stuck her tongue out at him. Graham instantly wrapped an arm around her waist and pulled her into his arms to place a quick kiss on her lips. Graham smiled down at his wife, then eyed Wyatt for a moment before he said, "Where have you been? I've been calling you for the last two hours. I want to invite a few friends over tonight. Grill outside, have some beers. A little pre-Christmas party. What do you think?"

Wyatt chanced a quick glance at Quinn, who was studiously avoiding his eyes. He could not see her tonight, or any night for that matter. He was going to incorporate a strictly no-Quinn policy from here on out. He just wished his lips would stop tingling, as if reliving every nip of her teeth and tug of her lips on his.

"We're having a party tonight?" Kendra asked sarcastically. "Oh, goodie. Cowboys, cowgirls and beer. What more could a girl ask for?"

"It'll be fun, Kendra," Graham said, with an annoyed glance in her direction before turning to Wyatt. "Won't it?"

"I can't make it tonight, Graham," Wyatt said, carefully avoiding Quinn's eyes. "I have some paperwork to finish at home. We're getting a new drain. And then Velma Spears wants to talk to me about changing her backyard. She wants to get away from the cactuses like

I've been suggesting for the past two years to drought-resistant flowers."

Wyatt knew that he was babbling when Graham's lips quirked into a smile and Kendra looked instantly annoyed.

"Anyway, so I need to work," Wyatt murmured in conclusion.

"That'll take two hours tops. Come on," Graham practically pleaded then glanced at the Sibley sisters and said in a stage whisper, "Frankly, I'm outnumbered here. I need some menfolk around to even things out."

Charlie playfully pushed Graham, who laughed, and began to tickle her in the mid-section. She shrieked and tried to evade his reach.

"I feel like I'm in a condom commercial," Kendra muttered dryly, rolling her eyes, before she turned to Wyatt and Quinn. Her gaze flickered from one to the other, suspicion written across her face.

"You two both were un-reachable at the same time and I distinctly saw Quinn get out of Wyatt's SUV, which could only lead to one conclusion—you two were together. Somewhere. Not answering your cell phones," Kendra said.

"We just went to lunch," Quinn said with a small shrug.

"Yeah, it was just lunch," Wyatt muttered, then glanced at his watch. "I've got to get back to work."

"Tonight, party, nine o'clock," Graham said.

Wyatt nodded reluctantly, then got into his SUV and sped away before he looked at Quinn again.

Chapter 10

"Talk. Now," Kendra demanded.

Quinn sighed at the sight of her two sisters standing over her on the back porch and set down the movie script next to her on the swing. She had been able to avoid her sisters for the last two hours since Charlie had been obsessed with torturing them all with Christmas cheer, and Kendra had been too busy complaining about that to deal with Quinn. But it looked as if Quinn's grace period had ended. She still wasn't ready to face them. Not when she was still recovering from That Kiss. She never would have thought that a cowboy mortician in the middle of Sibleyville could kiss like that—or that she would have been counting the seconds, minutes and hours until she could get him to do it again.

"What are we supposed to talk about?" Quinn asked,

batting her eyelashes at Kendra. Kendra frowned, while Charlie sat on the swing next to Quinn.

"We want to talk about exchanging Christmas gifts," Kendra said dryly, then snapped, "you and Wyatt, dork. The reason you ordered me to get my ass on a plane and fly here in the middle of Christmas."

Charlie's expression fell and she sounded hurt as she said to Kendra, "I thought you were here for Christmas because you wanted to spend time with us."

Kendra groaned and leaned against the porch railing, while crossing her arms. "I'm not a Christmas person, Charlie. You know that."

"But we only have each other now. You can't spend Christmas alone, without us," Charlie protested.

"You're not alone, Charlie. You have a husband," Kendra snarled.

Quinn was surprised by the venom and jealousy in Kendra's voice. She glanced at Charlie, who looked as surprised as she felt. There was an awkward silence in the air as Kendra stared at the hills in the distance.

"Kendra—"

Kendra cut off Charlie's hesitant tone and said, gruffly, "I'm sorry. It's just been a long day. I'm jet-lagged and I'm cranky and tired. I haven't been able to exercise, and you know what lack of exercise does to me."

Charlie looked uncertain, but nodded after a few seconds. Kendra cleared her throat and turned to Quinn. "Now, I need an explanation about you and Wyatt and why it looked like you two were ending a date rather than you blackmailing him to do your bidding."

"Blackmail?" Charlie squeaked, looking at Quinn with wide eyes. "You're blackmailing Wyatt?"

"Of course not," Quinn snapped with a pointed stare at Kendra. "Wyatt and I just have a small understanding and we had lunch to talk about that."

"All you did was have lunch?" Kendra asked, doubtfully.

"Do you think we had sex in the back of his SUV? Of course we just had lunch." She used every one of her acting skills to refrain from blushing or giggling. It was technically the truth. There had been no sex in the back of the SUV, but if Quinn and Wyatt had had another two seconds alone in that SUV, she would have had to lie.

"What is going on?" Charlie demanded, her voice rising in frustration.

Quinn sighed loudly, then explained, "Wyatt refuses to allow me to use his house in the movie, so I bet that… that he could not get Dorrie in a week."

Charlie's brows lowered into a frown. "Get Dorrie? What is that supposed to mean?"

"This is precisely why I didn't want to tell you. I knew you would blow it out of proportion," Quinn muttered.

"Well, what is it supposed to mean?" Charlie demanded.

Kendra waved a hand dismissively at Charlie and accused Quinn, "There was more going on between you two than just lunch."

"You know, I had the same feeling when I walked in on Quinn and Wyatt in the kitchen yesterday," Charlie said excitedly. "There were strong undercurrents. I felt like I had interrupted something. I don't know what, but something was going on."

"Wyatt Granger is not my type. Granted, he's not the unsophisticated country hick that I thought he was. And

I'll even admit that he's more attractive than I ever noticed. And maybe he has a cute smile and a great body but...but... What was I saying?"

Charlie giggled, while Kendra smirked and said dryly, "You were telling us how adorable, cute Wyatt with the great body is not your type."

"Precisely," Quinn said firmly. "And, even if he was my type—which he's not—he's made it very clear that I'm not his."

Kendra shook her head, annoyed. "This is what I don't understand. I thought Wyatt was in love with you. Every time we've seen him during the last year, he can barely keep his eyes off you and becomes tongue-tied. Now he wants to marry someone else?"

"Wyatt was not in love with me. And even if he was in love with me at some point, he's not anymore. In fact, he told me in no uncertain terms that I'm not Sibleyville wife material."

"You'd make just as good of a wife as any of the other women in this town," Kendra said defensively.

"A better wife because I would force Wyatt out of his safety zone and to take chances that he wouldn't want to take," Quinn snapped, annoyed all over again. There was no way that Dorrie Diamond would know how to handle a kiss from Wyatt. At least, not the kiss that he had laid on Quinn.

"You're forgetting something kind of important," Charlie pointed out calmly. "You don't even like Wyatt."

"That's not the point," Kendra snapped at Charlie.

"Then what is the point?"

"The point is that Quinn is just as good as anyone else, and who is Wyatt to tell her that she's not," Kendra said, warming to her subject. "In fact, he would be lucky to get Quinn."

"Agreed," Quinn said, crossing her arms over her chest.

"But Quinn doesn't want to marry Wyatt. She doesn't even want to date Wyatt, so why would she care one way or the other if he doesn't consider her wife material?" Charlie pointed out, sounding a little too logical for Quinn's taste.

Kendra and Quinn wordlessly stared at Charlie. Quinn narrowed her eyes at Charlie. Sometimes Charlie was too damn logical for her own good. It was decidedly un-Sibley-like. Their grandfather, Max, had believed in living life by his gut, which was precisely how he had become one of the wealthiest and most powerful black men in America.

"Who is this paragon of Sibleyville feminine virtue who Wyatt has deemed worthy of marriage?" Kendra asked dryly.

"Her name is Dorrie Diamond. She's an accountant."

"You're not serious?"

"I am," she responded, laughing. "She wears pearls and shirts with bows."

"Quinn," Charlie admonished.

"She does," Quinn said defensively.

"I bet she's a virgin, too," Kendra said, with a snort of irritation.

"Hey," Charlie protested, waving her hand in the air. "The only man I've ever slept with is my husband. Not all of us can be as…experienced as you two."

"Experienced, my ass. Just say it, Charlie. We're sluts. Good old-fashioned American sluts," Kendra said with a wicked grin.

"She can be a virgin," Quinn said, with a smile in Charlie's direction, then added, "But she can't be a virgin who wears pearls and has blouses with bows."

"If that's who Wyatt wants, then let him have her," Kendra said with a shrug. "They can have boring sex for the rest of their lives. It's too bad because I always thought Wyatt was kind of sexy…for a Sibleyville man. Too bad that he's a complete waste. He wouldn't know what to do with a real woman."

Quinn's entire face flushed with heat as she remembered his tongue in her mouth, the confident way that his hands positioned her just so for the taking. She had a feeling that Wyatt knew exactly what to do with a woman. And that woman would be shivering and screaming his name all night.

"So are you going to be able to rein Wyatt in before the end of the week?" Kendra asked Quinn.

"One way or another," Quinn said firmly.

"Wanna bet?" Kendra asked with a small smirk. Quinn rolled her eyes in response, while Kendra laughed maniacally.

"This family bets too much," Charlie muttered, then stood. "I have to check on the cookies, and then we need to start getting ready for tonight."

She walked into the house and Quinn waited until she heard Charlie's footsteps fade toward the front of the house before she asked Kendra, "Did she say *we?*"

"I distinctly heard *we.*"

"This is going to be a long night."

Kendra nodded in agreement, then sat in the spot on the porch swing that Charlie had just vacated. "So when did you realize that you were attracted to Wyatt?"

Quinn didn't even question how Kendra knew, it was scary the things Kendra knew. "Sometime over lunch."

"That's the first time?" Kendra asked suspiciously.

"Maybe it's been a while, but what does it matter? He lives here, I live in L.A. and never shall the two worlds meet."

"Except with Charlie and Graham?"

"They're a completely different case. Graham has lived in every major city in the world. He's sophisticated, completely independent from this town. He probably wouldn't return now, except to visit his parents occasionally, if Charlie didn't love it here so much. Wyatt loves Sibleyville. It's his identity. He lives with his mother, for God's sake. You know how much mothers don't like me."

Kendra laughed suddenly. "Remember Adam Siddeon's mother in tenth grade? She walked into the school dance, grabbed Adam off the dance floor while you were in the middle of doing the electric slide with him and dragged him out of the gym, all without one word."

"I haven't had much better luck with mothers since then," Quinn muttered.

"But you want Wyatt?"

Quinn hesitated, then admitted, "I do."

"Then what's stopping you?"

She hated how pathetic she sounded, but said through clenched teeth, "He doesn't want me."

"Of course he does."

"He's already committed himself to Wonder Accountant."

"He's not married yet, Quinn. He's not even dating her."

"I know." Quinn groaned and raked a hand through her hair, then automatically pulled her hair back over her ears, which instantly made her think of Wyatt. "I'm just horny. It's been a while since… In between moving from New York, trying to find a place to live, auditioning and stalking Helmut for a role in this movie, I haven't had time to deal with men. Not that I've had the chance since apparently every man in L.A. has decided that I'm not his type."

"I've never known you to have problems finding a date since most men seem to like fake breasts and fake hair."

"My hair is not fake," Quinn said, glaring at Kendra.

"The point is, some men like your type of obvious beauty."

Mollified, Quinn said, "All I had to do was breathe in New York, and I would have to beat the men off with a stick. In L.A…. Forget in L.A., in Sibleyville, I'm having problems. I mean, I have to pull out all the stops just to seduce someone like Wyatt." Quinn laughed in disbelief and muttered, "The fact that I'm even thinking of seducing Wyatt, to begin with, proves how far I've fallen."

"But seduce him you will, right?"

Quinn thought of Wyatt's dark eyes dropping to study her breasts with an intensity that always made her slightly nervous. "What could it hurt? We're two adults, and it can be his one last fling before matrimonial hell."

"You could do worse."

"This is Sibleyville. I could do much worse."

"And how will your plans affect your bet?" Kendra asked.

"Will Wyatt really be able to keep saying no once he's slept with me?" Quinn said, trying to sound casual. "He'll feel obligated to give me the house."

Kendra narrowed her eyes at Quinn and demanded, "But that's not the reason you want to sleep with him, is it?"

"Of course not, but if it helps me get something I want, that's just an added benefit."

"Sometimes I'm really proud to call you my sister," Kendra said with a sigh of maternal pride.

"Only you would think sleeping with a man to get something is a good thing."

"I'm a realist. It's one of my best qualities." Kendra's smile faded, and she stared at her nails for a moment before she asked, "Quinn, do you think the two of us will ever find what Charlie has?"

Quinn studied Kendra, surprised by the serious expression on her face. She had never known Kendra to want a man for anything other than sexual Olympics or to stand around while she outshone him in the boardroom. But, suddenly, Kendra looked unsure of herself. Vulnerable, even.

"Are you all right, Kendra?"

"Kendra! Quinn!" Charlie called from the kitchen. "I need help icing the cookies!"

Kendra grinned, seemingly relieved, as she brushed her hands on her skirt. "Duty calls."

"Kendra—"

Kendra ignored Quinn and walked into the house, closing the screen door behind her.

"How do I look?" Quinn asked Graham as she spun around the kitchen in a sparkling silver minidress that showed off her best assets and hid her flaws.

She had spent over an hour on her makeup and hair

and had washed, scrubbed and polished every inch of her body until she practically glowed. She had made up her mind. She wanted Wyatt. And whether he was ready or not, she was going to have him. Tonight. He was just another man; there was absolutely nothing special about him. Quinn would have slept with him a long time ago if she hadn't spent so much time being annoyed by his existence. He was gorgeous, had a great smile and was obviously interested in her. It was a wonder that she had held out this long.

"Great," he responded, absently. She noticed that he didn't even look at her as he continued to pour ice into a cooler on the kitchen floor.

"Do you need any help?" When Graham looked up at her in disbelief, she shrugged and said, "It's the thought that counts, right?"

"Sure, Quinn," he muttered, then began to stick various soda cans into the chest.

"So who did you invite to this soirée?"

"Half the town." Graham paused in his preparations to stare at her for a moment before he said, a tad too casually, "Wyatt left me a message on my cell phone that he's not coming tonight."

Quinn felt as if her entire body had deflated. She hadn't realized that she had spent the last two hours getting ready just to see Wyatt until that moment. Realizing that Wyatt would not be there made her feel there was no reason for her to go to the party. How pathetic was that.

"Did you invite Dorrie?" Quinn asked Graham.

"Of course."

"Did you tell Wyatt that you invited Dorrie?"

"Of course."

"And?"

"And he told me that he had a lot of work to do for the new drain," Graham said with a shrug, then went back to stocking the cooler. "I've known Wyatt a long time and I've never known him to pass up a chance for free beer and free food. Something or someone is keeping him away from the party tonight."

"Is that a hint?"

Graham laughed. "I didn't think I was being subtle enough to call it a hint. What exactly happened between you two this afternoon? He wouldn't tell me."

"That's because there's nothing to tell. We just ate lunch." She rolled her eyes, annoyed as Graham continued to stare at her. "If you want me to drag him to the party, just say so."

"He's my best friend. I don't get to spend enough time with him. I want him here."

"I need the keys to your car. My car is still downtown."

Graham grimaced, but dug into his jeans pocket to toss her a set of keys. "Be gentle. I just got this one."

Quinn waved a hand in dismissal and then walked out of the house, excitement once more humming through her body.

Wyatt stepped out the shower and began to towel himself off. He had spent an hour in the greenhouse, another hour in the backyard turning over the hard dirt and still he hadn't been able to distract himself. Every moment from that afternoon with Quinn continued to play through his head like a slow-motion movie. He couldn't go to the party, see her and not show how much he wanted her. Dorrie would know, Quinn would know. Damn, the entire town would know.

His plan was simple. He would let Quinn do whatever she wanted with the house, then ignore her for the rest of the holiday. She'd be gone in another two weeks and his life would return to normal.

His heart stalled in his chest at the sound of a knock on the front door of his apartment. He knew that knock. It had started this entire nightmare. He thought about ignoring her, but he knew that Quinn would probably figure out a way to pick the lock and barge into his apartment and Wyatt definitely didn't want her to find him cowering in his closet because he was too chicken to face her. He muttered a curse.

"Wyatt, I know you're in there," Quinn called through the door. "Open the door."

Wyatt gripped the towel tighter around his waist, then walked through the small apartment to the front door. He froze in his tracks in the middle of the living room when he saw Quinn standing on the other side of the glass door. Her hair was down and shiny and a mass of loose curls. And her dress... She was killing him in that dress. Every part of her body that he had imagined and caressed in his dreams for so long was on full display.

His breath caught in his throat, as every second from their kiss that afternoon replayed in his head. He could practically taste her even now on his lips. He had been able to taste her for hours afterwards. How in the world could any man ignore this woman?

"Open the door, Wyatt," Quinn commanded since he continued to stand like a gaping idiot in the middle of the living room.

Wyatt shook his head to clear his thoughts, quickly walked to the door and opened it. Quinn walked inside the house, brushing past him, leaving a lingering scent of…something delicious. It was a mixture of flowers and cookies and cakes and…motor oil for a high performance car. Every scent in the world that made him salivate.

Quinn pointedly glanced around the small living room. Her gaze lingered on the riot of green indoor plants throughout the living room, then she walked closer to the built-in bookshelves to examine the book titles. His gaze instantly dropped to her ass. The dress stopped just mere inches below that gorgeous, plump ass. He licked his lips and his hands tingled. If he had the time, the things he could do with that….

She turned to him, and he prayed that she hadn't seen him examining her ass in minute detail. Or notice that he had loosened the grip on the towel so that it would camouflage parts of him that were growing too hard too fast.

"You only have gardening books," she noted, appearing oblivious to his in-depth perusal.

"*A Tale of Two Cities* is up there, too," he said, defensively. He wouldn't tell her that he had gotten that book from the library in high school and had never returned it.

Quinn laughed in disbelief. "*A Tale of Two Cities?* I never did finish that one. I blame Jerry Buchalter for that." At the questioning arch of his eyebrow, she explained, "He sat next to me in senior English. He wrote a book report for himself and a book report for me for every book. He was very sweet."

"Poor slob. He never had a chance, did he?"

"No, he didn't." She studied his face, and Wyatt grew more and more self-conscious the longer she lingered on him without speaking. Quinn was not exactly known for enjoying silences.

"What?" he demanded, unable to stand it any longer.

"Why aren't you coming to the party tonight?"

"Because I'm not giving you an opportunity to humiliate Dorrie and sabotage my chances with her," he said simply. And he also hadn't wanted to see Quinn again until he could get his emotions under control. With visions of having his mouth on every single part of her body running through his mind every second, he decided it was best to probably stay as far away from her as possible.

"Is that really the reason?" she asked uncertainly, looking slightly guilty.

"Yes," he lied.

She crossed the living room and stood mere inches from his bare feet. For the first time, Wyatt noticed her stiletto sandals and bright red painted toenails. Whatever composure he had managed to gather in the last few seconds instantly disappeared.

"How about a truce for tonight?"

He drowned for a second in her beautiful eyes before he remembered that she had said something. He repeated dumbly, "A truce?"

"I'll stay out of your way, and you can use the night to try your charms on Dorrie."

"I don't believe you," he said suspiciously.

She frowned, then asked, "Why?"

"Because you wouldn't be wearing this dress if you were planning to stay out of any man's way."

Anger flared in her eyes and, for some reason that made Wyatt feel even more out of control. For so long, she had ignored him and now he had her attention. He felt his muscles tighten with the need to grab her and drag her to the nearest flat surface.

"Don't flatter yourself, Wyatt. I wore this dress because I like this dress."

"You wore that dress because you knew that I would not be able to take my eyes off you in that dress. Especially after that kiss you laid on me this afternoon. What was that about?"

She flushed slightly, then snapped, "If Dorrie is the love of your life as you claim, then you should have no problem having eyes only for her. And, if I recall correctly, you kissed me first."

"Work with me here, Quinn," he practically begged. "You know that your body…your body…" His voice trailed off as his eyes zeroed in on her breasts.

Quinn's jaw clenched, which he should have taken as a warning sign for the impending eruption and apologized. But it was too late.

"You ass," she spat out.

"Quinn—"

"If you don't want to sully your precious Dorrie with your dirty thoughts about me, then maybe you should find someone you can sully your thoughts with, instead of pretending that I'm this big temptation. I'm not the problem, Wyatt. You are. Instead of admitting that maybe, just maybe, you don't want Dorrie, and that you should find someone who you could have the picket fence and family without her being boring as plain toast, you blame me. This afternoon in her office, I had to resist the urge to take her pulse to make certain she was still breathing. My God, Wyatt, how do you stand it?"

"I take full responsibility for the fact that I am easily distracted by you in a dress like that. Any man would be. But you could also admit the truth. You wore that dress with me in mind."

She sputtered in outrage, "What do you want me to do, Wyatt? Should I wear jeans and a sweatshirt? Would that make you feel better? Maybe I could wear a pair of your overalls? You do have overalls, right? All cowboys have overalls—"

Wyatt couldn't take it anymore. Her eyes were flashing; her honey skin was flush with anger and maybe the same undeniable heat and lust that he was feeling. He cursed and closed the distance between them in two long strides. She must have seen the intent in his eyes because she looked momentarily panicked and tried to step back from him. Wyatt forgot the towel, grabbed her arms and slammed his mouth against hers at the same time that he molded her body against his.

Quinn gasped, and he took the opportunity to ram his tongue into her mouth. To plunder her mouth. To crush any resistance she may have thought of having. He was tired of being the nice guy around her. No more. Not until he had gotten a good taste of her. And he did. All the strawberries and honey he could want.

One second, Quinn had been fighting the need to run across the room to grab Wyatt's towel and see if the rest of his body matched his impossibly sculpted chest; the next, she was in his arms, with his tongue inside of her.

And it was like being quenched with water after being thirsty for years.

When she had walked into his apartment, she hadn't expected him to be half-nude and dripping with water, like her own private adult entertainment show. He had a body that should have made every personal trainer in Hollywood cry in envy. Miles of gleaming brown skin, well-defined arms, a narrow waist and long lean legs. He had hidden all of that underneath his denim and tacky shirts. The man had been rocking the towel like a Calvin Klein model and looked good enough to eat.

His mouth continued to devour her, his tongue continued to demand more. The muscles, the hardness under her hands. She moved her hands around to his chest. His pectoral muscles flinched under her touch, and his nipples beaded against the palm of her hand. She moved her hands lower to his stomach and realized that the towel had slipped and was in danger of slipping farther.

His hands moved to stop hers. "We should stop, Quinn. We have to stop," he groaned against her mouth, his voice impossibly deep and sending rumbles of ecstasy against her mouth.

"No," she whispered. He stared at her for a moment, then devoured her mouth once more with a passion that slightly scared her. No man had ever wanted her this much. No man had ever looked at her the way Wyatt had looked at her.

Wyatt plunged his hands into her hair, almost to the point of pain. His tongue plunged into her mouth over and over, his teeth nipped at her lips. His hands moved roughly from her arms to her back and down to squeeze her behind. Quinn moaned and moved closer to him, cursing the towel that prevented her from feeling every single inch of him.

Through mutual, unspoken consent, the two stumbled into the bedroom, lips and arms jumbled and entwined. The world shifted and they were in the middle of Wyatt's king-sized bed. Wyatt moved in between her legs, fitting perfectly, more perfectly than she thought possible. Her hands wrapped around his back to his lower back, to massage and knead, to push at that cursed towel.

Wyatt's mouth moved to her neck while she tried to breathe. He paid erotic homage to her neck, licking and nicking, as his hands made their way down her body, burning through the thin material of the dress. Her eyes squeezed closed, and she arched her back at the feel of his callused hands on her bare legs. His hands were so hard and her skin was so soft. The friction made her feet flex in sheer need.

His hands stopped their perusal of her body and landed on her breasts. He squeezed. Quinn instantly froze. He was touching her body. The private parts of her that were only hinted at in pictures and film. The parts that everyone thought were perfect, but they weren't. At all.

She bit her bottom lip to prevent the protest at the edge of her tongue. She cursed herself and told herself to enjoy him, to enjoy the feelings, but she suddenly felt self-conscious, uncertain. Soon, he would take off her clothes and he would notice that the reality of her didn't match the retouched, well-lit image on the screen or magazine covers. And he would compare, like all men inevitably did. The men never told her in the heat of the moment that she came up short, but she could always see it in their eyes the next morning, or in the fact that they never called again. Once a man slept with the infamous Quinn Sibley, what more did he need to brag about to his friends?

Wyatt continued to plant kisses on her neck and shoulders, then slipped the straps down her arms. Quinn squeezed her eyes shut. He was getting closer. He pushed the dress down past her breasts and to her waist. Cool air touched her already hard nipples, but now she just felt cold, instead of aroused. She clenched the cool sheets in her hands. She started thinking of ways to position herself, where the light would hit her just right. It was all about the lighting, after all.

She shifted on the bed and Wyatt mumbled something against her neck that sounded like a protest, then gently moved her back into the worst absolute position to hide her flaws, flat on her back. He moved back to her mouth, his tongue plunging inside, flickering the dying embers.

Quinn tried to be excited. She wanted to be excited. She dueled with his tongue. Wyatt was beautiful as he hovered above her in the moonlight. His jaw clenched, his eyes flowing with passion and his lips slightly plump from their ravenous kisses. His hips were undulating against hers and even through the towel, she could feel the hardness. He was long and thick. She prayed that she could, for once, just enjoy and be enjoyable and not be the "wet blanket," as one man had called her behind her back. Another man had told her to her face that, like most beautiful women, she was a bore in bed.

She suddenly realized how important Wyatt was to her because she didn't want him to think that about her.

She would die if he thought that about her. She forced herself to focus on his weight on her. She liked that. He felt warm and heavy, like a big ol' comforter.

"You okay.?" Wyatt whispered as he touched the tip of his tongue against one nipple. She heard the towel hit the floor. She flinched as she felt his hardness against her thigh.

Quinn faked a moan and glanced at the computer on the large desk in the corner of the room. She was just starting to twist to get a look at the other side of the room when Wyatt's eyes abruptly opened. She froze.

He stopped moving, hovering above her, staring directly into her eyes. He gently brushed hair from her face, and Quinn felt a small spark of something again under his gentle ministrations.

His voice was soft as he whispered, "Are you still with me, Quinn?"

Quinn gulped down her sudden nerves. He could see her. For the first time, a man could truly see her in bed.

"I'm here," she said, moving her arms back around his waist. She squeezed him to encourage him to continue.

He remained still even though she could feel the strain in his arms as he held himself above her. Sweat beaded on his forehead. "No, you're not. Talk to me."

"I'm really here, Wyatt. I promise."

He muttered a curse and dropped his head to her shoulder. He kissed her again, and she threw herself into the kiss, wrapping her arms around his neck, pulling him closer. Trying to remember how much she loved the feel of his slick tongue inside her mouth. It took him several seconds, but then he began to move again. His hand traveled up her leg and to her center. She hid her wince as one finger invaded her. Deep inside of her. Where she was completely dry.

She prayed that he wouldn't stop so they could go back to cuddling and kissing…fully clothed. Maybe he would allow her to turn on the light in the hallway to cast a better environment for her body. But he stopped. Wyatt rolled off her and onto his back next to her. He laid his arm across his eyes and took several deep breaths.

Quinn released her own deep breath and bit her bottom lip to squeeze back her tears. She had been called cold and not good in bed before, but she knew that it would hurt more coming from Wyatt.

Chapter 11

The moment Quinn froze under his touch, Wyatt was reminded how strange it was that he was in his bedroom with Quinn. His gaze dropped to her beautiful bare breasts and then to her flat stomach and her flared hips, where the dress was bunched. He swallowed the perpetual lump in his throat. This was either a dream or a nightmare and he would wake up hard as a rod and in need of a cold shower like he usually did whenever he thought of Quinn.

Except no matter how much he told himself to wake up, he was wide awake and Quinn was right here. She was right there, looking petrified and about as aroused as a woman at a gynecologist exam. She glanced at him, then quickly looked away. Wyatt's heart broke a little and something shifted in his heart. Quinn was gorgeous. No one could deny that, but there was so much more to her, and for the first time, Wyatt wondered if he had never noticed that.

"What's going on here, Quinn?" His voice in the still bedroom caused her to jump slightly.

She kept her gaze on the ceiling. Her hands clenched at her sides. "You're the one who stopped."

Wyatt wanted nothing more than to climb back on top of her and insert any part of his body inside of her, because as hard as he was, he didn't exactly need her active participation. But there was something in her eyes that stopped him. That dampened his own ardor. Maybe all this time he had been like every other man out there, just focusing on the outside, and that was why she had treated him like crap. He should have treated her like he did Dorrie. He should have started by getting to know her. Getting her comfortable with him. Wooing her.

Instead he had yelled at her, lusted after her, told her that she wasn't good enough for him and now he had treated her like a common slut. For a supposedly nice guy, he was an ass.

"Maybe we should try this another night," he said, gently.

She turned to him, surprised. "No. Let's finish. I'm ready."

"No, you're not."

Quinn started to move off the bed, but Wyatt grabbed her arm. She glared at him and tried to tug out of his grip. He gently tugged her back onto the bed and tucked her against his side, their barely clothed bodies fitting perfectly. He shifted his lower body slightly to move his still stiff penis away from her.

"We don't have to go so fast, Quinn," he whispered.

"Who's moving fast?"

He didn't answer but smoothed hair from her face then traced his way to her ears. She looked confused as he gently tugged on her ears.

"I don't think your ears are too big. In fact, I'm beginning to suspect that I'm one of those men who has an ear fetish," he confessed.

She gave him a begrudging smile like he wanted her to, and his chest grew tight. He realized in that instant that this woman could make him do anything with that smile.

Wyatt pressed a kiss on her forehead, then just laid next to her on the bed, staring out the window at the star-filled sky and the moon. Her breathing became soft and deep and her body relaxed against him until Wyatt almost feared that she was asleep.

He cursed himself. He had Quinn Sibley in his bedroom and he had stopped her from undressing. But as she snuggled closer to him, and her soft breasts pressed against his arm and her legs moved over his and she relaxed, Wyatt realized that was the point.

"I like all the plants and flowers in the apartment," she said, breaking the silence. "This interest in gardening… It's not just an interest, is it?"

"It's a business, whether I admit it or not."

"I heard you did all the landscaping on Main Street, and every house in town that has a beautiful lawn seems to have your handprint, too."

"My major in college was landscape architecture. I always thought I'd be traveling the world, creating green spaces for businesses and private residences, but then my dad died, and I had to drop out of college and return home to run the family business. The mortuary has been in the family for four generations."

"And you love flowers so much because growing something—anything—is exactly opposite from all the death you've dealt with your entire life," she guessed.

Wyatt paused for a moment, absently running his hand across the smooth skin of her shoulder.

"Maybe," he finally admitted.

"Why can't someone else run the mortuary? You obviously hate it."

"There is no one else. There's just me. The last male Granger in Sibleyville. Actually, the last of the Grangers this side of the Mississippi. We have a whole slew of relatives on the East Coast running their own Granger Funeral Home."

"A family of morticians? Just like some families are in show business generation after generation. Your family is in the funeral business?"

He abruptly laughed and said, "As crazy as this sounds, I don't want to talk about the mortuary business while I have you in my bed." He saw her smile in the moonlight and gently traced her plump lips with the pad of his thumb. "So you want to tell me what just happened here."

"The only thing that happened was you stopped."

He wanted to protest, but then she climbed on top of him and pressed her mouth against his. He heard a moan, not certain if it came from her or him, and her sharp fingernails dug into his shoulders. He slipped his tongue into her mouth and once more stroked the dark, moist places that he liked to think were reserved just for him. Her body sank into his and he remembered that she was completely bare, except for the dress bunched at her waist and the scrap of lace material that passed for her panties.

He gently flipped them over, with her on the bottom. He kept her mouth busy as his hands moved to her breasts. Like a repeat on television, she became completely still again. Wyatt stifled a curse of frustration and started to move off her again, but her hands moved to his, keeping them on their breasts.

"My breasts are fake," she blurted out.

He stared at her face, illuminated in the moonlight. He had expected to hear her say many things, but not that.

"What?" he croaked.

"My breasts are fake," she repeated, sounding close to tears.

He thought of multiple responses, then settled on, "I know, Quinn."

"And my thighs are flabby because I don't do enough lunges—okay, I don't do any lunges—and my stomach isn't as flat as it should be. In movies and on television, they can hide all that. The right light, the right shading, the right placement of a sheet or a prop. It makes everything look perfect. It makes me look perfect. And that swimsuit calendar was all retouched. And most men expect me to look like that. Most men expect me to act how I look. To act like this sex kitten, but I'm not. I'm just…me."

She finished and looked at him expectantly, almost as if she expected him to run screaming from the room.

"I don't go to the movies much, and I don't watch a lot of television, except sports. And I think you're beautiful just as you are, Quinn."

Quinn stared at him for a moment. Then tears filled her eyes as she whispered, "I'm also horrible in bed."

Wyatt coughed to hide his shock. "I find that very hard to believe."

"I am. I was labeled The Worst Lay in Daytime Television."

Wyatt instantly grew angry, but kept his voice gentle so as not to scare her, "What jackass called you that?"

She swiped at her eyes and said, warily, "Calm down, Wyatt."

"I am completely calm. I just want to know what jackass called you that so I can find him and shove my foot up his ass."

She giggled and gently punched him in the chest. "You're supposed to be the mild-mannered one."

He fought a grin as he said, "I'm as mild-mannered as Clark Kent."

"That's pretty mild-mannered," she agreed. She wrapped her arms around his neck, and her thighs widened a little to allow him more access.

Wyatt felt her body slowly relax. She ran her hands down his back, and he tried not to convey how unrelaxed he was. He was still between her creamy thighs, gradually growing hard as rock as heat and moisture radiated from her core. She stared at him with such trust in her eyes that he instantly felt like a Neanderthal for even thinking about moving.

"I want to try again," she said softly. "But I'm warning you that I'm pretty awful."

"There is no way you can be awful in this bed with me. We can either have a lot of fun or just plain ol' fun."

She sent him another full-watt smile, and her body relaxed another degree. "How do we have a lot of fun, instead of just plain ol' fun?"

"It's real simple. You tell me when I'm doing something you don't like, and you tell me when I'm doing something you like."

She sent him another full-watt smile. "You'll tell me the same thing?"

He choked out, "Count on it."

This time, Quinn made the first move. She reached up and pressed her lips to his. Wyatt groaned as her soft lips pressed against his. Kissing this woman was his new addiction. Her mouth opened under his, and he used the invitation to sweep his tongue inside of her mouth. He wanted to take things slowly. He wanted her swimming with so much honey that she wouldn't have time to get nervous or apprehensive. Instead, he became ravenous. The taste of her, the feel of her body welcoming him. Everything was working together to drive him insane.

His tongue dragged through her mouth, trying to inhale and taste every inch of her. And she matched his desire kiss by kiss. Her hands strained to break free, but he refused to release them, mostly to control his own actions. If he didn't hold her down, he would be touching her and moving things entirely too fast. Her hips pressed into his and he instantly grew hard, especially when he saw her hard nipples. He groaned again and took her mouth harder, squelching the urge to take that nipple into his mouth.

Quinn turned her head to break her mouth free. He buried his mouth against her neck. Their heavy breathing filled the room.

"I like this Wyatt. I really like this," she begged in a hoarse voice.

Wyatt considered himself a decent person, but he

was not a saint. He trailed his hands down her soft arms then over her breasts. She was perfect. Soft. He moved his hands down her bare thighs and legs, then reached the strap of her stilettos. She watched him with heated eyes as he slowly and carefully released one strap, then the other. He dropped her shoes on the ground, then moved back up her body until he was between her thighs and once more mere inches from her lips.

Their eyes held for a moment, and Wyatt felt a lump grow in his throat. He had been deluding himself into thinking that he could forget about her and move on with his life. How could he do that to himself, or to any other woman? He would think about and obsess about Quinn for the rest of his life.

Quinn smiled and caressed his face. "Why so serious?"

Instead of answering, Wyatt kissed her as if his life depended on it—because it did. And the best part was she responded with the same passion. Wyatt broke free of her lips and headed straight for that straining nipple. He took the whole nipple in his mouth and she whispered his name and placed her hand on the back of his head, urging him closer.

Wyatt tugged on the nipple with his lips, then licked it. Her breast was shaped perfectly, soft. He squeezed and molded the other breast as he continued to pay lavish oral worship to her left breast. She arched underneath him and made little mewling sounds that drove him crazy.

Wyatt finally moved to the other breast. He wanted to move slow, he wanted to be the world's best lover for her, but his mind was urging him to move lower, his body was urging him to just move and Quinn was arching and bucking beneath him. His head was buzzing and screaming. Wyatt tried to stop, but he couldn't. His hands moved down her stomach to lace and satin panties. He forced himself to stop sucking long enough to stare at her. Still no fear. That was all the authorization he needed.

Quinn didn't have time to freeze up or remember that this had never worked in the past because she was too busy trying not to scream down the house with the feelings that Wyatt evoked in her. He was so slow. So deliberate. So utterly delicious. Her body was on fire. Her soul was on fire.

Wyatt's hands were setting her body on fire. His tongue was swirling in her belly button, and his teeth nipped at her stomach. She wanted him inside of her. In fact, she had a feeling that if he didn't get inside of her soon, she would scream or yell or something.

He poised at the entrance of her entire being and she could feel the heat emanating from her. Wanting him.

His eyes glittered with desire and another emotion that she only hoped meant what she wanted it to mean. She dug her fingernails into his shoulders, wanting him inside her more than she ever wanted anything in her life. She arched against him, and his hardness brushed against her center. She opened her mouth to scream, but no sound came out.

"Please," she urged in a hoarse whisper. She didn't even recognize her own voice.

He sent her a grin that made her arch in pure desire. "I like having you at my mercy."

"Please, Wyatt," she whispered, unable to laugh or joke at this moment.

His expression became serious once more, as his hands caressed her thighs. He seemed incapable of not touching her, not caressing her. "If you want me to stop, just tell me. One word—"

"I don't want you to stop," she groaned. "Please, Wyatt. Stop being so damn nice. Just do it already."

"Do what?" he asked, lifting one side of his mouth in a sardonic smile.

"Kiss me, touch me, do something. *Anything*."

Wyatt grinned again. "Remember you asked for this," he said, then sank lower and touched his tongue to her.

Quinn screamed louder than she had before as pure desire shot through her body and ended directly in her brain. She didn't know if it was because it was a tongue on her, or because it was Wyatt, but she was in another plane of ecstasy. His tongue began to dally against her, soft, long, slow. She wanted to crawl away, she wanted to move closer. She just wanted it to never stop.

Wyatt grabbed her hips and pinned her down, even though she hadn't known that she had been moving. He began to kiss her in earnest, running his tongue over her, inside of her, around her. Quinn undulated against his tongue, squeezed the sheets trapped in her hands, screamed for mercy. She squeezed her eyelids shut, unable to handle the feelings and seeing at the same time. It was as if she could only concentrate on one sensation at a time.

"I want to finish you off, but I can't...I have to be inside of you," he moaned, giving her some relief, as he stopped to hover above her.

She tried to reply, but there was nothing she could do, except wordlessly moan. He pushed inside of her, filled her to capacity, and it was a momentary relief as she hugged him to her. He groaned her name through clenched teeth, then moved his mouth over hers as he began to pump. Firecrackers sparked throughout her body and flooded into a tight ball at the base of her. It overwhelmed her. Quinn screeched under his open mouth and dug her fingernails into his sweat-slickened back. She squeezed her eyes closed and matched his rhythm. Loved his rhythm. Wanted his rhythm.

It was as if they were the same person. Moving together as one. She opened her mouth to scream, but then she could only place a kiss on his shoulder and suck his skin. He tasted salty, delicious, like he was hers.

And then it started. It spiraled and moved into one force and then exploded inside the center of her. She arched and screamed his name, glorying in the feelings. Wyatt pumped faster, quicker, moaning her name, his arms quivering as he hovered above her. Then he shuddered and rushed into her.

And as if a storm blew by, Wyatt lowered himself next to her and became still. His chest moved up and down. Quinn was motionless, unmoving.

Wyatt moved toward her and she flinched. He didn't appear to notice, because he wrapped his arms around her, pressed a kiss on her shoulder and promptly fell asleep. Quinn told herself to move. But she was so warm and satisfied. She would just rest her eyes for a moment. Just sleep and bask in the glow of fabulous sex.

Chapter 12

Quinn opened her eyes at the sound of a telephone ringing. The sound abruptly ended and she snuggled back into the plump pillows surrounding her. There was a pleasant buzz in her bones, as if she had just eaten a really good, high-calorie meal…with dessert. She smiled and stretched her arms over her head, purring like a cat, and then Wyatt's clean, fresh scent stirred from the sheets.

She cursed, feeling a combination of renewed desire and utter fear. She had slept with Wyatt. Not just slept with him, but made love to him. Laughed with him. And shared her secrets. And he had told her his secrets, too. He had treated her like she had imagined men treated their girlfriends, not their trophies, as she usually was.

She glanced towards his side of the bed. It was empty. She looked out the window at the moon high in the sky, then at the clock radio on the nightstand. It was almost eleven o'clock. She had been at Wyatt's almost four hours. She cursed again and covered her face with her hands. She had to get home as soon as possible. She didn't want to face her sisters' knowing grins, but she also couldn't exactly face Wyatt. What was she supposed to say to him? She had never completely released herself in bed with anyone. She didn't know how to deal with the repercussions.

The bedroom door abruptly opened. Wyatt walked into the room, carrying a tray loaded down with food. He flipped on the lights with an elbow, then walked across the room towards her. She gulped at the sight of his muscled chest. He had pulled on a pair of dingy sweats that only made him look more adorable because he looked so at home and relaxed.

Quinn quickly sat up in bed, keeping the sheet tightly clutched between her breasts. She smoothed down her tangled hair, refusing to even picture what it might like. She tucked hair behind her ears because Wyatt truly didn't seem to care about her huge ears.

He grinned at her, noticing her movement, then placed the tray on the bed between them. He leaned over and traced the shape of one of her ears. Without a word, he pressed a quick kiss against her lips. He stared at her for a moment, then returned for another longer kiss. Then another one, until she opened her mouth. His tongue worked its way through her mouth, feeling foreign and familiar and erotic. She almost dropped the sheet to wrap her arms around him. Almost.

Wyatt pulled away from her with an even bigger grin, then pointed to the tray. "We missed dinner." She stared at the tray. He had made scrambled eggs, bacon, fried potatoes, biscuits and diced fresh fruit. There was enough food on the plate to feed a small army. "I'm not much of a cook, but I make a pretty mean breakfast."

"It looks delicious," she said and realized that she actually meant it.

He handed her a fork and she reached for the bowl of fruit, but then grabbed bacon. She hadn't had bacon in almost two years.

Wyatt grabbed another piece of bacon and laid across the bed on his side to stare at her.

"Did I hear the phone ring?" she asked as she swallowed a mouthful of eggs.

"It was Graham."

She nearly choked on the eggs and drained the glass of orange juice on the tray. "Graham called here? Please tell me that you didn't let him know I was here."

"Of course I did," Wyatt said, with a shrug. "He called to see if I knew where you were. He said no one had heard from you since you left four hours ago."

Quinn set down the glass and hung her head in shame. "I am never going to hear the end of this."

"The end of what?"

"This," she retorted, motioning wildly towards the bed and him. "As soon as Graham tells Charlie, which we both know he will because he can't keep anything from her, she'll tell Kendra and then I'll get a phone call." As if on cue, the sound of a cell phone ringing came from the living room. Quinn shook her head. "I knew it."

"Sisters," Wyatt said sympathetically. He took the other fork on the tray and dug into the eggs.

Quinn stared at him for a moment, annoyed with his

cavalier attitude. Then her stomach growled. She started on the fried potatoes.

"How's the party going?" Quinn asked.

"Graham says that half the town is there."

Quinn pretended to focus on the plate as she murmured, "You're missing a chance to score points with Dorrie. If you hurry, you can still catch her."

Wyatt froze, and anger flashed in his eyes as he stared at her. His voice was deep with barely concealed rage, "I don't know what type of men you've dated in the past, but I don't sleep with a woman and then pursue another woman the same night or the next day."

"She is your dream woman, remember? The mother of your future children?"

"Stop while you're ahead, Quinn," he said through clenched teeth.

"I'm just reminding us where we both stand. We slept together, but it doesn't change anything. You still want Dorrie, and I still want my movie filmed here. We just had a truce, like I said when I walked in."

"We just made love and you bring up Dorrie? Nice, Quinn. Very nice." With a look of disgust, he stormed out the room.

She heard the front door of the apartment slam closed. She quickly slipped from the bed, grabbed her clothes and sprinted across the hall to the bathroom, slamming the door. After she had relieved herself, thrown water on her face and wiggled into her clothes, she cautiously opened the bathroom door. The apartment was completely silent. Wyatt still hadn't come back.

Quinn grabbed her heels from the bedroom, then

hurried through the apartment and grabbed her handbag. She opened the front door and glanced down the stairs. The driveway was still empty, except for Graham's prized Porsche. The funeral home was still dark since Beatrice probably was at Charlie and Graham's party. The coast was clear.

Quinn ran down the stairs, then pulled on her heels. She walked on her toes to the car so her heels wouldn't clack on the cement driveway. She was home free until she noticed the lights on in the green-house that stood about two hundred yards in the field behind the house. Quinn hesitated with her hand on the car door.

Wyatt obviously didn't want to see her. She should just leave. Except Quinn released the door handle and headed toward the greenhouse. Maybe she was a glutton for punishment. Or maybe she just needed to see Wyatt one last time. To kiss him one last time. If he would let her.

She crossed the field on a stone walkway that had been placed into the manicured lawn. She opened the greenhouse door and was nearly overcome by the variety and colors of flowers and plants in the large building. It was like a fantasy, a tropical paradise. The air was slightly damp and warm, compared to the chill outside, and it smelled like wet dirt and fragrant flowers. Soft muted lights glowed on tracks on the ceiling. There were several aisles that led to each grouping of flowers. She took her time looking and oohing and aahing and gently touching delicate leaves.

Then she saw Wyatt. He stood at the back of the greenhouse at a large worktable that had a single, solitary lamp. He was potting bulbs of tulips into small clay pots. She stopped several feet from him, then saw him look up in the window at her reflection. She waited for him to acknowledge her, but he leaned back over and began to pack dirt in the pots.

"Wyatt," Quinn said softly.

He stopped moving and leaned on the table. "I thought you'd be gone by now."

"I wanted to say goodbye."

"And thanks for the memories," he muttered, dryly.

"Don't put words in my mouth, Wyatt." When he started working again, she sighed and walked to the table to stand next to him. He refused to look at her. "What do you want from me?" she asked desperately.

He turned to face her, and she stepped back at the hurt apparent in his eyes. "Just sex, Quinn. Isn't that what you think of me?" he snarled. "I just want sex. I've gotten it, so you can leave."

"I don't like your tone."

"Tough shit," he snapped. Her eyes widened and, in a burst of fury, he slapped a small ceramic pot off the table. It crashed into a wall and fell to the ground in numerous pieces. He glared at her. "I'm sick of tiptoeing around you, around us. The question isn't what I want. You know what I want. You've always known what I've wanted. The question is what do you want?"

"I don't know what you want, Wyatt," she retorted, her voice rising until she was screaming at the top of her lungs. "You've been panting after me since we first met. You didn't even know me. I was horrible to you, and the more awful I was to you, the more you seemed to want me. And when I finally talk to you like a human being, you tell me that you're in love with some woman you barely know—

who's allergic to flowers, I might add—and that I'm not good enough for you. What am I supposed to think?"

Wyatt took several deep breaths, then said calmly, "I never said that you weren't good enough for me."

"Oh, please," she snorted in disbelief. "That's exactly what you were telling me when you said that I was not Sibleyville wife material. Because like every other man I've known, you only wanted the image. The fake breasts, the short dresses and the high heels. You didn't want to get to know the real me and that's why I treated you like dirt, Wyatt. Not because you're a mortician, or because you're from Sibleyville, but because I expected more from you."

She cursed as tears blurred her vision. She turned her back to him and swiped at her tears. She did not cry over men, but that didn't change the fact that here she was crying over a man.

"You're right," he said softly. "You're exactly right." He gently grabbed her arms and turned her to face him. "And I'm sorry, Quinn. I didn't mean to hurt you."

She rolled her eyes in response and focused on a corner of the room to fight back more tears.

"That's how I felt in the beginning, but after tonight, you have to know that I don't feel like that anymore. I think you're amazing and funny and smart. And that's why I…that's why I want you even more now than the first moment I saw you."

She stared at him for a moment, not wanting to believe him. "It's been a joke between us for so long."

"Not anymore. I really care about you, Quinn."

Sephora would have walked out the greenhouse, never to look back, while delivering a cutting monologue that would have left Wyatt a trembling mess. But, of course, Sephora had a team of award-winning writers to help her, and Quinn… Well, Quinn didn't want Wyatt to be a trembling mess. She just wanted him.

She took a deep breath, then took his hand. He pulled her against his chest and wrapped his arms around her. He buried a kiss in her hair.

"I'm sorry, baby," he whispered.

"Me, too," she whispered, then buried her face in his chest.

He smoothed hair from her face to tuck behind her ears. "So, we're both sorry. What do we do now?"

She wiped at the tears on her face and said instantly, "You have to talk to Dorrie."

"That's the first order of business?" he asked with a teasing smile.

"Yes," she said firmly. "You have to tell her that you're interested in someone else."

"That would be you, right?" he asked, uncertainly, then laughed when she stared at him.

She hesitated, then plowed ahead, "And then we need to talk about the movie."

He smoothed his thumb across her lips, sparking butterflies of pleasure down her body. His voice was soft as he said, "You have to know by now that anything you want that is within my power to give you, you can have. If you want to film the movie here, you'll film the movie here."

Quinn felt the tears well up in her eyes again and she kissed him. Hard and fast. "Wyatt," she whispered, unable to say anything else through her surprise.

He lowered his mouth to hers. It was a kiss of

promise, of hope and a stake of ownership. And Quinn reveled in every second of it because she was his. She had never been anyone's before, because she had never wanted to be, but she wanted to be Wyatt's woman. His whatever. As long as she had the same claim to him.

One of his hands moved to her behind to press her closer to him. She moaned as he hardened against her and pressed into her center. His hot tongue and his hot length between her thighs were driving her insane.

She tore her mouth from his and whispered, "We need to go back to your bedroom."

"Too late," he muttered before claiming her mouth again in a deep, erotic kiss that instantly flooded her center.

Wyatt didn't break contact with her mouth, but swept the worktable clean. Clay pots and plants crashed to the floor. He lifted her onto the table and pushed up her dress. When he saw her bare, he laughed dryly.

"You kill me, Quinn. Where are your panties?"

"I couldn't find them," she admitted, then pulled him toward her for another kiss.

He ate her mouth raw. She didn't see him pull down his sweats, but suddenly he was inside of her. She screamed his name, then dug her nails into his lower back, urging him to go harder and faster.

Their moans and grunts filled the greenhouse, rising to the ceiling. He plowed into her without mercy, his expression tight, his eyes closed. Quinn forgot to be self-conscious, to think about her body. She matched his strokes, meeting his kisses when he remembered to kiss her, holding onto his bottom lip. And then she exploded in sheer ecstasy, screaming his name at the top of her lungs. Several more powerful strokes and Wyatt followed her over the edge, her name torn from his lips in a hoarse cry.

Chapter 13

"Well, well, well. Look at what the Porsche dragged in."

Quinn ignored Kendra's snide comment as she climbed from Graham's Porsche late the next morning. She slammed the car door and walked towards the front porch, where Kendra was dangling on the porch frame between pull-up sets.

Quinn collapsed onto one of the wicker chairs on the porch and set her handbag on the ground. She continued to ignore Kendra as she sniffed the bright red tulip that Wyatt had given her before she had left. He had kissed her at the same time he had handed her the tulip. The kiss had turned into a much longer kiss that had made her leave his apartment an hour later than she had intended. And she had loved every second of it. His hands mapping her body, his eyes hot on hers, his mouth claiming hers with a sense of own-

ership she had never thought she would allow anyone
to have over her.

"Earth to Quinn," Kendra snapped. "You look like
shit and you're dehydrated. It must have been quite a
night, you little slut."

Quinn snapped from the replay of that morning and
suddenly realized that it was cold and she was sitting
on the porch in a minidress. She grabbed Kendra's dis-
carded sweatshirt from the ground and slipped it on,
then drained a nearby water bottle in one gulp. She
wiped her mouth with the back of her hand.

She focused on Kendra, or, more accurately, on
Kendra's body. Kendra wore a pair of shorts that gave
the term *short shorts* a new meaning and a barely-there
sports bra, without any regard for the cold weather. On
any other woman, there would have been cellulite or
jiggle or something to show that the woman was real.
On Kendra it was all muscle and smooth dark brown
skin. There would be no need for touch-ups or special
lighting for Kendra.

"You're such a ray of sunshine in the morning,"
Quinn noted lightly.

"I've been told that once or twice."

"Where's Charlie?" Quinn asked.

"She and Graham went shopping for more tinsel or
something. All I know is that I don't have to watch their
coochie coo anymore. How do you live with them?
They are downright sickening," Kendra grunted through
clenched teeth, as each visible muscle strained from
another pull-up that would have made a lesser man cry.

"I don't live with them. I live in the poolhouse."

"Semantics, Quinn."

"As soon as this movie comes out, I'll find—"

"You're doing an indie movie, Quinn. Didn't you have to pay them to put you in?"

Quinn narrowed her eyes at Kendra. She leaned back in the chair and asked sweetly, "Kendra, I'm curious about something, too. Are you trying to look like a man, or does it just come naturally?"

Kendra dropped to the porch step, her chest heaving. She wiped her face with a nearby towel and frowned at the empty water bottle.

"You should try exercise sometime, Quinn. Then maybe you wouldn't have to use the eat-and-barf method to remain thin."

"I am not bulimic."

"Then that explains the new set of love handles that have filled in."

"And do the steroids explain the distinct Adam's apple I see developing?"

Kendra rolled her eyes, then she stood to stretch her arms overhead. "Are you going to tell me what happened last night and how you managed to miss the hoe-down here, or do you want to exchange some more insults?"

"I think I'd rather exchange insults with you all day than talk about something that special with you," Quinn shot back.

Kendra rolled her eyes then performed some complicated stretch that brought her right ankle to her right ear. "Quinn, I can tell that you're on the verge of bursting to tell someone, anyone, what happened to you last night. So just tell me what's wrong before I get really pissed off."

Quinn stared at her sister for a moment, then couldn't

prevent the grin that crossed her face. Kendra dropped into the chair next to Quinn and stared at her hard. "It was amazing," Kendra guessed.

"More than anything that has ever been hinted at in Sephora's scenes with the one true love of her life, Blake Banks," Quinn gushed, turning in her seat to face Kendra. "He was patient, gentle, funny. He made me feel beautiful and wanted me, not just for my body but for me. I've never felt that way in my life."

Kendra actually laughed, and for a moment Quinn was shaken from her own reverie to realize how beautiful Kendra was when she smiled.

"You are completely whipped," Kendra said, shaking her head, amused.

"Completely," Quinn agreed.

"So does this mean that your mission was successful? The movie will be filmed in the house?" Kendra asked, her perpetual frown returning.

Quinn's smile faded. She averted her gaze and murmured, "Yes."

"Then you won the bet."

She glared her sister. "Last night was not about that. Why would you say that?"

"That's not what you told me yesterday."

"What are you saying, Kendra?"

"I'm not saying anything, except what everyone will think. Quinn Sibley stops at nothing to get what she wants."

She jumped to her feet. "Last night with Wyatt had nothing to do with the movie."

"If it didn't, why are you getting so angry?"

"I knew I shouldn't have talked to you about this.

Go to hell," she shot back, then stormed toward the front door.

"By the way," Kendra called after her, "Helmut called. He wants to know your progress. He didn't not sound happy. I won't even tell you his exact message because it involved a few words that are not fit for your young, impressionable ears."

Quinn didn't acknowledge her sister and climbed up the stairs to her bedroom. She slammed the door closed and stared at her reflection in the mirror. She did not like what she saw.

"You look like a man who could use a lunch break."

Wyatt looked over his shoulder into the sun to see Graham standing over him. Wyatt pushed back the bill of his baseball cap and brushed his hands on his jeans. After leaving Quinn that morning, he had headed straight to city hall to replant the carnations lining the sidewalk. He hadn't been able to stop smiling. And he couldn't wait for the day to be over so he could see Quinn again and give himself even more reasons to smile.

"You buying?" Wyatt asked squinting at Graham.

"Haven't I been buying since we were fifteen?"

"I usually buy the beer," Wyatt said, defensively.

By mutual consent, the two walked toward Annie's Diner. Wyatt washed his hands in the bathroom, resisted the urge to call Quinn just to hear her voice, then joined Graham at their favorite booth at the front of the restaurant.

"So you know why I'm eating lunch with you, instead of cuddling with my wife in front of the fireplace at home," Graham said with a long sigh.

Wyatt bit his lower lip to prevent the laughter. "Quinn," he said simply.

"If this is what fatherhood is going to be like, I think I can wait another ten or twenty years," Graham muttered. "So, tell me that you don't have any nefarious plans for Quinn and I can face my wife with a clear conscience."

"You can face your wife with a clear conscience. I don't have any nefarious plans for Quinn." Then he hid his smile because he didn't think that Graham would want to hear about the plans that he did have for Quinn, which involved her naked in his bed and, maybe, whipped cream.

"Great," Graham said, relieved.

Annie walked over to the table and actually smiled at Wyatt. Wyatt had been coming to Annie's Diner his entire life, and Annie had never actually smiled at him. "Wyatt, you are quite the stud, aren't you?" she said, laughing.

Wyatt exchanged glances with Graham, who coughed over his laughter. Wyatt turned back to Annie. "Excuse me?"

"I heard that Quinn went to your house last night and didn't leave until late this morning. You've been holding out on us all these years, haven't you? I knew you weren't the Boy Scout your mother always claimed." She laughed loudly, then said, "Two house specials for you boys, my treat, in honor of Little Granger here finally getting some."

Annie walked away, still laughing to herself, while Wyatt sunk lower in his seat to avoid stares from the other diners.

"Annie just congratulated you on getting laid," Graham noted.

"I caught that," Wyatt muttered.

"I don't know whether to laugh with you or cry with you."

Wyatt hid his own laughter, then shrugged. "At least, we get lunch on the house."

Graham shook his head amused then muttered, "Living in a town like this, I now understand why you're in a rush to be married."

"It's not because of the town. I'm thirty-two years old. It's time."

Graham waved his hand dismissively. "There's no time line for starting a family."

Wyatt was surprised by the quickness and intensity of his anger. "I'm going to ignore that you said that."

Graham's eyes widened in surprise. "What's wrong?"

"You never wanted a family. You thought marriage was a fate worse than death. I was the one who wanted the wife and the stability…" Wyatt's voice trailed off and he ran both hands over his head. He took several deep breaths and forced himself to meet Graham's surprised gaze. "This is awkward," he admitted with a forced laugh. "I guess I'm a little jealous of you."

"Jealous?"

Wyatt felt awkward, uncomfortable, but now that he had started down the road, he had to finish. "Jealous of what you have, the potential for what you could have."

Graham stared at his hands for a moment, then looked at Wyatt, obviously at a loss for words.

Wyatt forced a laugh. "I actually rendered you speechless. I didn't think it could be done."

"I'm sorry."

"Don't apologize for falling in love. There is no one

in this town more happy for you that you found Charlie because you two are terrific together. It's just that I always thought that I'd be first. I always wanted it more than you did. Even when we were kids, you dated a new girl every month, and I was the one looking for the steady girlfriend. You couldn't wait to leave this town, to try new things, meet new people. I was always content here, to live the Sibleyville lifestyle."

"I tried to get you to visit me when I was living abroad—"

"It's not about leaving Sibleyville," Wyatt said, trying to keep the frustration out of his voice. "I've never wanted to leave here. I fit in here. It's just I never thought it would be this hard to find someone. I'm lonely, Graham."

"I didn't know," Graham said helplessly. "I thought you were happy."

"I live above a garage in the back of the funeral home I grew up in," Wyatt said, shaking his head in disbelief. "Why would you think I was happy?"

"You never seemed unhappy, I guess." The two men were silent for a moment, carefully avoiding each other's eyes.

Wyatt cleared his throat, then said, "You were right about Dorrie. She wasn't the one for me. Maybe the only thing worse than being alone is being in a marriage with a woman you don't love, who you constantly compare to someone else. It wouldn't have been fair to Dorrie or me. So it's back to the drawing board for now."

"What about Quinn?"

"What about her? She wants to be a movie star, and she can't be one in Sibleyville."

Graham shook his head, his expression more serious

than Wyatt had ever seen him. "If you love her, Wyatt, it doesn't matter. You'll make it work."

"Here you go, boys," Annie said, setting down plates of steaming turkey and mashed potatoes. She winked at Wyatt and said, "I added an extra helping of potatoes for you since you've been exerting so much energy and need to keep up your strength."

Wyatt dug into the food and hoped that Graham would change the subject. Graham watched him for a moment and when Wyatt didn't look up, Graham started to eat and, thankfully, did not bring up Quinn again.

Two hours later, Quinn felt refreshed after a shower and a short nap. She wore the only comfortable pair of jeans she owned and Graham's sweatshirt that she had decided to permanently co-opt. She combed out her damp hair in front of the mirror in her bedroom and mused about the last few days.

Ever since she had set foot in Sibleyville, things had been different. She had been different. And she blamed it all on Wyatt. She could hardly concentrate on her script. She hadn't returned any of the six voice mail messages that Helmut had left on her cell phone. And she had been more happy than an out-of-work actress should have been.

Her cell phone rang again. Quinn sat on the bed and stared at the telephone on the nightstand. It was Helmut. She had to break the "good news" at some point, except it suddenly didn't seem like good news anymore.

"Quinn," Helmut barked into the receiver as soon as she answered.

"Hello, Helmut," she said, forcing herself to sound remotely cheerful.

"Hello, Helmut? Hello, Helmut! I've been trying to reach you for two days and all I get is 'Hello, Helmut.' Tell me something, Quinn, anything. We need to start filming in five days, and I still don't have a location. I have producers breathing down my neck, actors telling me that they need to take other jobs if this one doesn't come through, a crew that is demanding start and stop dates. And it's too late to find a new location. Much too late. I need an answer, Quinn, and I need one now."

"I got it," she said simply.

There was a long silence as if Helmut were too overjoyed to speak. "Please tell me that this is not a joke," he said, his voice trembling with emotion.

"It's not a joke, Helmut."

"Quinn, I will never forget this."

"Just make me a star and we can consider ourselves even."

"You will be a star, Quinn," Helmut gushed. "I will do everything in my power to make certain that you come out of this movie with Oscar buzz. And you will."

"I have to go, Helmut. Merry Christmas. I'll see you next week."

"Next week? We'll be there tomorrow."

"Tomorrow? Christmas Eve is in three days," she protested.

"Did you hear the part where I told you that we have to start filming this movie as soon as possible? We have to rehearse and block scenes, and there have been revisions to the script. We'll be there tomorrow, ready to move at full speed. Be ready."

"I'll be ready. I'll see you—"

Her voice trailed off as she heard the dial tone singing in her ear. She tried to avoid the sinking feeling in her stomach that told her she had just made the biggest mistake of her life.

Chapter 14

"I love Christmas shopping. Don't you?" Charlie asked cheerfully as she linked one arm with a glowering Kendra and another arm with Quinn and dragged the two down Main Street.

Quinn straightened her sunglasses and her knit cap with her free hand and ignored Charlie. She wanted to be home, studying the script, memorizing her lines or, more accurately, reliving every moment of her night with Wyatt. She knew that she should have been excited about *On Livermore Road*. It was actually going to happen. Quinn Sibley was going to be in a movie. The first role in her comeback. But, like a high school girl after her first kiss, Quinn could only think about Wyatt. His smile. His hands. Every soft word he had spoken to her last night. Even now, in the cold weather, her entire body grew warm just thinking about last night. Or, even better, waking up all warm and cuddly against his smooth chest.

"And there's just something about Christmas in Sibley-ville," Charlie continued, an unstoppable force of good cheer. "The fresh air, the… Good morning, Harvey—"

"'Morning, Charlie," a man greeted with a smile, tipping his cowboy hat. Quinn exchanged a look of dis-belief with Kendra.

Charlie grinned and continued, "The friendliness, the tinsel…and they're lighting the tree tonight in the town square. Graham says it's an annual tradition. One of the best traditions, besides running around the maypole."

"Maypole?" Quinn questioned, confused, snapped from her own self-disgust. "Do people still do that?"

"What is that?" Kendra demanded, suspiciously.

"In Sibleyville, they do," Charlie said, cheerfully, squeezing their arms closer.

"Remind me again why I'm being tortured in Small-ville, when I could be in New York City, taking advan-tage of the Christmas sales," Kendra groaned.

"Because you don't have any money," Quinn sug-gested sweetly.

Kendra pinned her with a hard glare. "At least I can support myself, and I don't have to live off my sister and brother-in-law."

"Support yourself? You haven't worked in over six months, Kendra!"

"You haven't worked in twelve years, Quinn. And, yes, I'm including your time on *Diamond Valley* in that."

"Stop it," Charlie ordered, dragging her sisters to a halt in the middle of the sidewalk. She glared from one to the other, her brown cheeks flushed with anger. "It's Christmas, and we're going shopping to buy presents for each other. For once in our lives, we're going to have a good, normal holiday, with lots of good cheer and happiness, damn it, or I'll…I'll make you two string more popcorn for the tree."

"Enough said," Kendra said, pasting an obviously fake smile on her face. "I love Christmas. I love Christmas shopping. I love Sibleyville."

Behind Charlie's back, Kendra popped Quinn in the back of the head. Quinn automatically repeated in a monotone, "I love Christmas. I love Christmas shopping. I love Sibleyville."

Charlie's anger melted into a smile and she shook her head. "What am I going to do with you two?"

"Love us," Quinn said with a sweet smile.

Charlie grinned. "Of course, I do. Even though you two are a pain in the butt, I'm glad you're here."

"All right. Let's get this shopping out the way, so I can get back to the house and have a drink," Kendra said, cutting off anymore fuzzy feelings. She glanced at her watch. "We'll meet back here in half an hour."

"Half an hour—"

Kendra cut off Charlie's protest, "Half an hour, Mrs. Forbes, or you're hiking back home."

"Agreed," Quinn chimed in.

Charlie shot them both wounded looks, but Kendra had already stalked off in one direction.

"If she buys me another pair of gloves, I'll scream," Charlie muttered to Quinn.

Quinn laughed, always pleasantly surprised whenever Charlie said anything remotely bitchy. "I think she just walked into a store with a display case of Isotoners in the window."

Charlie groaned, then headed in the opposite direction from Kendra. Quinn smiled to herself and began to stroll down the street. She glanced in one store window after the other, but every time she tried to focus on something she thought of Wyatt, hovering above her, the look on his face when he entered her.

She gave up on looking for a gift with the current state of her horny thoughts. Not that she had money to buy her sisters presents anyway. The days of sending an expensive gift and a Christmas card were long over. Now Quinn had to actually spend time with her sisters and hope that was enough.

Quinn stopped in front of a jewelry store. Against her will, her gaze was drawn to several engagement rings laid out on the black velvet display. She chided herself to move on; instead, she took off her sunglasses for a closer look.

She was not the type of women who salivated over engagement rings. Diamonds, sure. Rubies, even better. Emeralds, she would kill for. But boring engagement rings? Still, here she was. Staring at the rings, holding her breath and trying not to make a wish.

"Merry Christmas, Quinn."

Quinn looked in the reflection of the window to see Dorrie Diamond. Judging from Dorrie's slightly distorted face in the window, Quinn definitely was not her favorite actress any longer. Wyatt had obviously told Dorrie about last night.

Quinn pasted a bright smile on her face and turned to face Dorrie. The image in color was even more transparent. Something akin to disgust flashed in Dorrie's eyes.

"Hi, Dorrie," Quinn said, brightly. "Merry Christmas to you, too." For some reason, Quinn decided to hug Dorrie. The two women awkwardly wrapped their arms around each other and patted once, while making certain that no part of their bodies touched the other.

Quinn quickly stepped back from Dorrie and smoothed down her coat. Dorrie stared at Quinn, then averted her gaze. The two women stood speechless for a moment.

Quinn cleared her throat, then said abruptly, "I have to meet my sisters, and I'm late. It was good running into you."

"I just wanted to talk to you for a second," Dorrie said quickly, moving to block Quinn's escape route.

"Oh? What about?" Quinn squeaked. She discreetly glanced around the suddenly deserted Main Street. Where were all the witnesses? Where was Kendra? Kendra could bench-press Dorrie. Sure, Dorrie didn't reach Quinn's shoulders, but she looked as if she would scratch and Quinn had a face to protect.

"You know what about," Dorrie said flatly. "Wyatt."

"Right."

"I know that you know that he's had a crush on you for a long time, but leading him on like you did yesterday in my office is not fair to him."

Quinn bit the inside of her lip and mentally smacked Wyatt upside the head. Apparently he had not spoken to Dorrie yet.

"I was not trying to lead him on," Quinn said honestly.

"Of course you were," Dorrie said simply. "And I almost understand it. You're stuck here in Sibleyville for the holidays. You don't have your usual entourage of admirers and you thought why not play with Wyatt a little? He's a decent guy. Even if he has a crush on you, you figure that he would never act on it, unless he had some encouragement."

Quinn shook her head in disbelief. "Dorrie, you are so wrong—"

Dorrie took a step closer to Quinn, until she was practically breathing in her face. Quinn gulped. She was a lover, not a fighter.

"I like Wyatt, and he and I might have a future together. I don't need you to confuse him. You have your pick of men anywhere you go. I just have Wyatt. Leave him alone."

Quinn straightened her shoulders and said in a dangerous voice that had made taller women tremble, "Maybe I like Wyatt, too. Did you ever think of that?"

"You couldn't possibly like him. He has nothing to offer you. He's a nobody."

Quinn felt a sharp stab of anger at Dorrie's description of Wyatt. "If that's how you think of someone you supposedly like, I'd hate to hear how you would describe someone you can't stand."

"Ask anyone in town how I describe you and you'll get your answer," Dorrie said in the same soft, dangerous tone.

Quinn smiled slightly at the not-so-hidden insult. "You're not as boring as you look," she noted casually. "How long do you think you can fool Wyatt?"

"Long enough," Dorrie said, with the same smile in return.

"Making friends already, Quinn?" Kendra purred, walking to stand next to Quinn and to tower over Dorrie.

The hard look she shot Dorrie made Dorrie take several steps back.

"Merry Christmas, Quinn," Dorrie said with her fake sweet smile, then quickly walked away.

"What did She-Elf want?" Kendra asked, looking after Dorrie.

"That's Dorrie Diamond."

Kendra's eyes widened in amusement. "*The* Dorrie Diamond?"

"The one and only," Quinn muttered.

"She looked like she wanted to kick your ass…if she could reach it from her low position on the ground. Did she hear about last night?"

"No," Quinn said, shaking her head and narrowing her eyes. "And now I have to kill Wyatt."

"You're in trouble," Graham sang to Wyatt as he opened the door for Wyatt to enter the house.

Wyatt grimaced and walked into the Sibleys' house. He had spent all day tending to his nursery clients and projects around town. He had barely gotten home in time to shower and change for dinner with Quinn at her house. But he had heard from several people in town that Dorrie and Quinn had had a showdown on Main Street and while no one had heard what was said, everyone had seen their expressions. World War III.

Wyatt and Graham walked into the dining room. Wyatt's stomach grumbled at the scent of pot roast and mashed potatoes on the small round dining table, and he was momentarily distracted from his impending doom. He hadn't eaten since lunch.

Then Graham nudged him. Wyatt looked up and saw

fire spewing from the eyes of all three Sibley sisters. Even Charlie.

"I'm not with him," Graham said, holding up his hands in self-defense. He took his seat next to Charlie. That left the one chair between Quinn and Kendra.

Kendra's eyes narrowed at him, while Quinn pursed her lips and glared at him. Wyatt carefully crossed the room and slid into the chair. He leaned over to kiss Quinn on the cheek, but she stopped him with a glare. He didn't care. It had been a long day, he hadn't seen her all day and he had missed the hell out of her. He gently grabbed her chin and pressed a kiss against her lips. He grinned against her mouth when she licked his bottom lip in return.

Kendra snorted in disgust. "Way to give him hell, Quinn," she muttered dryly.

Wyatt pulled back and grinned at Quinn. He saw the corners of her mouth slightly lift in a return smile even as she frowned at him.

"You didn't talk to Dorrie today," she said, flatly.

"I didn't talk to Dorrie," he confirmed.

"Why?"

"I was busy," he said, avoiding her gaze.

"And scared," Graham chimed in.

"It's not exactly easy to dump someone…especially when you never really started dating," Wyatt said, while shooting Graham a look that promised retribution at a later date. "It's a delicate situation."

Charlie began to spoon mashed potatoes onto her plate. "You should have told Dorrie, Wyatt," she said.

Wyatt grabbed a bowl of green beans and heaped some on his plate and a smaller mound on Quinn's plate. She gave him a nasty look.

"Yeah, Wyatt. I'm not sure if Dorrie knows that you two haven't started dating from the way she was warning off Quinn," Kendra said while passing him the plate of roast.

"She was warning you off?" Wyatt asked, surprised.

"You don't have to sound so pleased," Quinn snapped. "The little runt was on the verge of taking a swing at me."

"Dorrie?" he said in disbelief. "What did you say to her?"

Graham groaned and shook his head. "Wrong thing to say, brother."

Quinn ignored Graham and pinned Wyatt with a hard glare. "What? You think I had to say something to make your sweet Dorrie semiviolent? You think she's much too wonderful and perfect to come at me unprompted?"

"That's not what I meant," he quickly said.

Quinn snorted in disbelief, then stabbed a piece of roast on the platter and dropped it on her plate. She dropped several more pieces on his plate. "Let me tell you about your little Dorrie. She's a barracuda. A pit bull. Or some other obnoxious, small creature. There is nothing remotely sweet about her."

"Just agree, Wyatt," Graham suggested from across the table, then winced and glanced at Charlie, who obviously had kicked him under the table.

"I'll talk to her," Wyatt quietly said to Quinn. "I'm sorry you had to deal with that. I never thought she'd confront you."

She glared at him and then lightly pushed his arm, a smile playing at the edges of her mouth. "You better be glad I had time to calm down since it took you forever to get over here."

He grinned and took her hand to place a kiss on her knuckles. "I missed you today, too."

"I liked them better when they were fighting," Kendra chimed in.

Wyatt glared at Kendra but didn't comment. Instead, he concentrated on his food and didn't release Quinn's hand throughout the meal. Strangely enough, she didn't try to make him release it, either.

An hour later, Wyatt finally had Quinn alone in her bedroom. He lay on her bed, while she sat next to him with the script in her hands. He had another copy of the script in front of him. He was supposed to be reading lines with her, but instead, he was just enjoying watching her. Everything she did captivated him. Made his heart skip a beat. He couldn't remember any other woman intriguing him so much. The way she flipped her hair over her shoulder, how she crossed her eyes whenever she got a line wrong, the way she bit her bottom lip when she was trying to remember her line. Wyatt was slowly and inevitably falling in love with this woman, and trying to stop it was like trying to stop a runaway train.

"…You did it on purpose, Parker. You knew that I would find out…" Quinn's voice trailed off and she peeked at Wyatt. "Is that right?"

"It would be right in another six lines," he said with a sympathetic smile.

Quinn groaned and fell on the bed next to him. "It's been so long since I had to remember lines. We had tele-prompters on *Diamond Valley*."

"Let's try again," he said, nudging her in the side. She groaned again, but sat up. He looked at her seriously, then at the script. "Katherine," he pretended to read. "I beg of you not to hurt her. Place yourself in the poor girl's shoes—"

"Where are you?" she asked confused, flipping through her script.

"If you knew that you had lost me to Dorrie, you would flip out on her in the middle of Main Street, too," he finished dramatically.

Quinn screamed playfully, then attacked him, tickling him in every spot she could reach. Wyatt laughed and tried to twist out of her reach, but she showed him no mercy, her fingers poking into his stomach, finding the funny spots. He rolled on top of her and pinned her arms overhead. Their mutual laughter faded as they stared into each other's eyes.

"Hi," he murmured, placing a kiss on each eyelid, then on the tip of her nose. "Have I told you how much I missed you today?"

"Not nearly enough," she responded softly, her fingers curling into his.

"Each hour was torture."

"You sure took your sweet time getting over here."

He smiled. "You told me dinner was at six. I got here at five forty-five."

"I would think that a man who was tortured by each hour away from me would have been here at five-thirty."

Wyatt laughed, then released her hands to lie next to her and pull her into his arms. She cuddled against him. His heart clenched. He had never thought that he would be holding Quinn, or that she would willingly move into his arms. Her denim-covered legs twined with his.

"Are you going to admit that you missed me, too?" he prodded, stroking her hair.

Quinn moved from his arms and hovered above him with a mysterious smile. "I'm supposed to show, not tell," she whispered.

Her fingers went to the buttons of his shirt. He shifted nervously and glanced at the closed door.

"Let's go back to my place," he suggested in a hoarse whisper.

"You should have told Dorrie," she said with a dramatic sigh. "Now, I can't be seen at your house. Everyone will see my car in the driveway."

Her hands smoothed his shirt as she brushed aside the shirt halves and pulled them off his shoulders. He lifted to help her and she threw the shirt on the floor.

"I'll drive you there," he said, growing panicked as her hands tangled with his belt. "We'll take one car. I'll drive you home in the morning. Don't start this here, Quinn. Your sisters and Graham will know what we're doing."

"Not if you manage to keep your mouth closed," she said in a low, throaty voice designed to drive him crazy. She dropped the belt on the floor, then unbuckled his pants and pulled them down. She tugged at his boots and, after a grunt, pulled off one, then the other. The jeans followed. He trembled under her lithe body as he laid on the bed in his briefs.

Quinn crawled back up his body to plant a soft kiss on his mouth. "Of course, you never manage to keep your mouth closed."

"You're the vocal one," he protested, then groaned loudly when one of her hands cupped him.

"You were saying?" she teased.

"This isn't fair," he complained, but all speech stopped when Quinn pulled off the oversized sweatshirt she wore followed by the tank top underneath.

"What's not fair?" she prodded in a soft voice as she unhooked her bra.

Wyatt gulped as her breasts spilled free. "What?" he asked, blankly.

She smiled, then moved back down his body. Her fingers hooked on the waistband of his briefs. "You know, Wyatt, I've never liked giving oral sex. In fact, I haven't given a blow job since my third year on the soap."

"A guy can still dream, can't he?" he murmured.

"I mean, have you ever looked at a penis? Would you want to put your mouth on that?"

"Hey," he said defensively, looking at his still covered penis. "You're going to give him a complex."

"I mean, everyone can agree that a woman's body is beautiful. It's proportional. Nothing untoward hanging here or there, unless she has some sagging somewhere and then one trip to a plastic surgeon and everything is back where it's supposed to be. But a man. Things are okay, downright interesting, until you get to the penis. It's strange looking."

"I'm trying not to be insulted."

Quinn pulled off his briefs and his erection sprang free. Proud and heavy. "He doesn't seem to be suffering any low self-esteem," she noted.

"It takes a lot to get him down," he said, then reached for her. He was ready to end the game. He wanted her.

She evaded his hands and placed one hand around his length. He dug his heels into the bed and arched at the feel. He could have exploded from that one touch.

"The reason I bring up my blow job ban is because it's different with you. I want to taste you there. I think you're beautiful all over. Even here."

He tried to swallow, then gave up and stared at her, posing by his penis, one hand around him, her breasts swinging free and her hair loose and wild.

She suddenly looked worried as she said, "If I do something wrong—"

"You won't," he quickly assured her.

Her other hand massaged his right thigh. "You'll let me know."

He nodded quickly, energetically. Then she took him in her mouth. Wyatt grabbed the sheets and nearly tore them in half. She sucked the length of him, stroked him, licked him. Generally made him a slave to her mouth. Her soft, persistent pulls, her hard strokes, had him biting his lower lip, straining to scream her name. Sweat beaded on his forehead, on his chest, between his toes. She was claiming him as her own forever.

She licked the tip of his erection, then gave him a heavy-lidded look that almost sent him over the edge. Wyatt cursed and sprang from the bed, grabbing his jeans off the floor. He ripped open the condom packet and sheathed himself.

"I wasn't done," she said, disgruntled.

Wyatt didn't have time for talking. He ignored her protests and grabbed her waist, turning her onto her stomach. He ripped off the scrap of lace she called underwear and slammed into her so hard that they both grunted. She was dripping wet and ready. He paused as a force as powerful as a hurricane gathered in the base of his spine.

He absently rubbed her back, forcing himself to go slower. She wriggled against him, staring at him over her shoulder, pleading him with her eyes to go faster. And that was it. Wyatt lost all control. He pounded into her, holding on to her waist as she clung to him. She gasped at each invasion and begged him in between for more.

Wyatt smiled even through the madness and leaned close to her ear. "You're going to bring the whole house in here."

Quinn buried her face in a pillow, and her muffled screams made him move harder and faster. No matter where he went, she was there with him, clinging to him, driving him on and on. She quivered underneath him, and her body milked him unmercifully. Wyatt bit his bottom lip and finally exploded in a shower of emotion so intense that chills covered his body. He knew that nothing would never be the same after this woman. Nothing.

He still hadn't decided if that was a good or bad thing.

Chapter 15

Wyatt took a deep breath for courage, then opened the door to the mortuary the next afternoon. He had barely dragged himself from Quinn's bed early that morning and had started his rounds around town. He had a lot of work to do, but if was being honest with himself, he also had been avoiding his mother.

He passed through the viewing room and the chapel and headed to the living area in the back of the house. He was not looking forward to this conversation. In a perfect world, Wyatt would have been able to tell his mother about Quinn and the movie after taking her to dinner at her favorite steak house in Bentonville. But he lived in Sibleyville, not in a perfect world. And in Sibleyville, Beatrice probably knew that Wyatt had been at Quinn's house the night before, that Quinn had spent the night there, and that

On Livermore Road would be filmed at Granger Funeral Home.

Wyatt paused in the hallway when he heard voices coming from the dining room. He heard his mother's distinctive laugh, but the other person's voice was too quiet for him to hear. He walked into the dining room and inwardly cursed when he saw his mother and Dorrie sitting at the dining table amidst a banquet fit for a queen—or Beatrice's hoped-for future daughter-in-law.

"Wyatt, you're just in time," Beatrice said with a smile that was entirely too bright.

"Hi, Wyatt," Dorrie said with a shy smile.

"Dorrie," he said, gulping.

"I made your favorite for lunch, sweetheart. Chicken and dumplings," Beatrice said, motioning towards the chair next to her. "Have a seat."

Wyatt obeyed his mother's command and sat at the chair she indicated. He watched his mother cheerfully spoon a heaping mound of food onto a plate. She added mashed potatoes and mixed vegetables.

Wyatt noted the elaborately decorated table. The good china. The crystal glasses. A vase of while lilies mixed with white roses. And her best serving platters. His mother had gone all out for Operation: Any Woman But Quinn.

"This is nice, Mother," Wyatt said in a tone that let his mother know that he knew what she was doing. She had obviously heard the gossip about Wyatt and Quinn and had decided to handle the situation in her own way. Manipulation.

"Thank you, dear," Beatrice said, smiling.

"Dorrie, this certainly is a pleasant surprise, but… what are you doing here?" he asked.

"Beatrice invited me over," Dorrie said, almost apologetically.

Beatrice continued with the Clair Huxtable routine. "I heard that Dorrie would be in Bentonville all morning and I figured that she would be exhausted when she returned home, so I thought it would be nice if I invited her over. Since you and Dorrie are growing so close, it was time for the three of us to sit down to a nice meal. I'm not trying to imply anything or pressure you kids because I know young people move at their own pace, but maybe this will become a regular occurrence."

Dorrie's soft skin flushed and she stared down at her plate.

"That was very thoughtful of you, Mother, but you really shouldn't have," he said through clenched teeth.

Beatrice pretended to ignore Wyatt's pointed glare and, instead, said, "I also wanted to give Dorrie the recipe for my award-winning apple pie." Beatrice patted Dorrie's hand and sent her an encouraging smile. "It's rare to find a woman Dorrie's age who cares about things like baking the perfect apple pie. She's a find, Wyatt. Don't let her get away."

"Beatrice," Dorrie said, laughing in embarrassment.

Beatrice smiled, then stood to clear the plates from the table. "I'm just stating the obvious. I'm sure I don't need to tell my son what a great woman you are. Excuse me, kids, while I check on the pie."

Beatrice sent Dorrie a wink, then walked into the kitchen. Wyatt heard the telephone ring and shook his head in amusement, as his mother loudly asked her friend to hold while she took the phone call upstairs. She obviously wanted to give Wyatt and Dorrie time alone.

Beatrice's steps echoed on the stairs and then her bedroom door slammed closed. Wyatt stared at the plate of food that he had not touched, then forced himself to look at Dorrie. She shyly smiled, then ducked her head.

"Dorrie, I'm sorry about all of this," Wyatt murmured. "My mother can be pushy."

Dorrie shook her head and said, "Beatrice is sweet."

He couldn't prevent a burst of laughter. "My mother has been called many things, but I'm not sure if I've ever heard anyone use the word *sweet*."

Wyatt shifted uncomfortably in his chair and cleared his throat. "Dorrie, I'm actually glad you're here because I've been meaning to talk to you."

Her smile faded and she became very still. "What is it, Wyatt?"

"The last couple of weeks… What I said the other day… I really like you, Dorrie—"

"I like you, too," she said instantly.

Wyatt became more uncomfortable. "There was a time when I thought that the two of us…. You and I…. The things I said to you—"

"You're in love with Quinn," Dorrie said simply.

Wyatt couldn't hide his shock at her instant assessment and his relief that he didn't have to stutter through a breakup speech. "Sort of."

"You don't have to explain anything, Wyatt," she said with an obviously forced smile. "I'm not surprised that you're more attracted to Quinn than me. I mean, what man wouldn't be? She looks like herself and I look like me."

"It's not about looks," Wyatt said quickly. "I mean, yes, Quinn is very beautiful but she's not the reason that

I'm…. I just don't think that we're right for each other. We want a lot of the same things, but I don't think I'm stretching here by saying that neither one of us is in love with the other."

She stared at him for a moment with a confused expression on her face. Then she abruptly stood and walked into the kitchen. Wyatt quickly followed her. Her movements were jerky as she grabbed her purse and coat hanging on the coat hook near the back door.

"Dorrie, wait," Wyatt said. He held up his hands in self-defense when she whirled around to face him and rage shot from her eyes.

"What, Wyatt?" she demanded angrily.

"I hope that we can still be friends."

"Friends? Friends! You just dumped me," she screeched, then added, as an afterthought, "and we weren't even dating!"

"I really like you—"

"I am not a violent person, Wyatt, but if you say that one more time, I will not be responsible for my actions." Ice dripped from each word as her eyes shot lasers at Wyatt. She stuck her arms into her coat sleeves and said through clenched teeth, "I was prepared to walk out of here without another word and to preserve our supposed friendship, but why should I be the only one here to show some dignity?"

"Dorrie—"

"You pursued me, Wyatt. You chased after me from the diner. You made that speech about how you wanted to get to know me. What's changed in the last forty-eight, besides the fact that Quinn was seen leaving your house the other day and you were seen leaving her house this morning?"

Dorrie knew. Wyatt felt like an ass. "I didn't mean for this to happen."

"Of course you didn't," she snapped dryly. "Men like you never intend to fall for a woman you have no chance with until you actually have a chance with her. Then it's drop anyone and everyone as quick as possible."

"Dorrie, I swear that I never meant to hurt you. And this is not about Quinn. It's about you and me. You have to see that I'm right. We wouldn't have been happy with each other."

"Who said that a relationship is about happiness?" she demanded in a high-pitched voice of amazement. When Wyatt sputtered in response, she growled, "Marriage is not about love, Wyatt. It's about commitment and promises. We could have had a good life together. We both want the same things. And you had to ruin it."

"Dorrie—"

"I really thought you were different, but you're just like every other man. You want the unattainable. The Victoria's Secret size zero model who doesn't talk or think, but just flips her hair and pushes her fake breasts in your face. You want someone like Quinn, not a real woman."

"Quinn is a real woman," he protested before he could stop himself.

As the temperature in the kitchen officially dipped to freezing, Wyatt realized that was the wrong thing to say.

"I didn't mean to hurt your feelings—"

She flung open the kitchen door, then turned to glare at him. "You know, I always thought you were gay because you've been single for so long and never have a woman, but now I know the truth. You're an idiot. You think a woman like Quinn wants you? She'll eat you alive. Everyone in town knows about her stupid movie. And everyone in town knows that you agreed to let her use your house after she spent the night here. Do you really think that she's going to have any use for you now that she's gotten what she wants? Grow up, Wyatt."

"Quinn is not like that," he told her.

She gave a dry laugh of disbelief. "Of course she is! And the sad part is that you're the only one who can't see it. I'm almost glad this happened before I invested more time in you."

She stormed out the house, slamming the door behind her.

Wyatt could still hear the ringing in his ears from her shrill tone. He decided that he never wanted to have that conversation again. Hell hath no fury like a woman scorned, and he had just seen the pit of hell in Dorrie's eyes.

"What did you say to her to make her leave?" Beatrice demanded, walking into the kitchen.

"You shouldn't have invited her over here," he said quietly.

"I can invite whoever I want to lunch at my house."

Wyatt took a deep breath for calm, then said, "I'm in love with Quinn." He didn't know who was more surprised by his announcement—Beatrice or him. He had meant to tell his mother that he was dating someone else and that it was cruel to lead Dorrie on, but that hadn't come out. In fact, it sounded suspiciously as if he had just said that he was in love with Quinn.

Beatrice leaned on a nearby chair for balance. "What did you say?" she whispered.

Wyatt hesitated, then realized that it was true. He was in love with Quinn. He had been in love since he first laid eyes on her, since she first pounded on the front door, since she first challenged him to the bet.

"I'm in love with Quinn," he said firmly.

"You're in lust with her," Beatrice corrected.

"No, Mom, it's not lust. I'm in love with her."

"What about Dorrie? She's perfect for you."

"Dorrie is not the one for me. She never was," he said gently. "I would have been making a big mistake."

"Dorrie may not be the one for you, but Quinn isn't, either." She said, desperately. "Look at what she's already done to you. I had to hear at the beauty salon that my house is going to be featured in some movie. You went over my head without even bothering to tell me. The Wyatt I know never would have done that to me."

"I was going to tell you, Mom."

"Wyatt, this is my home and I refuse—"

"We both own this place, Mother," he reminded her gently. "Dad left me the mortuary."

"And I'm sure he's spinning in his grave at the travesty that is about to occur in these walls."

Wyatt took another deep breath for calm. "There won't be a travesty. I'll make sure that they don't disrupt your routine—"

"That's not the point," Beatrice exploded. "Disruption of my routine was never the point. I don't want a bunch of strangers traipsing through my house, making fun of my life."

"The movie is not about making fun of our lives."

"Of course it is. Every time Hollywood decides to make a movie about people like us, we're either tooth-

less and poverty-stricken or gun-toting fundamental-
ists. It's always a caricature. You know that, Wyatt.
You're helping those people tear us down. The son I
know never would have allowed this, and he never
would have done it behind my back."

"It was not behind your back—"

Beatrice shot him another disgusted look, then
walked out the room. Wyatt leaned against the wall and
rubbed his aching eyes. He had the sudden, almost
primal need to see Quinn. And he told himself that it had
nothing to do with the fact that he believed anything
Dorrie or his mother had said.

Wyatt pulled his SUV to a stop in front of the
Sibley home and stared in amazement. In under twelve
hours, the house had completely changed. There were
white Christmas lights lining the roof and porch of the
house. A brightly decorated Christmas tree shone
through one of the living room windows. And there
were a few blown-up plastic snowmen and candy
canes in the front yard, on top of the Santa Claus and
reindeer on the roof.

The holiday spectacle was nothing compared to the
circus in the front of the house. There were trailers
parked along the road, men and women moving around
the yard, carrying equipment and talking in headsets
like secret service agents, and there were bright lights
shining on the house, making the scene almost as
bright as day.

And in the thick of the whole thing stood Quinn. She
stood on the porch under the lights, sparkling and glittering, looking like the Hollywood star that she was. She

was in deep conversation with Helmut. She had never looked more out of reach than she did at that moment.

His mother's rants, and even Dorrie's rants, raced through his mind. Wyatt clenched his jaw and forced himself to get out of the truck. He loved Quinn, and she loved him. Well, she hadn't exactly said that, but he knew she did. It was in her touch last night. Her sighs. Not even an actress could have pretended that.

Wyatt slammed the door, causing several people to stare across the yard, irritated at the unwanted noise. Quinn looked up, too. For a moment, their gazes held, and Wyatt waited for that glimmer of recognition. That smile that she had given him last night.

Quinn waved to him and started toward him, but someone grabbed her arm, stopping her. A tall man all in black clothes that marked him as an *actor* stood next to her. Quinn's face lit up with a bright smile, and she threw herself into the man's arms. He grinned and picked her up, twirling her around the porch. The two laughed together and began to talk animatedly.

"They descended like a plague of locusts about an hour ago," Kendra muttered from behind Wyatt.

He turned to her and Charlie. He darted another quick glance at Quinn and her new friend then turned to the sisters.

He forced a smile and said, "Hello, ladies. I see the word has gotten out."

"I thought you would have held out a little longer," Kendra said, with a disappointed sigh.

He fought back a laugh, then said, "Sorry to disappoint."

Kendra rolled her eyes in response. Charlie smiled at

Wyatt and squeezed his hand. "Quinn should be done in a few minutes. They just want to finish up an interview and get Quinn's reactions to filming in her hometown."

"This is not her hometown."

"Filming in her hometown has a much better ring than filming in a shithole that Quinn hates and rarely visits," Kendra said with a shrug, then yawned. "This is even more boring than I thought it would be. When is it going to be over?"

Wyatt ignored Kendra and tried to sound casual as he asked Charlie, "Who is that man all over Quinn?"

Charlie's amused glance told him that he had not been quite as casual as he had intended.

"His name is Vaughn Cotton. He's an old friend," Charlie assured him. "Quinn worked with him on *Diamond Valley*—"

"Lots of hot, steamy closed bedroom door scenes between them," Kendra added.

Charlie shot an annoyed glance at her, then said to Wyatt, "They worked together, and they're old friends. You have nothing to worry about."

Wyatt glanced at Quinn once more. Now Vaughn was moving strands of hair from Quinn's face while she laughed. Giggled, actually. She was giggling.

"Who says I'm worried?" he muttered, more to himself than to Charlie.

"I do, cowboy," Kendra said flatly. He glared at her, but she was staring at Quinn and Vaughn. She murmured, "I never noticed how cute Vaughn is, or how good Quinn and Vaughn look together. Even their names sound good together."

"Kendra," Charlie snapped.

"Well, it's true. I mean, they were voted America's number one daytime couple and didn't one of those stupid fan sites vote them for one of the sexiest love scenes—"

"Thank you, Kendra," Wyatt said through clenched teeth.

"You wanted to know," she said defensively.

"Not all of that," he muttered.

"You have nothing to be worried about, Wyatt," Charlie reassured him, while not so discretely jabbing Kendra in the arm.

"I'm not worried," Wyatt said.

And because he was not worried, he walked through the thicket of people and lights and cameras toward Quinn.

Wyatt walked up the porch and a cameraman stopped him, placing a hand in the center of his chest. "This is a closed set," the man said, sounding irritated.

Wyatt stared down at the hand, wondering if he should break the entire hand or just a few of the fingers. The cameraman instantly removed his hand and stepped back.

"Wyatt!" Quinn said excitedly.

Wyatt shot the cameraman another hard look, then walked up the porch toward Quinn and Vaughn. Wyatt hadn't noticed how tall Vaughn was from across the yard. Vaughn towered at least two inches above him, and Wyatt usually found himself staring down at most men. Then there were his shoulders. Shoulders like that only came from intense time in a gym with a trainer every day.

Breaking through his thoughts, Quinn threw her arms around him and, more importantly, pressed her body against his, much closer than she had to Vaughn. That easily, Wyatt didn't care about Vaughn's shoulders or the muscles underneath his expensive clothes, because he had Quinn in his arms. And she wanted to be there.

"I'm glad you're here," she whispered only for him to hear. She pulled back from him, but held on to one of his hands as she turned to Vaughn. "I want to introduce you to an old friend. This is Vaughn Cotton. He and I worked together years ago on *Diamond Valley*."

Vaughn sent Wyatt a smile, with teeth bright enough to guide home a ship at night. "Quinn was the best thing that ever happened to that show. It hasn't been the same since she left. And the fans have noticed."

Quinn beamed and playfully pushed Vaughn in one of his broad shoulders. Wyatt gritted his teeth.

"I just found out that Vaughn is going to be in the movie," Quinn said to Wyatt, with excitement glittering in her eyes. "I didn't know until just now."

"I just got the call from Helmut yesterday about this movie. As soon as he told me that Quinn was in the movie, I didn't need to hear anything else. I would pay them to work with this beautiful woman."

"Vaughn, you're so full of crap," Quinn gushed, obviously enjoying the compliments.

"I'm telling the truth," Vaughn said, the picture of wide-eyed innocence. "I still blame you for my dating dry spell in New York while I was filming *Diamond Valley*. Every woman I went out with, I compared to you and, of course, they fell miserably short."

Quinn giggled again, turning into Wyatt's chest. Wyatt narrowed his eyes at Vaughn, who shrugged in response.

"You're so funny, Vaughn," Quinn said while shaking her head.

"Yeah, funny," Wyatt muttered, then said to Quinn, "Can you leave? Do you want to grab dinner?"

Quinn looked hesitant as she glanced at Vaughn, then at the cameras and lights. Helmut was in the yard, berating another man who was practically quivering in fear.

She turned back to Wyatt, and he knew what her answer was going to be before she opened her mouth.

"I can't," she said softly.

He told himself to nod in understanding and be an adult. Of course, he whispered, "Thirty minutes, Quinn. I haven't seen you all day."

She placed a hand on his face and said regretfully, "I can't leave. We still have to discuss the shooting schedule and the revised script and meet the rest of the cast. Helmut even mentioned something about doing a read-through tonight."

Wyatt clenched his teeth in response. She smiled and pressed a kiss against his unyielding mouth. "Don't be angry, sweetie," she cooed. "I'll come to your apartment as soon as we get done here."

"I'll see you tonight, right," he said, hating his need to be pacified.

"I'll see you tonight," she promised then kissed him again. A little too short and a little too sweet to be satisfactory, like a kiss she would give a chump who had won a date with her in some stupid radio contest. Wyatt felt effectively managed as she released his hand and gently turned him toward the porch steps.

He turned back to her, but she was already deep in conversation with Vaughn and Helmut. Wyatt clenched his teeth again and stalked toward his truck. Kendra and Charlie both stood right where he had left them.

"Don't say anything, Kendra," Wyatt warned through clenched teeth.

For once, Kendra kept her mouth shut.

Chapter 16

"This isn't *Diamond Valley*, Quinn. I need real emotion, not crocodile tears before the next Tide commercial," Helmut roared.

Quinn ducked in her seat as every eye in the barn stared at her. And there were a lot of eyes. The cast and crew had spent all night preparing to begin shooting. Quinn had gotten about three hours sleep, then had shown up at the barn at the Forbes property the first thing that morning to read through the script with the rest of the cast.

The barn, which was usually filled with animals, was now filled with high-tech equipment, sawdust, wood and computers. The barn still smelled like hay and animals, but now also had the scent of fresh paint and sweat. But even with all the activity in the barn, Helmut's loud voice had carried enough to freeze everyone in their places to look at her.

Vaughn cleared his throat in the deafening silence and said, "How about a half-hour break, Helmut? My allergies need a break from all the hay and dust."

Helmut threw down his script and glared at the actors assembled around the table. Taking that as their cue, most people in the barn quickly dropped their tools and walked or ran out of the barn.

Quinn quickly walked of out the barn, ignoring the sympathetic and amused glances in her direction. She tried not to break into a flat run to escape the gazes and, instead, quickly walked into the Forbes' house and headed straight to the guest bathroom on the ground floor, slamming the door. She slammed the lid on the toilet and sat.

There was a soft knock on the door. Quinn wiped at her tears and shouted, "The house is closed to cast and crew! Go back outside!"

"It's Vaughn, Quinn. Let me in," Vaughn's muffled voice came from the other side of the door.

Quinn sniffed and opened the door. Vaughn walked into the bathroom and closed the door. She returned to the closed toilet lid.

"Don't let Helmut get to you," he said gently. "You know he's all bark, no bite."

"He's scared of you. He doesn't talk to you the same way he talks to me. He doesn't talk to anyone the same way he talks to me."

Vaughn dropped to his knees until she would look at him. He took her hands and said, "He's harder on you because you're gorgeous. You intimidate him."

She rolled her eyes and laughed dryly. "Usually your insincere flattery makes me feel good, but can it for today, all right?" She sighed heavily and planted her chin in her hands. "I just didn't think it would be like this."

"What?"

"Making a movie. I thought it'd be...better. Fun."

Vaughn shook his head in confusion, then said, with his million-watt smile, "I'm not being insincere, Quinn. You are gorgeous, and seeing you after all this time only reminds me what an idiot I was to let you slip through my fingers."

Quinn instantly became uncomfortable at the sudden intensity flashing in his eyes. "Vaughn—"

His voice was gentle as he said, "Quinn, you have to know how I feel about you. You never returned my calls—"

She stood, uncharacteristically awkward, as she crashed into the counter. "We should get back to the reading. Helmut is probably ready—"

"Quinn, stop," Vaughn said gently, standing. She stopped moving and stared at him. "You and I were great together on screen, Quinn. You can't deny that. I think we'd be even better together off screen. What do you think?"

She cleared her throat and said, "I'm seeing someone else, Vaughn."

"The cowboy who was at the house yesterday," he said with a slight smile.

"He's not a cowboy. He's a mortician. Well, actually, he's a gardener or, maybe, a landscape architect...I'm not sure what he calls himself, but he's not a cowboy."

Vaughn appeared on the verge of arguing with her then shook his head dismissively and said, "I don't care what he does, or who he is. Helmut told me everything. You gave the cowboy—excuse me, the mortician slash landscape architect—a little taste of Quinn magic just to get the location, and it worked. You don't need him anymore."

"It's not like that with Wyatt," she said, shaking her head.

Vaughn smiled again and fingered her hair. "Of course it is, Quinn. I know that, everyone out there knows that, and you're beginning to realize it, too. Weren't you supposed to meet him last night?"

Quinn crossed her arms over her chest. "We were busy all night on set. I didn't want to wake him—"

"My advice is to pull the Band-Aid off quick. Don't let it linger."

"I care about Wyatt." She took a deep breath, then said something that she had never said in her life. "I think I love him."

"I'm sure you do," Vaughn said, sounding amused. "He's different than what you're used to. He probably still throws his coat on the sidewalk so you can cross puddles without getting your feet wet. But you're going to get bored. You know it. I know it. And the cowboy probably knows it, too.

"He's a cowboy, or mortician, or whatever. And you're about to become America's best actress. How long is he going to survive in a world like that? He almost attacked the camera crew because they told him not to come on the porch. What is he going to do to a paparazzo that sticks a camera in his face? You may as well end it now."

"Don't pretend to know about my relationship with Wyatt," she snapped. "You don't know anything about him, and you don't know anything about me."

"My God, Quinn, do you think he's ever seen—let alone dated—a woman like you before?" he asked in disbelief. "You're just a trophy to him."

Quinn rolled her eyes, ignoring the stab of uncertainty. "You don't know him."

"I don't need to know him to know that he's pinching himself every day wondering how in the world he has a woman like you giving him the time of day."

Quinn studied Vaughn's expression, the passion burning in his eyes. She had seen that expression on his face many times. On *Diamond Valley*, when he had been trying to act in a particularly emotional scene.

She crossed her arms over her chest and asked suspiciously, "Why do you care about my relationship with Wyatt?"

"I told you why—"

"I don't believe you," she said simply. "I'm not your type. I can read and buy alcohol without a fake ID. Tell me what's going on, Vaughn. Now."

He took a deep breath then admitted, "The phone hasn't exactly been ringing off the hook since I left the show."

"You've been in a couple of movies."

"Two movies. The first movie, I died in the first twenty minutes, and the second movie I was the third gang member from the right. My career is dying here, Quinn," he said desperately. "I lied about Helmut calling me. I called him. I begged, I pleaded, I...I blackmailed him."

"Now that sounds like the Vaughn I know and love," she muttered dryly, then demanded, "what does this have to do with me?"

"Helmut's movie could be a huge commercial

success, Quinn, but he wants to revel in the indie scene. About five people in America watch indie films, and none of those five are in the position to offer us multi-million-dollar film deals. But if you and I start dating, think of the press coverage we'll both get. The tabloids will love it, not to mention our old fans from *Diamond Valley*. Once we explain that we met on the set of *On Livermore Road*—due in theatres this fall—it'll create automatic interest in the movie. Studios have been doing these publicity stunts for years. Why not us? It'll be good for the movie, good for our careers. I don't see a downside to my plan."

"The downside is it will be a lie."

"As if you've never lied to the press before," he said, then pointedly stared at her breasts.

"And I'm in love with another man."

"You won't even remember his name once award season starts."

"Kiss my ass," she retorted.

"We don't have to take it that far, unless you want to," he said, with a flirtatious grin.

She shook her head in annoyance, then stalked out the bathroom because she was actually starting to contemplate his plan. Vaughn had a point. It was one small lie. It didn't mean that she couldn't still date Wyatt, who would be in Sibleyville anyway.

She ran into Graham, who smiled when he saw her. His smile faded when Vaughn walked out the same bathroom.

"Excuse me," Vaughn said to Graham, then nodded at Quinn before he walked down the hallway and out the house.

Quinn looked at Graham and the disappointed expression on his face made her feel momentarily guilty, even though absolutely nothing had happened.

"Graham—"

"I just stopped by to make certain you guys had everything you need," he said stiffly. "It seems like you do."

Without another word, Graham walked toward the front door and left the house. Quinn muttered a curse and started to go after him.

"Quinn, we need you out here," one of the production assistants said from the other side of the screen door.

Quinn groaned in frustration, then ran out the house toward the barn.

Wyatt inwardly groaned as Boyd Robbins walked into the greenhouse. Boyd didn't just walk into a room. He swept into a room like a hurricane and destroyed everything in its path. And this morning, he apparently had decided to pick on Wyatt.

Well, he could try, at least. Wyatt had been in a foul mood since he had gone to sleep alone last night and had woken up this morning even more alone. Quinn hadn't even called last night. In fact, he hadn't heard anything from her since he told her that she could use the house. He didn't even count his visit to her house last night since he hadn't been able to get her alone and she had essentially brushed him off.

Instead of doing some of the jobs around town that he had been scheduled to do that morning, Wyatt had gone straight to the greenhouse. He did not want to see the I-told-you-so looks.

"I came for my wife's roses," Boyd bellowed.

Wyatt set down the spade and walked across the

greenhouse to the box of potted red and yellow roses he had prepared for Alma Robbins. He set the box on the table near the door, ignoring Boyd the whole time, then went back to the potted hydrangeas.

Boyd didn't touch the flowers. Instead, he stared at Wyatt. "I heard that your girlfriend dropped you like a hot potato as soon as you gave her access to the house."

Wyatt told himself not to react, but then again it had been a hell of a morning. He glared at Boyd. "I don't know what you're talking about."

"Really?" Boyd said in disbelief. "I think it's pretty simple. Quinn Sibley wanted something from you, would do whatever she needed to in order to get it, she got it and now she's thrown you away like trash."

"As enlightening as this conversation is, as usual you have no idea what the hell you're talking about and, even more important, it's none of your business," Wyatt said calmly even as he clenched the spade handle in his hand.

Anger flashed in Boyd's blue eyes, and he took several steps closer to Wyatt. "That's where you're wrong, Wyatt," Boyd snarled. "Because I gave you more credit than you're worth, I based my decision to allow those people to film in town on your decision to let them use the mortuary. I thought your relationship with your mother would be worth more to you than a pair of tits—"

Wyatt instantly went toe-to-toe with Boyd and said through clenched teeth, "Shut your mouth, Boyd, or I'll shut it for you."

The two men stared at each other for a moment. Boyd looked away first and made a show of picking up the box of roses. It was the first time that Wyatt had ever seen Boyd back down from a confrontation, but Wyatt took no pleasure in the scene. In fact, he felt like a bigger ass.

He dragged a hand down his face tiredly. He had just threatened the mayor of the town. And not only that, but Wyatt had known Boyd most of his life. Boyd was an arrogant ass, but he was well-intentioned most times. Wyatt could just imagine what his mother would say when she found out—and Wyatt had no doubt that his mother would find out.

"Boyd—"

Boyd whirled around to face Wyatt, the anger flashing in his eyes. "It's clear what path you've chosen, Wyatt, and that's too bad. I always thought you were one of the good ones in town. I had always hoped that Graham Forbes hadn't rubbed off on you. But, it looks like I was wrong about you. I just hope the town doesn't suffer too much because of it."

Boyd walked out the greenhouse, using his foot to kick the door closed. Wyatt had to give it to the old man. He knew how to make a more dramatic exit than Quinn.

Chapter 17

"**W**ake up, Wyatt," a gentle voice sang into his ear.

Wyatt smiled in his dream as Quinn's soft hips filled his hands and her breasts pressed against his chest. He had gone to sleep alone and hard last night, but she was in his dream and the rest didn't matter for now.

He squeezed her hips, then molded her fabulous butt that he had not paid nearly enough attention to the one night they had been together.

Quinn moaned with pleasure, then placed a butter-fly soft kiss on his neck. "Wyatt, wake up. Please."

Wyatt's entire body hardened at the break in her voice because he realized that he wasn't dreaming. Quinn was in his bed, in his arms. He opened his eyes and stared straight into her beautiful hazel eyes. She smiled.

"I like how you look in the morning," she whispered, while caressing the short bristles of his night's growth of beard.

He moved her loose curls behind her ears and tugged on the soft, fleshy lobes. "I like how you look in the morning, the afternoon and the evening."

She sent him another sweet smile, then kissed him in response. Wyatt instantly gave her access to his mouth. With her on top, she was in control and her tongue swept through his mouth, sweetly dominating him. She ate his mouth, then began to gently nip at his lips. Wyatt opened his legs and her lower body instantly slipped into the space reserved just for her against his hardness. His pajama bottoms weren't even an impediment against feeling every inch of her.

He groaned in her mouth, then dragged one hand up her body to caress her breast through the thin fabric of the dress she wore. He arched his hips when he felt her nipple bead through the material like a soft pebble against his hand. He went into overdrive and flipped her over so that she was underneath him.

Quinn laughed against his mouth, then put both hands on his chest, stopping him from moving to her mouth again. "Wyatt, stop," she said, laughing.

For the first time, Wyatt noticed that she held papers in one hand. Papers that were now seriously wrinkled.

"What is that?" he asked, nodding to the papers.

She squirmed out from under his arms to get off the bed. She studied her reflection in the dresser mirror and began to rake her fingers through her hair as she said, "It's the contract that I need you to sign for us to use the house in the movie. Helmut wants to take a few establishing shots tomorrow."

Wyatt stared at the papers she had left on the bed, as something ugly and nasty twisted in his gut. She hadn't come to see him. It was about the movie. Of course. He shook his head, disappointed with himself and annoyed with her.

She turned to face him, obviously excited. "We're doing some test shoots tonight on Main Street. Apparently, word has gotten around town and half of the town plans to show up to watch. I think the town is actually excited about the movie being shot here."

"They are?" he asked tonelessly.

Quinn wiped at her mouth, then turned to him with a bright smile. "I knew they would be. Deep down inside, everyone is a camera hog." She sat back on the bed next to him and grabbed the papers. Of course, she already had a pen, too. "I just need you to sign this and then I have to head to Main Street. You would not believe how long it takes us to block one scene. It's going to be a long night, but I'm excited. This is moviemaking at its finest, right?"

Wyatt stared at her for a moment. She was so beautiful, she literally made his heart ache. And of course he had been stupid to think that she could be his. Dorrie was probably laughing with glee.

Wyatt took the pen from her and laid the paper on the bed to sign it. Quinn laughed and stilled his hands with hers. "You're not even going to read it? Get a lawyer to read it?"

Wyatt stared at her, then signed the paper. Without another word, he stood from the bed and walked toward the kitchen. He needed a cup of coffee to deal with this day. He had a feeling that it was going to be a long one.

He heard the slap of Quinn's stiletto heels on the hard-wood floor as she followed him.

"Thank you," she said.

He didn't respond and pulled a bag of coffee grounds from the refrigerator. He measured a few spoonfuls into the coffee machine. Quinn continued to linger in the kitchen door frame.

She cleared her throat then said, "Wyatt, filming this movie has been such a learning experience. Helmut has been hard on me, but I think it's because Helmut thinks I'm the best actress and he wants to push me. It's not exactly what I imagined, but…it'll change. As soon as the cameras start rolling, this is going to be so much fun."

Wyatt ignored the stabbing in his stomach and stared at the coffee dripping into the pot. His throat felt thick with emotion. He was hot. He was cold. He didn't know. But he wanted her to leave him alone. It was almost more painful that she was trying to let him down easy.

Quinn walked across the kitchen to stand next to him. She sounded suspiciously close to tears as she said, "Could you look at me?"

Wyatt forced himself to look at her and he nearly lost his breath. He instantly looked away again.

"What's wrong, Wyatt?" she whispered, touching his arm.

He jerked his arm from her touch and the hurt that flooded into her face made him almost relent and let her play out her scene. "Where were you last night?" he asked coldly.

"I told you how busy the schedule has been," she said softly.

"And where were you the night before?" he demanded.

"We didn't stop until four o'clock in the morning and Helmut wanted us back there at seven. I didn't want to wake you."

"You didn't want to wake me? That was thoughtful of you," he said with a dry laugh.

He waited for her to get angry with him, to scream and yell like the old Quinn would have done. Call him a jerk and storm out. But she didn't get angry. Instead, tears filled her eyes. And she looked more guilty than she did when he accused her of sabotaging his relationship with Dorrie. What a first-rate fool he had been. Everyone had been right.

He cursed and said in a low voice, "I hope it's all worth it. I hope you get that Oscar that you've already worked so hard for."

"What are you talking about?"

"Just stop it, Quinn," he said, trying to keep his voice calm, even though his blood raged. "I know what this was all about. I guess I knew it all along, but I didn't want to believe it because I was so in love with you. What a stupid jerk I've been."

"You think I slept with you to get the filming rights?"

"Your innocent act is really old."

She still looked confused as she said, "Wyatt—"

Whatever she was about to stay was cut off by the sound of someone walking into the apartment and calling her name. Wyatt's heart froze in his chest as Vaughn walked into the kitchen. He didn't miss Vaughn's quick glance around the small kitchen. Wyatt imagined that his kitchen was probably the size of Vaughn's closet.

Vaughn glanced at Wyatt's bare chest and pajama

bottoms and cleared his throat. "I didn't mean to interrupt," he said, attempting to sound sympathetic. "But, Quinn, we need to get going. You know that Helmut will flip if we're more than two minutes late."

Quinn glanced at Vaughn, then turned back to Wyatt. Wyatt's anger was roaring to break out of his chest. He wanted to launch himself at Vaughn and knock the arrogant expression off the man's face.

"Just go, Quinn," Wyatt snapped, since she was still staring at him with that wounded expression.

"Hey," Vaughn warned defensively. "You can't talk to her like that."

Wyatt smiled because he had been waiting for Vaughn to give him a reason to knock him out. "What did you say?" he growled.

"Wyatt, please," Quinn said, grabbing his arm.

"I can handle him, Quinn," Vaughn said, obviously offended. "I'm not scared of this Neanderthal."

"Yes, Quinn, he can handle me," Wyatt said, with a nasty smile in Vaughn's direction. "So let him handle me."

"Wyatt, this isn't like you," Quinn said, shaking her head in disappointment. "Why are you acting this way?"

"What way?" he snapped, turning to her. "Like a man who's been treated like a mark."

"You can't believe that," she whispered in disbelief.

"Quinn, you don't need this," Vaughn said, walking to stand by her side. "Let's go."

"Yeah, go with him," Wyatt muttered. "You know you want to anyway."

"You don't know what I want," Quinn retorted, suddenly becoming angry. "You've never known."

"I know that you want this movie and, as soon as you

got it, you couldn't drop me fast enough. I know that you made me look like a fool in front of this entire town. And I know that I will never forgive you for it."

Tears filled her eyes as she stared at him with a gaping mouth. Beatrice burst into the kitchen, looking panicked and worried. Wyatt stepped around Quinn and Vaughn to grab his mother. She was trembling.

"Mom, what's wrong?" he asked, concerned.

Beatrice calmed slightly when she saw Quinn and Vaughn. She looked back at Wyatt and said, urgently, "Mrs. Woods died last night."

Wyatt felt all the blood drain from his face and the air grow cold. He rubbed his suddenly tight throat. "How?" he croaked.

"Cancer. She had been sick for a while," Beatrice whispered, clutching his arms. "The family wants the burial to take place tomorrow before Christmas."

"Tomorrow?" he repeated, feeling the cold sweat break out on his forehead.

"Wyatt, are you okay?" Quinn whispered, closing the distance between them to stand at his side.

"He's fine," Beatrice snapped in response. "What are you doing here? Didn't you already get what you wanted from us?

"Mother, stop," Wyatt warned.

Beatrice ignored him and glared at Vaughn. She demanded, "And who are you?"

"I'm Vaughn Cotton," Vaughn said, while puffing his chest in indignation that she didn't know who he was.

Wyatt looked down at Quinn, who was watching him. He couldn't read her expression. She appeared concerned for him but then again, he had thought she was in love with him. Or maybe he had just hoped that she had been falling in love with him because he had finally accepted that he was in love with her.

"Just leave, Quinn," Wyatt said, hoarsely, barely able to support his own weight. If he fainted in front of Quinn, he would never be able to look her in the eye again. He cursed his weakness. And he cursed Vaughn for witnessing it all, even though he looked more confused than triumphant.

Quinn stared at Wyatt for a moment, her expression unreadable. Then she shook her head and muttered, "Fine."

She walked out the house, with Vaughn following on her heels. As his legs gave out, Wyatt fell onto the nearest chair. Beatrice began to rub his shoulders.

"It'll be fine, Wyatt," she said gently.

Wyatt tuned out his mother and tried to breathe. No, it wouldn't be fine. With Quinn out of his life, he had a feeling that nothing would be fine again.

"I just love Christmas. Don't you?" Kendra muttered dryly, through clattering teeth.

Quinn ignored Kendra and continued to read the lines she had to recite "with feeling" in ten minutes. She and her two sisters stood in the town square, in front of the giant professionally decorated Christmas tree that Helmut had brought in to replace the town's smallish and lopsided tree that the town had decorated with children's ornaments made in school.

Half of the town had showed up to watch the rehearsals. Some people had even brought lawn chairs and hot chocolate and popcorn. Their excited chatter annoyed Helmut, but it did lend a festive environment and made

Quinn almost forget about the things that Wyatt had said to her that morning. No man, actually, no person, had ever hurt her that deeply. Even now, her eyes filled with tears as she recalled the disgust that had shone in his eyes when he looked at her.

She should have been angry at him. And she was. She was furious that he didn't have faith in her and that he believed town gossip. Maybe Quinn had briefly thought that sleeping with him would be good for her and good for the movie, but, movie or not, she would have slept with Wyatt Granger. But even after all that, another part of her just wanted to see his familiar face and have him send her that smile that was meant just for her.

"How long is Helmut going to have you out here?" Charlie asked worriedly, while burrowing deeper into Graham's chest and arms. Graham had pulled his over-sized winter coat open and around Charlie. "It's freezing."

"He said about fifteen more minutes," Quinn responded.

"He said that two hours ago," Kendra shot back as she adjusted the knit cap on her head.

"I'm actually with Kendra on this one," Graham chimed in. "It's freezing cold and you're dead on your feet. You haven't gotten a decent night's sleep since Helmut got here. It's time to call it a night, Quinn."

Charlie studied Quinn closely and said, "You really do look tired, honey. I know this movie is important to you, but what good will you be when they start filming, if you're sick?"

"I'm fine," Quinn practically shouted. She lowered her voice when several townspeople glanced curiously at them. "I'm fine. If you all want to go home, feel free, but I can't leave."

"Pity," Kendra said with a fake show of sympathy, then turned to Charlie and Graham excitedly. "Let's go."

"We're not leaving Quinn," Charlie said firmly, shooting Kendra her patented look of death.

"At least, not until Wyatt gets here," Graham said irritably, then glanced around the town square. "Where is he anyway? It's getting late."

Quinn bit her bottom lip as tears threatened to spill out of her eyes. "He's not going to be here tonight," Quinn said, surprised by how unaffected she sounded. "There's been a death in town. Mrs. Woods."

Graham's eyes widened. "Mrs. Woods?"

"Her family wants her buried by tomorrow, before Christmas," Quinn said, worriedly gnawing at her bottom lip, not caring that she was ruining her makeup.

"Did you know Mrs. Woods well?" Charlie asked Graham, sympathetically.

"Not really," Graham said, shaking his head. "But Wyatt does not deal well with death."

"Isn't that kind of in a mortician's job description? Dealing with death?" Kendra asked, amused.

"Shut up," Quinn snapped angrily. Kendra flinched in surprise while Graham and Charlie exchanged glances. Quinn cleared her throat and said to Kendra, "Death is very serious. You shouldn't joke about it."

"How is Wyatt doing?" Graham asked Quinn, a worried expression on his face.

"He didn't look so well when I left."

"I bet."

"If you could check on him for me...." Her voice

trailed off when she noticed Graham's eyes zero in on her, as if he sensed that something was wrong.

"Why can't you check on him yourself?" Charlie asked.

"Once we finish filming for the night, we have more script revisions to go over. It'll be really late before I get out of here," she lied.

Graham and Charlie didn't appear convinced. Kendra openly snorted in disbelief.

"I highly doubt that Wyatt would care what time you show up at his house as long as you show up," Kendra muttered.

"He needs his sleep, especially with Mrs. Woods," she replied lamely.

"If anything, Wyatt needs you now more than ever," Graham said, shaking his head. "The last time there was a death in town, I sat in the basement with him while he prepared the body for viewing. All night."

Kendra shivered in disgust and asked, with wide eyes, "Do you expect Quinn to sit in a basement with a dead body all night?"

"If it's good enough for Wyatt, it's good enough for Quinn," Graham shot back, offended.

"Graham, is that even legal?" Charlie murmured, concerned. "I don't think Quinn should be inhaling all of those fumes—"

Quinn rolled her eyes in disbelief at her sisters' overprotective streak. "It doesn't matter. Wyatt doesn't want me there." She inwardly cursed when three sets of eyes stared at her surprised. She muttered, "Can we pretend that I didn't say that?"

"Did you and Wyatt have an argument?" Charlie asked, concerned.

"Of course not. Everything is going perfectly," Quinn asked, brightly. "I'm in the middle of filming my comeback movie. I'm going to win an Oscar. And Wyatt and I are friends. Good friends. Things couldn't be more perfect. The PA is waving for me. Wish me luck."

She ignored their concerned glances and walked across the town square to avoid her family.

Chapter 18

Wyatt wiped at the sweat on his forehead with the back of his hand, then focused on the covered body on the table in front of him. It was just a slab of meat, he told himself. A slab of meat.

He pulled the sheet down and folded it just under Mrs. Woods' wrinkled, still face. He couldn't help himself and stared at her face. She had given him candy at Halloween when he had been a kid. She used to pinch his cheek. She had been… He took several deep breaths and told himself to focus on the job. Embalm Mrs. Woods, then call Kiki Landsman to perform her makeup magic. He could do that. He had to do that.

He looked up at the knock on the door of the embalming room. He was surprised that his mother would venture anywhere near this room, knowing that a dead body was inside.

"Come in," he said.

Dorrie opened the door and walked into the room. She opened her mouth to speak, but her gaze became focused on the body on the table. Wyatt grimaced and tore off his gloves and protective gown. He threw it in a biohazard bin, then quickly ushered Dorrie out of the room and into the hallway. He closed the door.

"Thank you," she murmured, leaning against the wall. "I…I've never seen a dead person before. My grandmother at her funeral. But my father made them close the casket before I entered the room."

"I'm sorry you had to see that," he said softly. "Do you want some water?"

She shook her head then focused on him. "Your mother told me that… She told me about Mrs. Woods and how you…I came to keep you company."

"You did?" he said, surprised.

She smiled for the first time. "I don't blame you for being confused. The last time we saw each other, I didn't exactly give you the impression that I would be making house calls.

"I understand—"

"I was out of line," Dorrie interrupted him. "I never should have said those things to you. I also saw Quinn on Main Street, and I was pretty out of line with her, too. I was just jealous."

"You shouldn't have been. Quinn had nothing to do with it," he said quietly.

"I believe you, but it's just no man has ever looked at me the way you looked at her in my office. I guess I was hoping that one day you would look at me that way."

"I'm sorry, Dorrie."

"I know you are. I also know that you never thought you had a chance with her, and that's why you asked me out—"

"That's not true," he protested.

"I'm not angry about it," she said quickly, holding up a hand to stop his protest. "The thing is, Wyatt, for me it wasn't just about the fact that we both wanted the same things. I really like you. I still really like you. And I just want you to know that…whatever happens between you and Quinn, I'm still here for you. No matter what."

Wyatt suddenly felt nervous about the hope that lingered in Dorrie's eyes. He tried to make himself feel something. To feel anything. But, it was useless. He was in love with Quinn, and Wyatt didn't want to hurt Dorrie—or himself, for that matter—by pretending that he wasn't.

He hesitated, then said, "Dorrie, it wouldn't be fair to either one of us—"

She smiled and shook her head, stopping him from saying what they both didn't want to hear. "I should go…unless you want some company…in there."

Her expression was filled with hope and dread. Wyatt shook his head and said, "I can handle it on my own."

She tried to hide her relief, but it was apparent that she would rather go to the dentist than sit in that room with him. "If the offer is still open, I'd like to be friends. You can never have too many friends, right?"

He smiled. "I'd like that."

She hugged him with a nervous laugh. Wyatt grinned and patted her back. They jumped apart at the sound of a throat being cleared. Wyatt couldn't help but smile at the sight of Graham standing at the base of the stairs leading from the main floor.

"I didn't mean to interrupt," Graham said, holding up his hands.

Dorrie's face colored with embarrassment, as she shook her head. "No, I was just leaving." She glanced at Wyatt once more and sent him a small smile. "I'll see you around."

Wyatt nodded, and she walked toward the stairs. Wyatt nodded at Graham, then walked back into the room. The smell of heavy chemicals made him wince. He would never get used to that smell. Graham followed him into the room and openly grimaced at the sight of the covered body on the table.

"Is that Mrs. Woods?" Graham asked, sitting on a table on the other side of the room.

"Yes." Wyatt pulled on another robe and gloves, then went back to Mrs. Woods' body. He hesitated before pulling down the sheet and looked at Graham. "You know that you don't have to be here, right? In fact, you shouldn't be here since you're not licensed."

"I know," Graham said with a sigh, then settled back in the chair and crossed an ankle over the other knee.

Wyatt tried not to smile, but he failed miserably. He turned back to Mrs. Woods' body. She was a slab of meat, but she was also someone's mother and a grandmother and someone's friend. And they deserved to see her as they remembered her in life. He once more rolled down the sheet to under her chin.

"Aren't you curious as to how I knew that you'd be down here?" Graham asked.

"Since this is Sibleyville, I figured you just heard it through the grapevine."

"Well, it is headline news that the Woods are

planning a Christmas Eve burial and service, but I got my news from a more reliable source."

Wyatt paused then said, flatly, "Quinn."

"Quinn," Graham said, nodding. "And not that I don't want to spend this cozy time with you, but why isn't Quinn here?"

"I don't want to talk about Quinn."

"Uh-oh."

"I *really* don't want to talk about Quinn."

"What did you do?"

"What makes you think I did anything?" he asked defensively.

"Because Quinn looked close to tears every time she opened her mouth and you're about as cuddly as a bear coming out of hibernation."

Wyatt sighed tiredly and muttered, "It's not going to work."

"Why?"

He laughed in disbelief. "Do I really need to list the reasons? You, more than anyone, should know why it's better this way."

"I know that you have loved Quinn since the first moment you saw her—"

"Oh, please—"

"Don't bother to deny it, Wyatt. You haven't stopped thinking about her since you first met her two years ago. You don't think I noticed how you always perked up whenever her name was mentioned, how you pretended not to notice her when she was in the same room, how you always stared at her pictures in our house a little too long whenever you visited. I've known you too long to be fooled. You've wanted her for a long time, and now you have her. I don't understand why she's crying on Main Street and you're here alone."

"She wanted me for the house," Wyatt blurted out. When Graham stared at him in speechless surprise, Wyatt shook his head. "That's right. Your innocent, sweet sister-in-law slept with me so I would let her film her movie in the funeral home. And now that I've given her authorization to do that, I haven't heard from her since."

"That is a load of bullshit," Graham blurted out.

"No, it's not, Graham. As soon as I told her the mortuary was hers, I didn't hear from her. Oh, wait, I didn't hear from her until she needed me to sign some papers to make it legal. I was played. As a former player yourself, I'm surprised you're not applauding her moves. They were flawless."

Graham jumped to his feet, his chest heaving with outrage. "You're my best friend, Wyatt, but if you don't stop this shit right now, I will knock you out."

"What are you getting so upset about?"

"Why am I getting so upset?" Graham repeated, shaking his head in disbelief. "I have spent the last year living with Quinn, and I have seen the way men treat her. She's smart and funny and next to my wife, one of the most loyal women I know, and men don't recognize that. They view her as an object. You have no idea the things men say to her when she's walking down the street. It actually embarrasses me, and this is coming from a guy who has done his fair share of things to keep men's reputation as dogs alive and well. But I never thought that I would count you in that list."

"I'm the asshole now? I'm the one who was used,

Graham," Wyatt reminded him angrily. "I'm the injured party."

Graham abruptly sagged back into the chair, while shaking his head. "You don't deserve her."

"You'll find no argument there."

"Is that what this is all about?" Graham asked, narrowing his eyes suspiciously. "You're trying to push Quinn away because you don't think that you deserve her?"

Wyatt rolled his eyes, annoyed. "What are you talking about?"

"You're scared," Graham accused. "You don't believe that Quinn used you. Admit it. You're just scared that maybe she actually loves you."

"That makes sense," he muttered, dryly, refusing for an instant to believe Graham was right.

"Because if she does love you, then that means you'll have to stop pining for her and acting like the martyr you want everyone to believe you are and actually live your life. You can't hide behind your father's memory, or this mortuary, or family tradition. You'd actually have to put yourself out there and make some really hard choices and decisions about your life. You're not lonely because you live in Sibleyville, Wyatt. You're lonely because you're scared."

Wyatt threw down his tools on a nearby tray with a loud clatter and stalked across the room to stand toe-to-toe with Graham. "I'm not scared of anything, Graham. I'm a mortician. Once you've seen enough dead bodies, you realize that there's nothing left to be scared of."

"Maybe that's the problem," Graham said quietly. "You've seen too much death, and it scares the hell out of you. And, so, you don't even try. All of your talk about having a family and babies was just talk. If you wanted all of that, you would have married Dorrie as soon as she stepped foot in town. But you were scared of that, too. Whether it's Dorrie, or Quinn, or some other woman, you're never going to leave that little apartment over the garage or this mortuary because it's safe."

Wyatt averted his gaze, unable to handle the sympathy and pity in Graham's eyes. He clenched his jaw, then said tonelessly, "I don't need you here after all. I'll see you tomorrow."

Graham sighed, then walked to the door. He looked at Wyatt, but Wyatt turned his back on Graham and refocused on Mrs. Woods. He didn't release his breath until he heard Graham walk out the room and close the door.

Quinn opened her eyes and stared at the morning sunlight steaming through the windows of her bedroom. She could already hear Christmas music coming from the first floor. Charlie's off-key voice also drifted through Quinn's closed bedroom door. She wouldn't be surprised if Charlie had been awake since five o'clock that morning, baking Christmas cookies and in a general Christmas frenzy.

Quinn turned over in her bed and stared out the window. The green trees and grass had a white covering of frost, almost as if even nature understood how she felt. Cold. As if she would never be warm again. She laid a hand across her eyes as tears once more filled her eyes.

She had never really had her heart broken by a man. Now she had. And it sucked.

"Kill me now" came Kendra's annoyed voice as she walked into Quinn's room without knocking.

Quinn quickly wiped at her eyes and sat up in the bed. "Do you know what the plan is for today?"

Kendra fell on the bed with a dramatic sigh. "If it involves caroling, I'm catching the first thing smoking back to New York."

Quinn forced a smile and asked, "Dinner at Graham's parents' house?"

"I think so…." Kendra's annoyed expression morphed into concern as she stared at Quinn for the first time since entering the room.

Quinn hoped to avoid an inquisition about her crying and motioned to Kendra's leggings and form-fitting athletic top and asked, through a sniffle, "Have you already worked out this morning?"

Kendra sat on the bed and asked, concerned, "Have you been crying?"

"Of course not," Quinn lied, then shrugged at Kendra's laser stare. "Maybe a little. I just hate Christmas."

"Charlie would make anyone hate Christmas, but that's not the reason you're crying."

"I'm not crying," she said, blinking away more tears.

Kendra crossed her arms over her chest and said flatly, "This is about Wyatt, isn't it?"

"I have never cried over a man in my life, and I definitely would not cry over a mortician," she said, straightening her shoulders. When Kendra only stared at her, obviously unconvinced, Quinn tried again. "I'm just stressed. I have a lot of things going on. Helmut is a nightmare. We're getting rewrites on the script every day, and I'm just trying to keep up with everything."

Kendra waved her hand, effectively dismissing everything Quinn said, and demanded, "What happened?"

"Kendra—"

"Quinn, whether we like it or not, God made us sisters. And since Charlie, the one you usually would talk to about this, is downstairs possessed by the Ghost of Christmas Cookies, you're left with me." Kendra's voice gentled as she squeezed Quinn's hand. "Talk to me. What happened with you and Wyatt?"

"Nothing happened," Quinn muttered, shaking her head. "He broke up with me…I think. I'm not even sure we were dating. We slept together and the next thing I know he's kicking me out of his house because he thinks I used him to get the location for the movie."

"You kind of did, though, didn't you?"

"No," Quinn snapped, then raked hands through her tangled hair as she admitted, "maybe I did in the beginning, but… He makes me feel safe, Kendra. I feel like I can say anything to him, and tell him anything, and he'll accept it. Accept me. And do you know how hard it is to find a man like that? Who you can talk to about anything and he'll treat it like it's a serious subject? No man has ever treated me that way."

Kendra looked uncomfortable as she said, "Maybe I should get Charlie. She's much better at this pouring-out-the-heart thing—"

"I'm in love with him, Kendra," Quinn said helplessly. "I'm in love with a man who doesn't love me and that has never happened to me in my life. Usually, men fall in love with me and want me, and I use them for whatever I can, but Wyatt is different. Or, at least, I thought he was.

"But he's not. He's like everyone else. And I'm starting to think that it's not everyone else. It's me.

Maybe I am a horrible actress, and maybe that's why no one takes my calls. And maybe I am just a run-of-the-mill black woman, and maybe that's why no man wants me. And maybe…maybe Dorrie Diamond would make a better wife and mother than I would—"

"Quit your whining. Please. My ears hurt," Kendra snapped, annoyed.

Quinn glared at Kendra through her tears. "You're right. You're not good at this pouring-out-the-heart thing."

Kendra sighed impatiently and said, "I just meant that you don't believe that. You're a damn good actress and you know that. And you're gorgeous, Quinn. Hell, you make old blind men whistle when you walk by. And, if Wyatt Granger thinks that Dorrie is better than you, then he's an idiot."

Quinn smiled as she wiped at her nose with the sleeve of her pajamas. "You just complimented me," she noted.

Kendra's glower turned severe. "I did not compliment you. I just stated facts. For instance, your thighs are bigger than an elephant's. Do you consider that a compliment, too? No, it's just a fact." Quinn frowned, and Kendra waved her hands dismissively. "The point is, Quinn, you're obviously feeling sorry for yourself and I'm not going to allow it. This has been going on for far too long. You are Quinn Sibley. The woman who brought Sephora Barstow to life. People love you, and you can do whatever you want. If you want to win an Academy Award, you will. And if you want Wyatt Granger, you will have him."

"He doesn't want me there," Quinn whispered, then hung her head in shame. "He kicked me out of his apartment last night. He never wants to see me again."

"When you've been looking for work over the last year, you've been kicked out of much better places by much more powerful men, but that didn't stop you."

"It's different."

"No, it's not." Kendra sighed again then said, softly. "You love him, Quinn, and no matter what he says, he loves you, too. It's just like in *Diamond Valley* when—"

"This is my life, we're talking about, Kendra, not some soap," Quinn snapped irritably.

She noted a strange look that crossed Kendra's expression before she nodded and said, "You're right, Quinn. And in this life, you usually get one chance. If you've found someone who makes you feel the way Wyatt makes you feel, then use all your God-given and silicone-enhanced assets and get him. Or, at least, make him think twice before letting you go."

"I'm not going to beg. I didn't do anything wrong. Maybe, just maybe, I had a few thoughts about sleeping with him for the house, but in the end it was about him. I could have cared less about the movie. He should have had more faith in me."

"You're totally right, but…this man loves your big-ass ears, Quinn. When you going to find that again?"

Quinn sighed because Kendra had a point. It looked as if Quinn had some begging to do.

Chapter 19

Wyatt kept a solemn expression on his face as the family of Lenora Woods filed into the viewing room. He held his breath as her daughter and son slowly approached the open casket. The two stopped at the edge, then clung to each other. Myrtle abruptly sobbed and turned into her brother's arms. Wyatt averted his gaze to the highly polished wood floor. There was something so private about grief.

He forced himself to turn back to the scene. He could just make out one of Mrs. Woods' silver curls. He loosened his tie and swiped at the sweat on his brow, then forced himself to remain calm. Mourners were looking to him for direction, for answers. His father had been great at this, but Wyatt had to get out of here.

Just when he thought that he would have to leave

the room to breathe, he felt a soft hand slip into his and squeeze.

Wyatt glanced over and choked when he saw Quinn standing next to him. He gulped in disbelief. He hadn't known she owned such a somber dress. She wore a black dress that stopped at a respectable length at her knees, her usually wild riot of curls was tamed into an understated bun at the top of her head, and there was not a speck of makeup on her face.

She looked like the picture of a mortician's wife, or at least a mortician's girlfriend. And then he saw her black stiletto heels. He fought his grin.

Quinn sent him a soft smile, then turned toward the front of the room. Wyatt followed her gaze, suddenly feeling as if he could stand the sadness and the grief. With her by his side, it all seemed…almost bearable.

Wyatt followed the program as much as he could, but he was more focused on Quinn. She never took her attention away from the speakers, and she never took her hand from his. She was like a still, composed statue. Wyatt couldn't even remember his mother standing with his father like this.

As soon as the last speaker sat down, Wyatt dropped Quinn's hands and walked to the front of the room.

He kept his voice soft as he said, "We have prepared refreshments in the drawing room. When you're ready, please feel free to head in that direction. Thank you."

The few people who did look at him looked as if they were underwater, drowning. He cleared his throat, then walked back to Quinn, who, if it was possible, was giving him support without one word. He took her hand and led her to an empty viewing room and closed the door.

Before he could open his mouth, she said abruptly, "I'm sure you want to know what I'm doing here, and I'm kind of wondering the same thing, except I think…I think we decided in the middle of all of this that we were friends, and as your friend I wanted to be here. For you."

The two stared at each other for a moment, as Wyatt tried to think of how to respond. He should have been cool, calm and collected. Uncaring. Except that wasn't how he felt.

He said softly, "I'm glad you're here, Quinn. I could really use a friend right now."

She smiled and moved toward him, as if to hug him. Then she hesitated, no doubt replaying his little performance from yesterday. Wyatt silently cursed because even though he knew he shouldn't, he wanted to kiss her. He wanted to touch her. He just wanted her. He took one step closer to her, and then the door opened. The two jumped apart like teenagers caught in a dark basement.

Beatrice walked into the room, the disapproval apparent in her eyes and her pursed lips. She glanced at Quinn and stiffly nodded, then turned to Wyatt.

"Ron is asking for you," Beatrice said.

Wyatt nodded, then glanced at Quinn. She sent him a small smile, but Wyatt saw the hesitation in her eyes. She did not want to be alone with Beatrice and, frankly, Wyatt didn't blame her.

"Hurry up, Wyatt. We don't keep our customers waiting," Beatrice said.

Wyatt squeezed Quinn's hand, then walked out the room. He stared at the ceiling for a moment, praying that his mother wouldn't run Quinn off, then hurried down the hall.

* * *

Quinn gulped over the sudden lump in her throat as she stood alone in the room with Beatrice. A man's mother. The natural enemy of Quinn Sibley. Quinn forced a smile at Beatrice, who only stared at her in response. Beatrice's gaze dropped to Quinn's hands, and Quinn realized that she was nervously wringing her hands. Quinn instantly clenched her hands into fists and dropped them to her sides.

Quinn did not imagine the corner of Beatrice's mouth slightly lifted in a smile, as if reveling in Quinn's show of nerves. Beatrice gave Quinn the same look of triumph that Sephora's archenemy, Phoebe Childress, had given her numerous times over the years, then turned to the door.

"Beatrice, wait," Quinn said, abruptly. Beatrice turned to her, her expression cold and forbidding.

Quinn gulped again. Now that she had Beatrice's attention, she didn't know what she was supposed to say. She wasn't Wyatt's girlfriend. She was barely his friend. Wyatt had practically thrown her out of his house yesterday.

"Yes?" Beatrice said, and that one word nearly froze the room over.

Quinn cleared her throat, then said, "I know that you don't exactly like me. I get it. But I like your son. I think I actually love him. I don't know if he loves me. In fact, I doubt that he does. But that doesn't change how I feel. So, I hope that you know that I want nothing but the best for him, and you have nothing to fear from me because I would never hurt Wyatt."

"That's a touching speech," Beatrice said, sarcasm dripping from her voice. "I've heard it before somewhere... Ah, yes. Didn't you give that speech on

Diamond Valley two years ago when Sephora first met the mother of the riverboat captain?"

Quinn's face burned with humiliation. "You didn't tell me that you watched the show," she stuttered.

"Once or twice," Beatrice snapped.

"Maybe the words are the same, but the sentiment is real," Quinn said, hastily. "I really care for Wyatt."

"You have a funny way of showing it. For instance, why did you bring another man to my son's home in the morning? Did you just want to rub his face in your affairs?"

"I wasn't rubbing his face in anything," Quinn retorted angrily. "Vaughn is a friend."

"Oh, really? Is that why he told everyone who would listen in the diner this morning that you and he were thinking of moving in together when you returned to Los Angeles?"

"What?"

"I know your typo. The Hollywood type," Beatrice said heatedly. "You collect men like trophies."

"I think you have to be able to get a job in Hollywood to be the Hollywood type, so, trust me, I am not the Hollywood type. Maybe the Burbank type, or the—"

Beatrice's eyes narrowed and she demanded, "Are you making fun of me?"

"No," Quinn said uncertainly, then more firmly, "No."

"You think you're better than everyone else in this town—"

"Stop it," Quinn shouted. She flinched surprised at the volume of her own voice. Beatrice's eyes widened in shock. Quinn cleared her throat and said quietly, "I don't want to argue with you, Beatrice. But I want you to know that I'm not the enemy. I love Wyatt, and I want him to be happy. And whether that's with me or not is for him to decide, not you.

"I can't help if you like me or not, but I just ask that you give me a chance. Because in the end, we both want the same thing—for Wyatt to be happy."

Beatrice stared at her for a moment, then averted her gaze. Quinn was surprised. She had actually won a staring contest with her.

Beatrice finally looked back at Quinn, then said stiffly, "I can accept that."

Quinn sagged against the door, then straightened when Beatrice rolled her eyes in disbelief.

Beatrice asked, "Have you said everything you've wanted to say?"

"Yes."

"Then can I leave?"

"Of course," Quinn said, confused, then realized that she was bodily blocking the door. She quickly jumped out the way.

Beatrice opened the door, then turned to Quinn and said, with a slight smile, "I recognized that last speech, too, Quinn. For the record, you delivered it much better than you did on *Diamond Valley.*"

Beatrice walked out the room. Quinn shook her head in disbelief, then softly laughed.

"Long day?" Quinn murmured as she and Wyatt walked into his apartment.

Wyatt didn't bother to turn on the lights in his apartment, but turned to face Quinn. She looked even more beautiful in the fading sunlight that streamed through the windows. He wanted to touch her. Instead of pushing his luck, he closed the door, then leaned against it to stare at her.

"You were there for every moment," he said, the awe apparent in his voice. "I think I even saw Mom smile at you once."

Quinn smiled, but only said, "Let's just say that your mother and I have reached an understanding."

The two continued to stare at each other. There was something that happened when he made eye contact with her. There were sparks, a jolt of something that hit him every time he met her beautiful eyes.

He looked away for a moment, just to be able to come up with a coherent sentence. "I've ruined your entire Christmas Eve."

"It's not over yet," she whispered, something unreadable flashing across her face.

For some reason, his voice lowered, too. "If you hurry, you can make it in time for the dinner at the Forbes'."

She stared at him for a moment, then took two steps closer to him. "I'm right where I want to be."

He shook his head, confused, about the certainty in her eyes. She loved him. It was obvious. Once more, he felt as if he were the last one in this town to know anything.

He suddenly felt like he was standing on the edge of a cliff. Maybe Graham was right. Wyatt was scared. All of the emotions racing through his body, the emotions visible on Quinn's face. How was he supposed to handle that? They were too different, too combustible together. He had never experienced anything like it, and he couldn't fathom how he would live with this every day, the expectations in her eyes. The love. No wonder he was alone. He couldn't disappoint anyone when he was alone.

"Quinn—"

She interrupted him, as if sensing that he was about to end things. "Wyatt, you were right. A part of me did think that sleeping with you would make the issue of using the house disappear, but that's not why I slept with you. I slept with you because you make me feel like no other man has ever made me feel. Cherished."

Tears surprisingly clogged his throat as he said, "I'm sorry I said those horrible things to you."

"You should be," she said with a slight smile, then wrapped her arms around his neck. "But, I forgive you."

"You shouldn't. You could have any man you want, Quinn."

"I do have any man I want."

Wyatt couldn't believe her. His mind warred with his heart. She would come to her senses soon enough and then where would Wyatt be? Not only alone, but alone and completely ruined. That scared him more than any funeral ever had.

He decided tonight would be it. He would spend one night saying goodbye, then he would cut himself off cold turkey. Quinn would be hurt, at first. But it was for the best. For her, because she had her whole career ahead of her. And for him, because he wouldn't have to face the inevitable rejection and pain.

"I didn't even buy you a Christmas present," he murmured.

"I never thought I'd say this, but the best things in life are free. And you're one of the best things to ever happen to me."

Before he whispered how much he loved her, Wyatt kissed her.

Quinn's eyes slid closed of their own accord as Wyatt's mouth covered hers. She immediately noticed something different in his kiss tonight. He was practically desperate. His hands clung to her shoulders. His hips ground against hers. His tongue owned her mouth, subduing her. Saying goodbye.

"Wyatt?" she whispered, staring at him uncertainly.

"Shh, baby. I want to remember tonight. Every detail," he said in that passion-roughened voice that always drove her crazy.

His hands found the zipper on the back of her dress, and the soft whir of the zipper being released filled the air. His gaze never left hers as he slowly slid the dress down her body. His expression alone could have brought her to completion. He released the band in her hair and ran his hands through the strands, loosening them. She sighed as his hands massaged her head. His touch was magical, soothing. She never wanted any other woman to know his touch.

She shuddered as he finally looked at her breasts covered with lace and the center of her panties that had already grown damp.

"Lie down," he said, taking her hand and leading her to the sofa.

She complied and laid on the sofa for him. He stood over her, staring at her from head to toe, as if memorizing every detail. She saw her own perfection in his gaze. She would never think of herself as ugly and fat, even if she gained one hundred pounds. In Wyatt's eyes, she was perfect however she was.

Like silk, he finally moved on top of her, spreading her thighs to position himself directly against her center.

She shuddered again as the coarse material of his slacks rubbed against her bare thighs. She was completely nude, while he remained clothed in his suit and tie.

She reached for him, but he evaded her hands and slid down her body, planting kisses against bare skin. She bit her bottom lip as his tongue dipped into her belly button. Something akin to a nuclear bomb started at that spot and spread to her feet and toes.

"Wyatt," she whispered.

"You're so beautiful, Quinn. I will never forget you as long as I live."

For a brief moment, she was drawn out of the cocoon he had created. She wanted to ask him what he meant, but then he kissed her. Licked her. Suckled her until she was writhing uncontrollably and tears slid from the corners of her eyes. He still did not show her mercy. Instead, he clamped down on her thighs and spread them even farther apart for better access.

"Please," she begged, but his questing, seeking tongue never paused. He was trying to kill her.

Just when Quinn was on the verge of hurtling over the edge of sanity, Wyatt stopped. His eyes were dazed as he ripped off his suit and shoes. He came back to her, and she clung to his shoulders

No sound came out of her open mouth when he slowly and torturously pushed inside her. He was too big. She was so tight. He pulled out, then slowly moved in again. His face was the picture of unfettered pleasure.

Quinn held on for dear life, loving the feel of him. Needing him. She wrapped her legs around him, chaining him to her in case he ever thought of escaping.

He continued to stroke as he drove his tongue into

her mouth. She responded with her entire soul, unable to breathe on her own, without his kisses giving her much-needed oxygen. She tore her mouth from his and squeezed her eyes closed, unable to handle the feelings anymore. It was all too much.

She screamed his name and went over the edge. Wyatt soon followed, then fell on top of her, breathing hard. He was so heavy. Too big. But she wrapped her arms around him anyway, needing to feel every inch of him.

"Let's move to the bed," Wyatt murmured against her ear. "I'm crushing you, and this sofa is not exactly comfortable."

"I don't want to move," she whispered. "I want to stay right here until we hear Santa Claus go by."

She felt more than heard his laughter. "There is no Santa Claus, Quinn."

"Just for tonight, I'm going to believe in miracles."

He rolled off her, ignoring her protests. But he pulled her into his arms, wrapping a blanket lying on a nearby chair around them. As she settled against his chest, she heard him whisper, "For tonight, I do, too, baby. I do, too."

Chapter 20

Quinn woke up to complete silence and sunlight streaming through Wyatt's bedroom windows. At some point, they had moved to his bedroom and had continued to make love to each other. Eventually, Wyatt had foraged food from the refrigerator and they had fed each other, then made love again. Quinn had never particularly cared one way or the other about Christmas Eve, but now it was her favorite holiday. Then again, any holiday with Wyatt was going to be her favorite holiday.

For the first time, Quinn allowed herself to think of a future with him. She could imagine him with silver hair and those same twinkling brown eyes surrounded by a few more smile lines. She wasn't quite ready to think of herself in the same light, but she would be right by his side. Children would come at some point, and who knew where they'd live, but all of that could be worked out.

She smiled at her reflection in the mirror and combed down her tangled hair. She had looked better, but she still climbed out the bed and grabbed the man's robe on the closet door to find Wyatt. No makeup or hair brush in sight. It was funny when she thought about it. The adoration of millions meant nothing, but one man loved her and she was ready to eat everything in sight and proclaim her weight to any magazine that would listen.

She found him in the kitchen, sitting at the table, sipping a cup of coffee and staring out the window. He looked at her when she walked into the kitchen, but he didn't smile like he usually did. Instead, he looked sad. Scared, almost. Quinn decided to ignore his strange behavior and crossed the kitchen to plant a kiss on his lips. A kiss that he didn't return.

"Merry Christmas," she said, smiling.

He gave a forced smile, then stood and walked across the kitchen. Away from her. "Do you want some coffee? Something to eat?"

"Coffee would be nice." She sat in the chair he had vacated and stretched her arms over her head. "I bet my sisters are gossiping about us right now. I probably should have called them last night. I was supposed to meet them at Graham's parents' house for dinner. We'll make it up to them today at Christmas dinner. You are planning to come over for Christmas dinner, right? You and Beatrice? Although to be honest, I wouldn't mind spending Christmas alone with you here. Although, Charlie would kill us, so we'd probably have to make a brief appearance at dinner. Don't you think?"

Wyatt set a cup of steaming coffee in front of her

on the table. He sat across from her and stared at her for a moment.

Quinn took a sip of coffee, then set the cup down and met his gaze. She stopped smiling and said, "You're scaring me, Wyatt. What's wrong?"

He averted his gaze, then seemed to force himself to look at her. "Quinn…last night…I…I can't do this."

She blinked in confusion. "You can't do what? Go to Christmas dinner? I don't want to go, either—"

"No, Quinn," he said quietly. "You and me. It's not going to work."

She froze. Every single muscle in her body froze for one second. Then she blinked and whispered hoarsely, "What are you talking about?"

"You want to be a movie star, and we both know that's not going to happen here."

"We'll work something out, Wyatt. Charlie and Graham have."

"We're not Charlie and Graham," he said, shaking his head. "My life is here at the funeral home—"

"You hate it," she protested, before she could stop herself. "Why do you fight so hard to stay here when we both know you hate it?"

"I don't hate it."

"Yes, you do, Wyatt. I saw your face yesterday. You hate seeing people's tears and their pain. That's not who you are."

"Yes, it is, Quinn, and you can't change it," he insisted. "I'm a small-town mortician, and we both know that I would only get in the way. You're going to be a huge star. You're going to have so many opportunities. I would just be in the way."

She stared at him for a moment, unable to speak. She had woken up this morning with so much hope for her future, for them. And in an instant it had disappeared. And there was nothing she could do to change it.

"Why are you doing this?" she whispered in disbelief.

"I'm just being a realist. You love me now, here, in Sibleyville, with no distractions. But, the moment we set foot in Hollywood, everything will change. I just want to end it before we hurt each other. At least, now, we can still be friends."

"You still think I'm a vapid Hollywood actress," she accused, no longer sad but quivering with anger.

"That's not true."

"First, you don't think I'm good enough to marry. And now you're telling me that you don't trust me to love you once I have some other options. You know what? Forget everything I said. You're right. We are different. I'm willing to risk everything, compromise everything, to be with you. And you can't even stomach the thought of spending Christmas with me," she said through clenched teeth.

She jumped to her feet and hurried toward the living room, where her dress and underwear still lay on the floor. Her heart broke a little as the scattered clothing reminded her of last night, of the way she had felt last night. She had known Wyatt was saying goodbye then, but she had ignored her own intuition.

"Quinn," he said softly, coming behind her.

She whirled around to face him. "Don't touch me. Don't you ever touch me again. What was last night about? One last screw for old time's sake?"

His eyes were bright with unshed tears. "You know that's not true."

She told herself not to beg. Quinn Sibley didn't beg, but then she said, "I am standing here with my heart open to you. Don't throw this in my face."

"It's better this happens now, Quinn, before we get too close."

"I'm already close, you bastard," she screamed. She turned her back to him to yank on her clothes. She threw the robe on the sofa, then slipped on her shoes.

Wyatt still watched her, with a ravaged expression. She almost thought that he was in as much pain as she was, but it wasn't possible because her heart was falling apart. Breaking into one hundred pieces.

"Quinn, please try to understand. I'm doing this for you. You deserve someone like you. Someone like Vaughn. He can fit in your world. I would just…I don't know anything but Sibleyville and dead people. I would embarrass you. If you ever looked at me with shame in your eyes, I…I just think it's better to end this now."

"I tried so hard to be different than what everyone thought, what I even thought," she said, attempting to speak through her tears. "And I just can't do it anymore. I'm tired of trying. I've never been more tired in my life. I love you, Wyatt."

He inhaled as if he had been punched in the gut. "No, you don't. You think you do—"

"Don't tell me what I believe," she warned through clenched teeth. "I love you, Wyatt. And if you're too scared to admit that you love me back, then you're not the man I thought you were." He watched her for a moment, then averted his gaze, as if he could not look at her anymore.

Quinn laughed, even though there was nothing funny.

She swiped at her tears, then whispered, "I hope you get that white picket fence and the babies. There has to be some woman out there safe enough for you love."

He still wouldn't look at her. She thought about jumping up and down or screaming to force him to say something. But she couldn't do anything but walk out the apartment and down the stairs toward her car. It was going to be a long drive home.

"Merry Christmas," Charlie and Graham sang in unison as Quinn walked into the house.

Quinn accepted her sister's hug, with a forced smile, then hugged Graham. Quinn gave herself much more credit for her acting skills because neither Charlie nor Graham noticed that she had been crying.

"Where's Wyatt? We thought he'd come over with you," Graham said.

"He'll be by later," Quinn said with a bright smile.

The sound of glass crashing caused Quinn to turn to the living room. Kendra was precariously perched on the top of the living room coffee table, swinging her arms around while singing to "Jingle Bell Rock." She held a tall glass of eggnog in one hand and was sending eggnog flying across the living room the more she gyrated to the music.

"Ignore her," Graham said to Quinn. "She's been swilling eggnog for the last two hours and I think I saw her eat a cookie. I don't think her body knows how to handle the sugar."

"Y'know, Graham, it really annoys me when you talk about me like I'm not here," Kendra slurred in reply.

"How about some nice, strong, black coffee?" Quinn said to Kendra.

"I could use something nice, strong and black. And it sure as hell ain't coffee," Kendra shot back. Graham coughed over his laughter, while Charlie frowned in concern.

Kendra began to dance again. Charlie and Quinn ducked a missile of eggnog headed towards them. "Graham, put on the Motown Christmas album. I want to hear some Temptations and Jackson Five. Did I ever tell you guys that I can moonwalk? Watch!"

Kendra jumped off the coffee table and collapsed onto the floor. Kendra laughed uproariously, then drained the rest of her glass that had remained mostly full.

"You two, get the coffee, and I'll make certain she's not bleeding," Graham muttered.

Quinn and Charlie walked into the kitchen. The smell of dessert and dinner mingled in the small kitchen. For some reason, those smells made Quinn want to cry even more. She would never survive Christmas dinner, especially sitting across from Wyatt, since he and his mother always spent Christmas with the Forbes.

Quinn shook her head and grabbed a mug from the drying rack on the counter to pour a cup of coffee for Kendra.

"At this rate, Kendra will be passed out by lunchtime," Quinn said, grateful that her voice didn't crack from the emotion she was clamping down.

"I think that's her plan. I'm really worried about her," Charlie said quietly.

Quinn's laughter faded. "Kendra is just blowing off steam. She lives like a monk three hundred and sixty-four days of the year. So, she drinks alcohol and eats a little sugar—"

"I'm not talking about today, although it is concerning that she can't spend a sober Christmas with her family. I'm just worried about her, period. She's out there in New York, by herself, without any support. She never mentions any friends or boyfriends, and whenever I try to ask her about her personal life, she changes the subject or ignores me."

"You worry too much. Kendra is fine."

"She's not fine, Quinn. She got blackballed by the entire financial industry last year, and she still hasn't been able to find a job. My God, it's Christmas morning and she's stumbling drink. And have you noticed how late she's been sleeping? The old Kendra never slept past five o'clock in the morning. I've been having to drag out her out of bed at eleven."

Quinn studied Charlie's worried expression and said softly, "If something is wrong, Kendra would never tell us. All we can do is just be there for her, and let her know that we're here if she ever needs to talk." Quinn poured coffee into another mug, then realized that Charlie was staring at her with a shocked expression. "What?"

Charlie shook her head confused then said, "That's right."

"What's right?"

"What you said about being there for Kendra. You just said something that made sense and was reasonable and wasn't related to your acting career or your weight."

"Is that what you think of me? That I only talk about things related to my acting career or my weight?" Quinn whispered, almost as hurt as she had been by Wyatt.

Charlie looked momentarily guilty before she said, "Well…yes, actually."

"I'm not like that, and I'm sick of everyone saying that!" Quinn slammed the mug on the counter, then cried out when specks of hot coffee flew on her hand.

Now she had a reason to cry at the sting of pain on the back of her hand. Charlie quickly ran over and tugged Quinn to the faucet where she turned on cold water. She massaged Quinn's hand and held it under the cold water.

Quinn sniffed and studied her hand as if her life depended on it because Charlie was studying her.

A few moments later, Charlie turned off the faucet and closely inspected Quinn's hand. There were two pinpoint spots of red on her honey skin. Charlie made soothing noises, then pulled calamine lotion from a drawer and gently massaged it into Quinn's skin.

"All better?" Charlie asked softly. Quinn nodded and wiped at her tears. Charlie didn't release her hand, but held on tighter as she said, "You're my sister, and nothing you do or say will make me stop loving you, but sometimes…you're a lot to handle."

Quinn frowned and stared at Charlie. "I am?"

Charlie hesitated, then said, "Sometimes you can be self-centered. And sometimes you can be one-track about the acting, about your glory days as Sephora. It gets a little old…sometimes."

"That doesn't mean I'm a bad person," Quinn said, close to tears again.

"Of course not, baby," Charlie said softly. "But it does mean that it takes a lot for someone to know the real Quinn. I know you don't mean to hurt me when you talk about my perfect, bland marriage to Graham, but it hurts just the same. And I know you think that Kendra can take your insults, but I notice that sometimes you hit a little too close to the heart for her."

Quinn sniffed, suddenly feeling ashamed of herself. She never meant to hurt her sisters. Okay, sometimes she meant to hurt Kendra, but not any permanent damage. "Charlie, I'm sorry if I hurt you, and I'll apologize to Kendra, too—"

"You don't have to apologize. But, maybe—just maybe—it's time to grow up a little and start thinking about the effect you have on other people, that what you say matters, whether you want it to or not."

"But who listens to me? I'm just an out-of-work actress. I don't even have a college degree."

"You're somebody, Quinn, whether you're working or not. And, believe it or not, there is more to life than acting. There's a whole world out there. It's why I'm so happy that things are working out with you and Wyatt. I think he's probably the one man on Earth who can show you that there are other things out there besides acting. I mean, he has gotten you to eat barbecue and French fries. Who else could do that?"

"I'm not changing for any man. If he can't handle my career—"

"That's not what I meant, Quinn," Charlie said with a bemused smile. "I just mean that work can't be everything because when work goes away, and it will some day either because you get bored with it and decide to tackle something else, or the industry gets bored with you, all you have left is your family. I would have thought you had learned that by now after this last year."

A loud crash from the other side of the kitchen door caused Charlie to flinch.

"A little help in here" came Graham's panicked voice followed by Kendra's maniacal laugh of glee.

Charlie stood, laughing. "Kendra's coffee." She walked out the kitchen and Quinn stared at the wall, her sister's words echoing in her head.

Charlie was right. Quinn had learned a lot over the last year. She had been yelling at Wyatt about taking charge of his life, but she needed to take her own advice. It was time to grow up.

The dining room was so quiet that Wyatt heard the second hand on the grandfather clock in the hallway tick each second away. Beatrice had gone all out for Christmas dinner. She had made a perfect golden turkey, mashed potatoes *and* dressing, corn bread, green beans, candied yams…. Wyatt didn't even want to think about the number of desserts he had seen lined up in the kitchen. There was enough food to feed the entire town.

Except the meal was for just her and Wyatt because Wyatt had talked his mother into staying home for Christmas dinner instead of going to the Forbes home as they had done every year since Wyatt had been born. But, then again, the idea of seeing Quinn… Wyatt clenched the fork in his hand even harder as he thought of the look in her eyes when she had walked out of his apartment. He kept telling himself that it had been for the best, but hours later, that mantra was starting to sound hollow to his own ears.

"You haven't said anything about the food," Beatrice said, breaking the heavy silence for the first time since they had sat down for dinner.

"It's delicious, Mom," he said automatically.

When his mother didn't respond, he looked up to find her watching him. Beatrice abruptly set down her fork and rubbed her eyes. She looked at him again and demanded, "Are you going to tell me the real reason we aren't having dinner with the Forbes tonight?"

"I told you, I wanted to have a quiet Christmas," Wyatt lied. "There's usually close to forty people over there, and I didn't want to deal with the mayhem."

Beatrice studied him for a moment, then said abruptly, "Did I ever tell you that your father lived in New York City for eight weeks?"

Wyatt's fork clattered to the table. He instantly picked it back up, so the food on the back of the fork would not stain the beige lace tablecloth.

"Dad lived in New York City?" he sputtered. "I thought he spent his whole life in Sibleyville. That's what he always said."

"He lied," she said. "He lived in New York City eight months before we were married and before you were born."

Wyatt quickly did the math in his head. "I was born—"

"Yes, I was pregnant with you before your father and I got married. Jim and I were dating and one day out of the blue, he comes to me and says, 'Let's move to New York City.' New York City? It was insane. I'd never been outside Sibleyville. To move from here to New York sounded about as realistic as moving from here to the moon.

"I laughed at him. I told him that he was living in a fantasy world if he thought two country hicks like us could survive in New York City. I will never forget the look on his face...." Her voice trailed off and Wyatt realized that there were tears in her eyes. He reached across the table to grab her hand. She squeezed his hand, then continued, "I shouldn't have laughed at him. I should have listened to him. He said that he wanted to leave, had to leave, to know what was outside Sibleyville. To know what he was like outside of Sibleyville."

"So, he left without you?"

Beatrice nodded and wiped at her eyes. "He left. Moved to New York. Got a job at an after-school program in Harlem, nothing to do with the funeral business. His parents were furious. His father didn't speak to him for months. And then I found out I was pregnant...." Her voice trailed off again, and she stared at her plate.

"And Dad came home."

"He was never the same," Beatrice whispered. "He tried to pretend that this was the life he wanted. He never complained, but he always said that when you left home, we'd close down the funeral home and buy an RV and drive across America. And...and then he died. So young. He never got the chance."

"Dad wanted to sell the mortuary?" Wyatt asked in disbelief.

"He hated it."

"But, you always told me...*he* always told me that there was nothing more honorable in life than to help others deal with death."

"His father told him that," Beatrice said, shaking her head. "Apparently, your grandfather hated the mortuary business, too, and came up with that little phrase to make himself feel better."

"What?" Wyatt didn't know whether to laugh or cry. Three generations of Granger men stuck in the funeral business, suffering for the sake of a legacy that no one wanted.

Beatrice reached across the table to stroke Wyatt's cheek. "You were the only thing that made his life bearable."

"He loved you, Mom."

"I know he did, but I will never forgive myself for making him come back here before he got a chance to explore. I made him take over the business because I thought it would make him feel more connected to this town and our life in it, but instead he pulled away from me more and more every day. I didn't know how much until he died."

Wyatt just stared at her, unable to focus on the numerous questions swirling around his head to ask just one. His father had hated the funeral business too?

"Jim was so happy when you went away to school and majored in landscape architecture. He thought you were going to finally break free of the Granger tradition."

"I thought...since he never mentioned it, I thought he was ashamed of me. Angry that I wasn't planning to take over the business."

"No, Wyatt. He thought you were brave."

Wyatt's eyes watered and he quickly swiped at his tears. "I never knew. All this time I thought..." His voice trailed off and he couldn't hide the spurt of anger as he demanded, "Why didn't you tell me this sooner? You knew how much I hate doing this. I could have gone back to college. I could have opened my own landscape architecture firm in San Francisco or Los Angles... All this time I've wasted here." He reached for a glass of water with a trembling hand and took a swig before he said something he'd regret.

Because I needed you," Beatrice blurted out. Wyatt looked at her shocked. Even she looked surprised by her admission. She stared at the table as she repeated more softly. "Because I needed you."

His anger instantly faded, as he caught a rare glimpse of his mother's hidden vulnerability. "Mom—"

She held up her hand to interrupt him. "Let me get this out because you deserve the truth after all this time. After your father died, do you remember what I was like?" Wyatt couldn't meet her eyes, but nodded in response. "I couldn't get out of bed. I didn't eat, I didn't shower, I gave up. I felt as if my world had ended, and I had nothing left to give anyone.

"And then you came home from college and you told me that you would take care of everything. Suddenly, I had a reason to get out of bed. To help you run this place. To keep Jim's legacy alive around this town. As time went on and you became more comfortable with the funeral home, I came to reply on you to provide that ray of sunshine I lost when Jim died. And you seemed to fit in so well around here. I thought you were relatively happy with your greenhouse and the landscape architecture you've done around town. I knew the mortuary was not your favorite place in the world, but the death rate around here meant you didn't have to deal with it too often. And when Dorrie moved to town and I saw you take an interest in her...I thought that things were going to go fine between you two and for me." She laughed dryly, "I had your whole life planned for you."

"I would have been miserable," he said, simply.

Beatrice exhaled then nodded. "I know that now, and I'm sorry, Wyatt."

"It's not your fault," he admitted, reluctantly. "If I really wanted to leave and take a chance, I would have done it, regardless of Granger tradition."

"Maybe, maybe not," Beatrice said, quietly. "I will never forgive myself for stealing those years from you. I should have encouraged you to find your own way, outside of this. Like Graham's parents. Lance and Eliza raised Graham with love and respect for this town, with the expectation that he would find his way back when the time came. And he has. I should have trusted you like that. You deserved it."

"Stop blaming yourself. Please," he said, softly.

"I'm finally taking responsibility for my actions. It's time for both of us to get out of this rut I've created for us. Jim would not want us to live like this. He was one of the most alive people I knew, and it would break his heart to know how we've been running in place these last years, trying to keep everything the same as the day he died, I mean, my God, I haven't even changed the wallpaper in this dining room, and I never liked this wallpaper, even when your father picked it out thirty years ago."

"Why are you telling me all of this now?"

She blotted her cheeks with the napkin and said, with a huge smile, "Because I want you to leave Sibleyville without any guilt."

"Leave Sibleyville," he said, surprised then laughed in disbelief. "I'm not going anywhere."

"You are, Wyatt," she responded, forcefully. "Because you'll have nothing holding you to this town once we sell the mortuary."

He thought her first little bomb about his father living

in New York was last thing she could have said to render him speechless. He had been wrong.

"What? Sell the mortuary?"

Beatrice nodded and said firmly, "Let's face it, son. You and I aren't cut out for the funeral business. You faint at the sight of dead bodies, and I get sick at the smell of blood. What are the two of us doing with this place?"

"Because we're the last of the Grangers this side of the Mississippi."

"Then maybe it's time for the Grangers this side of the Mississippi to try something else."

Wyatt sputtered in disbelief for a moment then choked out, "But where will you live? Where will I live?"

Something akin to a blush crossed Beatrice's face as she murmured, "Angus has been trying to get me to move in with him for years now."

Now Wyatt thought he had gone mute. "Angus Affleck?"

"We've been dating for two years."

"Two years?" Wyatt shouted in a mixture of surprise and anger. He shook his head in disbelief. "Why didn't you tell me?"

"I wasn't sure how you'd handle it. I was waiting for the right time."

"The right time," Wyatt repeated in disbelief. He opened his mouth to shout some more, then noticed his mother's anxious expression. He abruptly laughed and muttered, "This town can't keep a secret, except the one that actually involves my mother and Angus Affleck."

"You like him, don't you?" Beatrice asked, sounding nervous.

"Angus is one of the best men I know," Wyatt said truthfully.

She sighed in relief, then said, cheerfully, "As for where you'll live, I'm not worried. I've always wanted to be able to say that my son lives in Los Angeles."

Wyatt thought of Quinn, and his smile instantly disappeared. "Mom, this is a lot to think about. I don't think we should make such a rash decision—"

"It's not rash. And what's there to think about? We can't stay here, living like this forever. I want you to be happy, son. I want you to make mistakes. Try new things. After all, even if it means you leaving Sibleyville, we know better than anyone, Wyatt, how short life really is."

Wyatt flinched as the mark hit home. He thought about his life the last few years. The monotonous cycle of waking up, going to sleep, dreading people dying, the occasional fainting. And throughout everything, he had been followed by loneliness and fear. Maybe the two emotions even went hand in hand. Only a scared man would reject Quinn Sibley. Or a really stupid one.

"Quinn is a good girl, Wyatt," she said softly, almost as if she had been reading his thoughts. "You're going to be very happy with her, if you allow yourself to be. It was seeing you with her these last few days that made me finally come to grips with the mess I've made."

"You did not make a mess. I did that on my own. And Quinn is…great, but she's not exactly Sibleyville wife material."

"And why not?" Beatrice demanded.

Wyatt's eyes widened in surprise. "Weren't you vowing never to allow *that woman* to step foot in your house just a few days ago?"

"That was before she told me in no uncertain terms that she loved my son and that there was nothing I could do about it."

Wyatt almost thought his mother was smiling at the memory. But he couldn't believe that. He also couldn't believe that Quinn was walking around in one piece after telling his mother that piece of news.

"When did this happen?"

"Right after Mrs. Woods' funeral. I think I actually like her, Wyatt. Much better than I thought I would. And I think she can handle me. Anyway, if you think that Dorrie makes better Sibleyville wife material than Quinn, then you haven't been paying attention to who Sibleyville wives are. They're not shrinking violets and they're not quiet women. They stand beside their husbands and they fight to protect what's theirs. That's sounds a lot like Quinn to me."

Wyatt laughed and shook his head, suddenly feeling as if a weight had been lifted off his shoulders.

"We're really going to do this."

Beatrice beamed at him. "Yes we are," she said. She stood and began to clear away the dishes.

The doorbell rang and for a moment his heart sped up enough to practically leap from his chest. Maybe it was Quinn. He hoped it was Quinn, because his mother was right. It was time to start cleaning up his messes.

Wyatt ran through the house and opened the door, prepared to beg for forgiveness or pay for forgiveness. Whatever. Except it wasn't Quinn on the other side of the door. It was Angus Affleck.

Angus stared at Wyatt uncertainly, then took off his creased and worn cowboy hat. Wyatt had to admit that he liked seeing Angus nervous, but that lasted about two seconds. Angus was a good man, and Wyatt was glad that his mother had someone.

"Come in," Wyatt said, with a big show of reluctance.

Angus walked into the house and Wyatt closed the door. The two men stared at each other. Sized each other up.

"I guess your mother finally told you," Angus muttered, ducking Wyatt's gaze.

"I guess," Wyatt said, fighting back his smile.

"I wanted her to tell you sooner, Wyatt, but she—"

Wyatt abruptly laughed and the dread eased from Angus's face and turned into irritation.

He swatted at Wyatt with his hat. "You spoiled brat," he accused.

"You old country hick," Wyatt shot back, still laughing. "You could have told me. Two years?"

"Beatrice said not to, and you've lived with her long enough to know that no one challenges her. Not even me," Angus said with a bashful lift of his shoulders.

"Boys, come eat some dessert," Beatrice called from the back room.

Angus swatted at Wyatt with his hat again, then hurried toward the dining room. Wyatt stared after them for a moment, then smiled at their sound of their mingled laughter. Life never did make any promises. It was the first lesson most morticians learned, but Wyatt had missed that one. And now he had a feeling that it was too late.

Chapter 21

Quinn took a deep breath, then knocked on the door of the trailer parked in front of the Sibley house, the next morning.

"What!" came Helmut's enraged bark.

Quinn walked into the trailer, not surprised to find Helmut hunched over a laptop at the table in the middle of the cramped surroundings. Most of the cast and crew had gone home for the holidays, but had been slowly trickling back into work that morning. She would have believed it if Helmut had spent the past two days hunched over his laptop doing more rewrites. She hadn't thought to knock on the trailer door to see if anyone was left.

"What do you want?" Helmut demanded, glaring at her. "Shouldn't you be memorizing your lines since you've shown an innate ability to forget them at precisely the most inconvenient moment?"

"Helmut, I quit." She briefly wondered if he had heard her since he didn't instantly react. She tried again, "Helmut, I'm quitting the movie. I'm going back to L.A."

Helmut's chubby fingers stopping moving across the keyboard. He glanced at the trailer ceiling and muttered, "Why are the pretty ones always the most dramatic?" He turned to her and said in a monotone, "No, no, Quinn. Please don't quit. There, I have begged you. You are invaluable. Now, go get ready for rehearsals this afternoon."

"This isn't a ploy for attention. I'm quitting." When he only continued to stare at her blankly, she explained, "I'm going back to Los Angeles tomorrow. One of the few friends I have left in this industry has a small part on a TV sitcom he's directing. Second best friend from the right. The actress who read for the part broke her arm in a tragic in-line skating accident.

"Believe me, Helmut, I'm as surprised as you that I'm going to do this. After I left *Diamond Valley*, I turned up my nose at doing any type of TV, but filming this movie made me realize how…how much I really don't want to make movies. Especially depressing ones like this. I like making people laugh and giving them an escape. It's why I act—"

"You ungrateful little bitch," Helmut exploded, jumping to his feet. "You are nothing in this industry! No one touched you until I came along! And you want to know why? Because you're nothing! Nothing but a pair of fake titties!"

"Well, since I'm such a talentless hack, as you described me the other day, I'm sure whoever you find will be much better than I am."

"You signed a contract," he retorted smugly. "I own you."

"Actually, I didn't sign a contract," she said with a feigned "whoops" air. "You told me that you wouldn't give me one to sign until I got the deal sealed on the location, and I guess with all the excitement, everyone forgot."

"You will never work in this town again. I will make sure of it!"

"Much bigger and better people have said that to me, Helmut. And I'm still here." As his face grew more and more red, she smiled. "Good luck on your movie."

She waved, then walked out the trailer. She would probably never get that Oscar, but it was almost worth it to put that Napoleon in his place. She walked back across the yard to the house, planning to follow her vow to be more adult as soon as she finished relaying the story to Kendra.

"Are you sure you can't wait to leave until after New Year's?" Charlie whined as Quinn shoved her last suitcase in the trunk of her car.

Quinn slammed the trunk closed, then turned to Charlie, Graham and Kendra. She really was tempted to stay another few days, but if she ran into Wyatt, her heart wouldn't be able to handle it.

"I wish I could, but filming starts in two days and I need to learn my lines," Quinn said truthfully.

"I'm just glad you finally told Helmut to shove it," Kendra said, then moaned in pain and placed both hands on her stomach. "I think I just alluded to food. I'm going to be sick."

Quinn laughed. Charlie sniffed and hugged Quinn. "Drive safely. We'll see you in L.A."

"I checked the tires and oil. Remember to take it slow on the highway. Cops love to patrol during the holidays," Graham warned, hugging her.

Quinn waved as Charlie and Graham walked back into the house. She turned to Kendra, who was watching her closely through bloodshot eyes.

"Now, are you going to tell me what is really going on," Kendra demanded.

"I told you, the sitcom—"

"Who's making TV right now in the middle of the holidays? Even TV actors get the holidays off."

Quinn sighed heavily, then leaned against the car. "I can't risk running into Wyatt."

"You two make me so tired. What happened now?"

"He doesn't have any faith in me, and he never will. He told me that it was better to end things now before I grew tired of him. Of course I'd grow tired him. I don't know any couple that doesn't grow tired of each other at some point, but I love him. I don't feel complete without him. But he doesn't believe me. He said that I only think that I love him. He thinks I'm deluding myself into thinking I love him because I'm stuck here in Sibleyville without any other options." Quinn cursed as tears spilled from her eyes. "I've waited my entire life for him, Kendra, without even knowing that I was waiting for him. To think that he dismisses it all as the ramblings of a woman-child. No man has ever hurt me the way this man has."

"The condescending jerk. He doesn't deserve you," Kendra said fiercely, wrapping her arms around Quinn.

"I told him that."

"Good for you."

"I want to hate him. I want to think 'good riddance.' But, I can't," Quinn whispered. "I want him in my life. I was willing to commute to L.A. from Sibleyville."

Kendra's eyes widened in disbelief. "Really," she whispered, amazed.

"I have never lost myself before, Kendra, but I was willing to lose myself in him. I still am."

"Oh, Quinn," Kendra said softly, stroking her hair. "I'm so sorry."

Quinn allowed herself to be comforted for a moment, then stood and wiped at her tears and smoothed down her hair. "But, I'm not going to. I remembered something the other night. I'm pretty amazing, if I do say so myself. I moved to New York at eighteen years old, and I survived. I can do it again."

"I know you can," her sister said, squeezing her hand.

"But, I can't see Wyatt again."

"I understand. Do you want me to come with you? We could have fun. Wreaking havoc on L.A. On Charlie and Graham's big ol' house."

Quinn smiled, but shook her head. "I need to lick my wounds. Regroup. The sitcom films in two weeks, and I need to be ready."

Kendra hugged Quinn and said, "You're going to be okay, Quinn. I promise."

Quinn wanted to believe her sister, but she couldn't. Because no matter how much she regrouped or licked her wounds, she would never recover from loving Wyatt.

* * *

Wyatt looked up from digging in the flower bed in front of the mortuary and quickly shot to his feet when he saw Kendra. Or, at least, he thought it was Kendra. He had never seen her outside of her exercise clothes or some type of expensive, too-tight suit. This Kendra wore jeans and a sloppy sweatshirt and a baseball cap. Either way, Wyatt did not want to be on his knees in front of her. There was no telling what she might do.

Kendra stared him for a moment, then snorted in disgust. Wyatt stuffed his hands in his jeans pockets, then asked nervously, "Is there something you wanted, Kendra?"

Since Kendra declined to answer, Wyatt said, "I'm getting the house ready for the film crew. They'll be here tomorrow morning."

"Quinn left town this morning," she finally said.

Blood drained from his face. It was already too late. "What?"

"If you cared so much, why are you here playing in the dirt?"

"I didn't know she was leaving. I thought she was supposed to be filming the movie here for the next five weeks. That and I was kind of working up the nerve to talk to her. She was not exactly happy the last time I saw her." Wyatt hesitated then muttered more to himself than Kendra.

"So, you thought you'd mosey over to her at some point in the next five weeks and apologize for acting like an ass?" Kendra demanded.

"Not exactly, but—"

"My sister was crying over you," she spat out. "Crying! Over you!"

Wyatt averted his gaze, as his heart broke a little more. He thought it hurt to see Quinn crying. It hurt even more to hear that she had been crying from someone else.

"I'll never forgive you for that," Kendra informed him. "Quinn probably will because she's crazy in love with you. But fifty years from now, when you two are surrounded by grandchildren and great-grandchildren, I'll still be giving you hell for making her worry about your love for her."

Wyatt started to speak but Kendra cut him off.

"Shut up," she snapped, then demanded, "Do you love my sister?" He stared at her in response. She prodded, annoyed, "Do you?"

"I thought I was shutting up."

"Don't get cute with me, Granger. Do you love Quinn or not?"

"I do," he said, softly.

"Are you threatened by her career?"

"No," he said, surprised. "I want the best for her. Whether that's an Oscar, returning to *Diamond Valley*, whatever it is she wants, that's what I want for her."

"Are you going to turn into a jealous prick every time a man looks at her?"

"No. She's gorgeous. Who wouldn't look at her?"

"Do you think she's just a pretty face?"

"God, no. She's one of the sweetest, most loyal and courageous people I've ever known."

"Good," Kendra said simply, then snarled, "then get your act together and win her back."

Wyatt coughed over his surprise. "It's not that easy, Kendra."

"Why?"

He was suddenly speechless. He always had the mortuary to fall back on. He couldn't leave Sibleyville because of the mortuary. But if he and Beatrice had their way, there wouldn't be a mortuary anymore. Or if there was, it wouldn't have the Granger name on it.

"Because I'm scared," he admitted, more to himself than to Kendra.

Kendra's expression softened. A fraction. "Believe it or not, Wyatt, I know how you feel. I'm scared too. I haven't told my sisters, but I'm having financial problems. I have less than nothing and probably at the end of the month the only place I'll have to live is this town. I'm scared as hell."

"I'm sorry, Kendra. If you need anything—"

"I didn't tell you that because I want your sympathy," she snapped. She took several deep breaths and Wyatt was amazed to see tears fill her eyes. "I'm telling you this because I don't want you to end up like me. For most of my adult life, I used work to block out everyone and everything. I can look at you and see that you do the same thing. But now you have a chance, a real chance, to grab hold of life. Quinn is one of the bravest people I know. If you're scared, just hold on to her. She'll help you through it."

Wyatt stared at her wordlessly. Kendra shrugged and muttered, "I said what I have to say."

She turned to Graham's Porsche parked on the street, but Wyatt stopped her.

"You're not alone, Kendra. You have your sisters, you have Graham and you have me. I mean it."

She smiled at him, but kept walking to the car. Wyatt watched her leave, then turned to stare at the mortuary. Kendra was right, his mother was right. Even Graham was right. Wyatt had to start taking control of his own life. He had to offer Quinn everything she was offering him. And then he smiled. Because he suddenly had a plan.

Chapter 22

Six weeks later

"Ta-da! What do you think?" Quinn asked Charlie as she dramatically motioned around the one-bedroom apartment.

Charlie glanced around the beige walls, beige carpet and—even—beige chair in the center of the living room, then at the kitchen only two steps away and turned to Quinn. "I think you should stay in the pool house."

Quinn laughed and walked into the kitchen where she was unpacking the last of her stuff—a box of pots and pans. Not that she had any use for them since she never cooked, but Charlie had insisted on giving them to her for her new apartment. Her new apartment in North Hollywood. Quinn shuddered in disgust just thinking of the name of her city. She never thought she would be a resident of the San Fernando Valley, that sprawling metropolis over the mountain from the heart of Los Angeles where most out-of-work actors and actresses lived in cookie-cutter apartments, instead of flea-infested slums in the heart of Los Angeles.

But Quinn was being an adult. She couldn't stay in Charlie's pool house, mooching off Charlie and Graham, and she couldn't pretend that she didn't like cleanliness. So she had compromised and moved to the Valley. Her guest role on her friend's sitcom had turned into a multi-episode story line and Quinn finally had an agent. Her agent had just been an intern less than four weeks ago, but Natalie believed in Quinn. Natalie was much too green to lie convincingly yet, so Quinn believed her.

Charlie moved to the counter that separated the kitchen from the living room. "I don't understand why you're moving. Graham and I love having you around."

"I appreciate it, Charlie, but I have to stand on my own two feet. I'm getting a fairly steady paycheck from the sitcom, and there's the promise of more work. Doors are still closing in my face, but not quite with the same gusto."

Charlie studied her for a moment, then said begrudgingly, "All right, if this is what you want."

"It is," Quinn said firmly, then laughed. "The place is a dump, isn't it?"

Charlie laughed then set down her purse and suit jacket. "All it needs is a little TLC. We'll hang some pictures, get some more furniture from the pool house and…plants. Lots of plants."

Quinn's smile faded. Wyatt. As usual, the little burst

of pain at the thought of him exploded in her heart. She had thought it would have faded by now, but it hadn't.

It had been six weeks. He hadn't called, written, e-mailed. Nothing. He obviously had forgotten about her, probably moved on to Dorrie again. Quinn had gone through the stages of anger, sadness, back to anger and now she was just numb. She went through her day, did her job, laughed with newfound friends and her sister. She even had gone on a date that had ended in total disaster when she had burst into tears in the middle of the meal after noticing a vase of tulips on the table.

Nothing was the same without Wyatt. And no matter how tried, she could not stop thinking about him, dreaming about him. Nights were particularly cruel. Because then she had uninterrupted time to think about every kiss and every touch. The way he had felt in her mouth, blanketing her. She had never felt more lonely in her life.

"I saw a nursery on my way over here," Charlie was saying, oblivious to Quinn's musings as she opened another box on the counter. "In the Miracle Mile. On the corner of La Brea and 3rd Street."

Quinn forced herself to focus on the conversation. "The Miracle Mile? In Sunday traffic, it'll take me an hour to get there. There's probably a closer nursery around here."

"This nursery was advertising a bunch of specials," Charlie said. "I think you'll be able to find some really good deals."

"I'm tired. I'll go later this week."

"You have to go today," Charlie insisted. "The deals will probably be over after the weekend and on your budget you can't afford to pass this up. What do you say?"

Quinn sighed, annoyed, and glared at her sister. "You're not going to let this go, are you?"

Charlie dangled car keys from her hand. "I brought Graham's Porsche. I'll even let you drive."

Quinn snatched the car keys and forced a smile because she knew Charlie expected it. "Let's go."

An hour and a half later, Charlie pulled into the dirt parking lot of a nursery. Or what appeared to be the beginning stages of a nursery. Wooden beams lay in the parking lot, while their counterparts hung in half-finished arrangements around the giant lot, supported by scaffolding and ladders. Work tables were littered throughout the space, and the lone building on the property was chained closed and had several broken windows.

She saw row after row of green plants and colorful flowers on one side of the lot, but the other side of the lot was completely empty, as if waiting for more flowers.

Quinn looked at Charlie, who appeared unfazed by the condition of the place, and stood from the car.

"Charlie, I don't think anyone is here," Quinn said.

"Of course—" The sound of Charlie's ringing telephone had her digging around in her purse. She flipped it open. "This is Charlie Forbes." There was a long pause, then Charlie motioned for Quinn to walk into the nursery as she said, "Hello, Mrs. DeGault. Yes, we received the shipment of your collection, and we are greatly indebted to you."

Quinn ignored Charlie's droning and walked through the open fence into the nursery. Broken glass and pebbles crunched under her flip-flops as she glanced around. She fingered the petal of a red tulip sitting on the edge of a row of tulips.

"Hello," she called out.

No answer. She frowned and turned back to the parking lot. Charlie was nowhere in sight. Quinn muttered a curse about seriously deluded sisters, then started deeper into the nursery toward the tree plants in the back. There were beautiful and green. Exactly what she needed in her apartment.

And then she stopped in her tracks because she saw a large sign propped on the fence. The type of sign that the owner would no doubt display on the outside of the building once he opened the nursery for business. On a white board, in professionally blocked black letters, it read, *Quinn's Place.*

"It took me a long time to come up with a name, but I finally decided on that one because I wanted everyone to know that no matter where your filming took you, that you'd always have this place to come back to and call your home," said a deep, familiar voice behind her.

Quinn briefly closed her eyes as goose bumps covered her entire body in one rush of emotion. Wyatt. She didn't want to see him. She was aching to see him. Her body trembled as she turned to face him, and she instantly inhaled. He was gorgeous. Standing in blue jeans, a dirty white T-shirt and a baseball cap, he was beautiful and tall and strong. Just like in her dreams. Only better. Her body cried out for him, and she almost took a step toward him before she realized what she was doing.

Her stomach dropped, and she thought that she would, too, but only pride kept her standing. Pride, and the fact that body was frozen in place from sheer shock at seeing him in the middle of Los Angeles. It had been six weeks since she had last seen him, and it had felt like a lifetime. Her body cried at her to run to him, but she only stood in her spot, staring at him. Wanting him with every fiber of her being. It should have been illegal to want someone this much, especially when that person didn't want her.

But he was here. In L.A. With a nursery. That had to mean something.

"What are you doing here?" she whispered.

Wyatt closed the distance between them and stared at her expectantly. She hadn't forgotten how he looked at her as if he wanted to devour every inch of her, but that didn't make the effect even less overpowering.

"Isn't it obvious, Quinn? I came for you. I love you."

She shook her head, the anger finally kicking in. "No," she said, tears filling her eyes. "You can't just show up after all this time and expect to pick up where we left off. You gave up on us first, remember?"

He stepped closer and framed her face with his hands. At his touch, the flood dam broke, and tears rolled down her cheeks. "I remember, and I have regretted every word I've said since that night. I never should have doubted you, doubted your love."

She jerked away from his touch, hating that he was saying everything, she had been wanting him to say for six weeks. "You should have called before you did all this."

Wyatt's expression fell, and he stuffed his hands in his pockets. "I thought you'd hang up on me."

"And you would have been right," she retorted. She looked around the nursery in amazement, seeing it in a new light, now that she knew it was his. She had never seen anything more beautiful. "Did you really buy this place?"

"Lock, stock and barrel." He laughed. 'The ink is barely dry on the ownership papers."

"What about the funeral home? What about your mother?"

"Mom and I finally accepted that we were the worst funeral home owners this state has ever seen. We sold it. She moved in with Angus—"

"*Angus Affleck?* Lance's friend?"

Wyatt smiled slightly and her heart dipped. She had missed the smile so much. "Angus Affleck. They're getting married next month."

"So, you moved to L.A. just like that?" she asked, shaking her head.

"Just like that," he agreed, staring at her. "Although I'm still living I a rental unit."

"But what if I'm involved with someone else? What if I'm on the verge of moving to Paris for a three-month movie shoot? What if I never want to see you again?" she demanded.

"Then I'd wait," he said simply.

She snorted in disbelief. "You'd wait?"

"I'd wait," he repeated, then once more closed the distance between them. This time, he didn't touch her, but she could tell that he longed to because she wanted the same thing. The two of them never could be close to each other without touching. "These past six weeks, I've done a lot of thinking. I didn't want to just show up here with nothing to offer you. I want to be the man you think I am. Part of it was getting rid of the mortuary. Another part was leaving Sibleyville. And the last thing was starting to build this dream that I've wanted so long. I figured once I was happy and secure in what I was doing, I could be there for you like you need. So, I'll wait for you, however long it takes, because all of this is for you."

The tears that she thought had dried up returned with full vengeance. "I can't deal with this," she whispered.

"Yes, you can. You're the strongest person I know, much stronger than me, and if I can do this, then you can definitely do this."

"I thought you didn't love me."

He instantly pulled her into his arms. Her tears fell harder because it was as if she had never left. His comforting smell, the hard feel of him. The way he touched her like she was something precious.

"I love you so much that it scares me the hell out of me," he said softly. "But, I've also realized that's what love is all about. Being scared out of your mind. You just grab on and hope that the person you love is just as scared you are. And there's no one else I want to be scared with."

She pulled from his arms and swiped at her tears. "Just like that, you expect me to just…to just forgive you and… no, Wyatt. You really hurt me. You had your chance."

He wrapped his arms around her again, refusing to give her space. "I know, baby, and I'll never forgive myself for making you cry."

"I hate you," she said, without much heat. She bit her bottom lip as his eyes shone with so much love that a different type tears filled her eyes. "I really hate you."

"I deserve it, but I'm going to spend the rest of my life making it up to you. I promise."

Quinn clung to his shoulders, scared that she was imagining it and would wake up slapping her alarm clock. But his shirt felt real under her hands, and his body felt warm against hers.

"The rest of your life?" she questioned, shaking her head. "What about your perfect Sibleyville wife? I mean, I don't bake. I wouldn't know a nursery rhyme if it bit me on the ass. And…I'm about as far from your vision of the little wife you could possibly conceive. Although, I do want kids and I don't appreciate your insinuating that I don't. Just not yet. Or not within the next few months."

"Funny thing. Everything you just said fits all the qualities of a perfect Sibleyville wife."

She wanted to scream some more, to throw a big tantrum, but then he smiled at her again. That ridiculous, beautiful smile and he touched her bottom lip with his thumb. It was his touch that did it every time.

"Oh, hell," she muttered, then grabbed his shirt and dragged him to her mouth. He responded with a kiss full of promises and apologies that made her toes curl and her heart sputter back to life.

Quinn heard the sound of a car engine roar to life and she looked over her shoulder to see Charlie driving the Porsche out of the lot.

"That little sneak," she muttered.

"I bribed her. Box after box of chocolates."

Quinn laughed, then shook her head in amazement. "You're really here. I've dreamed about this and imagined, but I can't believe you're really here."

"I'm really here. For as long as you—and the L.A. gardening and landscape design community—will have me."

"For a lifetime, Wyatt, for a lifetime." She threw her

arms around him and squeezed. Hard. "Don't ever walk out on me again. My heart can't take it."

"Mine can't, either," he whispered then kissed her again. And just like in Diamond Valley, Quinn heard the sound of swirling violins signaling the sweet beginning.

USA TODAY Bestselling Author

BRENDA JACKSON

invites you to discover the always sexy and always satisfying Madaris Men.

Experience where it all started…

Tonight and Forever
December 2007

Whispered Promises
January 2008

Eternally Yours
February 2008

One Special Moment
March 2008

ARABESQUE®

www.kimanipress.com   KPBJREISSUES08

USA TODAY bestselling author

BRENDA JACKSON

TONIGHT AND FOREVER

A Madaris Family novel.

Just what the doctor ordered…

After a bitter divorce, Lorren Jacobs has vowed to never give
her heart again. But then she meets Justin Madaris, a handsome
doctor who carries his own heartache. The spark between
them is undeniable, but sharing a life means letting go of the
past. Can they fight through the painful memories of yesterday
to fulfill the passionate promise of tomorrow?

"Brenda Jackson has written another sensational novel…
sensual and sexy—all the things a romance reader
could want in a love story."
—*Romantic Times BOOKreviews* on *Whispered Promises*

Available the first week of December
wherever books are sold.

ARABESQUE®

www.kimanipress.com   KPBJ0231207

following LOVE

Award-winning author

CELESTE O. NORFLEET

Desperate for a job, single mom Dena Graham only has
one option—work for sexy, charismatic Julian Hamilton.
Julian has had enough of relationships and is focused
strictly on business…until Dena walks into his life.
Now these two, who've sworn never to gamble with
their hearts again, find that when red-hot attraction
enters the picture, all bets are off!

"A story that warrants reading over and over again!"
—*Romantic Times BOOKreviews* on *One Sure Thing*

Available the first week of December
wherever books are sold.

ARABESQUE®

www.kimanipress.com

KPCON0241207

He was like a new man...

TO *LOVE* A
STRANGER

Award-winning author

ADRIANNE BYRD

When aspiring fashion designer Madeline Stone's husband
returns after being lost at sea, Madeline is amazed that
Russell is no longer the womanizing rascal she married.
He's considerate, romantic...and very sexy.
Now Madeline faces a dilemma....

"Byrd proves once again that she's a wonderful storyteller."
—*Romantic Times BOOKreviews* on *The Beautiful Ones*

*Available the first week of December
wherever books are sold.*

KIMANI™
ROMANCE

www.kimanipress.com

KPAB0441207

Sometimes parents do know best!

Essence bestselling author

LINDA HUDSON-SMITH

*F*ORSAKING
ALL
OTHERS

They remembered each other as gawky teenagers and
had resisted their parents' meddlesome matchmaking.
But years later, when Jessica and Weston share a family ski
weekend, they discover a sizzling attraction between them.
Only, how long can romance last once they've left their
winter wonderland behind?

"A truly inspiring novel!"
—*Romantic Times BOOKreviews* on *Secrets and Silence*

*Coming the first week of December
wherever books are sold.*

"Devon pens a good story."
—*Romantic Times BOOKreviews* on *Love Once Again*

Favorite author

DEVON VAUGHN ARCHER

CHRISTMAS HEAT

The emotional painting of his late father seared
Aaron Pearson's soul and compelled him to meet the
artist, Deana Lamour. But her beauty and grace reawakened
in him a lust for life and enabled him to finally confront
the ghosts of his past.

*Coming the first week of December
wherever books are sold.*